Ask Him Why

Also by Catherine Ryan Hyde

CATHERINE RYAN HYDE

NEW YORK TIMES BESTSELLING AUTHOR

Ask Him Why

A Novel

LAKE UNION
PUBLISHING

Text copyright © 2015 by Catherine Ryan Hyde

Published by Lake Union Publishing, Seattle

www.apub.com

Amazon, the Amazon logo, and Lake Union Publishing are trademarks of Amazon.com, Inc., or its affiliates.

ISBN-13: 9781503950894 (hardcover)
ISBN-10: 1503950891 (hardcover)
ISBN-13: 9781503948907 (paperback)
ISBN-10: 1503948900 (paperback)

Cover design by Shasti O'Leary-Soudant / SOS CREATIVE LLC

Printed in the United States of America

First edition

Part One

Your Brother Knows

Remembering Spring 2003

Chapter One: Ruth

I was fifteen when our brother Joseph was shipped overseas to fight, and I was fifteen when he came home, uninjured, three and a half months later.

Yeah, I know what you're thinking. The army doesn't tend to have deployments that last only three and a half months.

That was the heart of our problem right there.

It was more than ten years ago, this part of things, but I still have a lot of clear mental snapshots. It wasn't one of those days you're likely to forget. Although sometimes I think we imprint only certain parts of it, like a series of snapshots, and then the rest falls away.

I wonder sometimes if the parts I kept are really the most important parts.

Anyway, when I got home from school there was a yellow cab parked in front of our house. I had no idea what was going on, but I knew it was something out of the ordinary, because that cab thing just didn't happen in my world. That would have been almost like leaving ourselves open to new people or something.

The cab was sitting at the curb in front of our gate, the engine running, and I was walking down the street, getting closer to it in a way that seemed too gradual. Like time was stretching out. The whole thing seemed to be taking forever. It felt like one of those moving walkways at the airport, only in reverse—instead of making me feel like I could walk powerfully fast, this felt like I couldn't get anywhere, no matter how hard I tried.

Nobody got in or out of the cab, which seemed weird.

When I got up to it, I saw there was nobody inside except the driver. He was about forty and had jet-black hair with a bald spot right in the middle. Right on top, which didn't seem to be the way most bald spots are destined to behave. He was smoking a cigarette with the windows rolled up, so the smoke was just roiling around in there with no place to go. He wasn't using his hands, either. His hands were both on the top of the steering wheel, like they hadn't gotten the message that he wasn't actively driving. I could see him use his lips and facial muscles to draw in and exhale the smoke.

I walked around to the street side and rapped on his window, and he jumped like I'd taken a shot at him.

He opened the driver's-side window, and I could see by the motion of his shoulder that he still had those old-fashioned windows with cranks. Smoke rolled out, smelling nasty and stale.

See, this is what I meant about the snapshots. Maybe the cab driver wasn't the real heart of the thing, but he got imprinted.

"What?" he asked, grumpy and challenging, like I had already put him out quite a bit, and now I'd best make this good.

"How can you do that?"

"Do what?"

"What if the next person in your cab is allergic to smoke? Or is a pregnant woman or something? Or just doesn't want to breathe all that?"

A silence.

I watched him purse his lips and inhale, then push the smoke out through his nose. A light breeze carried it right into my face and I waved it away violently, and probably more dramatically than necessary.

Hey, I was fifteen. Drama was my contribution to the world.

His eyes narrowed. "Who *are* you?" he asked around the filter of the cigarette.

"I live here," I said, thrusting my chin in the direction of my family's enormous house. "I just wondered why you were sitting out here at our curb."

"That's a logical thing to wonder," he said. "Especially compared to what you've been wondering so far, like why I do the things I do, or what my next fare'll want. I'm waiting to get paid."

"From . . . somebody . . . in there?" I indicated the house again with my chin.

"No, somebody at the airport. I just thought the view was nicer here. Yes, from somebody in your house. Anything else you're wondering?"

"I'll see if I can get something going with that," I said.

"Fine."

"I'll be as fast as I can."

"Take your time," he said. Then, when the look on my face seemed to communicate that he was being uncharacteristically kind, he added, "Meter's running."

I walked up to my front door carefully, if such a thing were possible.

When I stepped into the living room, Joseph was sitting on the couch. He was in his uniform, and I was struck by how handsome he looked in it, how put-together. And being put-together was never his claim to fame before the army got their hands on him.

Mom was sitting on one side of him, Dad on the other, all of which was even more wrong than a yellow cab at the curb. Because my mom should have had her book group on Friday afternoon, and my dad was at work—pretty much every day—from the first light of morning until he knew the coast must have been cleared by the last of us going to bed. Even my mom was somebody he tried to avoid bumping into any more often than necessary.

The minute they looked up and saw me, they stopped talking.

Now, there are silences, and there are *silences*, especially in the house where we grew up. If we'd ever talked about the silences out loud, I'm sure we'd have had a hundred different words to identify them like the Eskimos do with snow. But then, if we'd talked about the silences there wouldn't have been so many of them. I think I took myself around in a circle just then, which I blame on the silences. They don't take you anywhere but back to where you started.

This silence was electrical. It had a dark crackle to it, but that kind of electricity can be upbeat and exciting at times. This wasn't. This was heavy and sickening, like when the teacher's wall phone rings in class and it's me they're looking for—me getting called down to the office.

When the weight of it got to be too much, I said something blunt and obvious: "Joseph. You're home."

Then I just waited.

Of course, Joseph knew he was home. I'm sure he didn't need me to point it out to him. But that was another one of our silence types: the one where you state something brutally evident because you don't understand it, and then stand there and say nothing and hope someone will explain voluntarily, because you can't bring yourself to ask.

Fifteen and a half years on the planet, in that household, and I still hadn't found a word for that one.

Joseph seemed to have nothing to say. Joseph rarely said much, but I remember feeling that a word or two would have been nice in this case. I think he was locked down by the electrical patterns between my two staticky parents.

"Honey, go upstairs," my mom said. "We're having a conversation with your brother."

I opened my mouth to say something, but I'm not sure precisely what it would have been. I mean, I didn't have it planned out word for word. But I know the first word would have been "why." Then I got smart—or at least self-protective—and closed my mouth again.

I started up the long, curvy, carpeted staircase—slowly, in case I could catch a few of their words. But they were onto me—they waited until they heard my footsteps shuffle all the way up to the second-floor landing. Then they started again, but in whispers.

I waited, one hand on the polished mahogany banister, but I couldn't hear what they said. I could hear voices, but not words. Still, I stood there, looking down at the photos.

All the way down the staircase, hung on a spiral of wall and sloping with the pitch of the stairs, were framed photos of our family. My mom, Janet, and my dad, Brad. Yes, Brad and Janet, like in *The Rocky Horror Picture Show*. To this very day, it's hard to say their names at the same time without breaking into song. And Joseph as a child—who's really our half brother, not that it matters—and my full brother Aubrey, who's younger. And me, of course. In the photos, we were such a happy family. You could see it. It was shiny and warm. It even seemed to have depth. It was just what pictures of a happy family should be.

I guess my dad got them to add the "happy" in the photo processing or the framing. He had a way of buying what he needed. Even revisions of reality can be purchased if you have the cash and you want it badly enough.

I climbed the rest of the way up the stairs and down the hall to Aubrey's room to see if he was home yet, but his door was wide open, which it never in a million years would have been if he'd been around. Not even for a matter of seconds. I walked into his room, through the hanging stars and planets and solar systems. Walking through Aubrey's room was like space travel through the galaxy. I looked out his window at the front yard, but nothing moved out there.

Then I realized what I'd forgotten.

I trotted back down the stairs and stuck my head into the static electricity that was this freshly horrible moment in our family.

My father yelled at me, right away, before I'd even had a chance to say a word in my own defense.

"I thought we told you we needed to talk to your brother privately!" he shouted.

He was a big man, too thick in the middle, with a great barrel chest and a deep voice. He seemed to pride himself on anything that was manly, like bulky size and baritone speaking.

"This is important," I said.

"Fine. What?" my mom snapped.

"You forgot to pay the cab driver. He's still out there with the meter running."

My father leaped to his feet. For such a large man, he sure could be agile when there were savings involved. He was the kind of guy who would walk all over the house—which was quite a time-consuming patrol in that sprawling place—just to correct a stray lamp somebody might have left on. Just to save a few pennies. When he had so many.

"I'll take care of this," he said, and stomped out the door.

Our mom got to her feet. She looked down at Joseph. "I'm getting coffee. Don't so much as move." Then she disappeared into the kitchen.

I looked at Joseph and he looked at me. I guess I expected some kind of pleasant recognition, because we hadn't seen each other in months. But I think he didn't have the time or attention

for that. He had a look in his eyes like I'd caught him on the way
to his execution.

"Nice that you're home," I said.

"*Is* it now?" he said in return. Joseph had a wry way of looking
at the world. Almost everything he said was sardonic at some level.

"Do you have to go back?"

"No."

"How did you manage that?"

"It's kind of a complicated story," he said, flipping his head
in the direction of the kitchen and my mom, indicating that she
would never give him time to tell it.

Then my mom came back with a cup of coffee for herself, in
that fine bone china we're not allowed to use. I wondered if Joseph
might have liked a cup. I was thinking the coffee must be much
better here than on an army post in a war-torn Middle Eastern
country. But she hadn't bothered to offer any to anyone else, which
didn't seem all that surprising.

She stopped and shot me a look, and I ran up the stairs two at
a time without anything more needing to be said.

———

When things got weird at the dinner table, my little brother,
Aubrey, would focus on the chandelier. We had this enormous,
fancy chandelier with all these dangling pieces of cut glass that
caught the light like prisms. Or . . . well, I guess they *were* prisms.

I always wondered if it didn't hurt his eyes to stare up into
those lights. When I tried to do it, the bulbs burned these little
white spots into my eyes that I kept seeing for minutes after I
averted my gaze.

But Aubrey seemed to find something up there—something
he needed enough, I guess, to make it worth the sacrifice.

Usually dinner at our house was a stony silence. Sometimes it was broken up by weirdly generic and meaningless questions from my mom. Questions that, on the surface, reflected an interest in our lives, but if you were paying close enough attention, you might note that she sounded like she was reading lines from a memorized script.

And that was the tension, right there. That was the aspect of family dinners that was ruining my little brother's corneas—not what was said at dinner, but what wasn't. Or what was said but not deeply meant.

This dinner was different.

Joseph was stabbing his prime rib with his fork. Isabella, our housekeeper and cook, made terrific dinners. I had to imagine that the food on his plate was about a million times better than those premeasured army mess meals the taxpayers were paying Halliburton—or whoever was delivering meals at that point—to serve in the field. But Joseph had apparently lost his appetite but good.

He looked small to me, my big brother. Well, he *was* small. Bigger than I was, but small for a grown man. But that day he looked smaller than usual. Maybe even small compared to me.

The silence was so loud that it rang in my ears like noise. Then my father startled everybody with a hurled comment that sounded like the middle of a conversation, not the beginning of one. I swear, it didn't sound like the first sentence of anything.

"I just keep wondering what you were thinking, Joseph. How does a thing like this happen?"

Joseph opened his mouth to answer, but my father shouted him down.

"I don't want to hear a word from you! I've had quite enough of you for one day."

We were all smart enough not to point out that you shouldn't ask questions of someone if you don't want to hear a word from them.

Then all went quiet again for a long time, and my appetite started to go wherever Joseph's had gone.

"You won't be able to get a job!" my father shouted. "Nobody's going to hire you. How do you expect to make something of your life if you can't get hired anywhere?"

Joseph looked up at him briefly but said nothing, as instructed. Aubrey stared at the chandelier.

"I just want to know if you thought of that first. Did it occur to you that you were making a decision that could bring your whole life to a halt?"

Joseph set down his fork. It's not like it had been doing him much good anyway. "Am I supposed to answer that?"

Amazingly, our mom spoke up for the first time that meal. "Brad, the decision's been made. It's done. The time to ask these questions was before he did what he did. It's too late now."

"I know that!" my father bellowed. "Don't you think I know that?"

"But the point I'm making, Brad, is that it's not very useful to ask."

"Especially if you're not going to let him answer," I said.

It was brave, and it froze me, and everybody stared at me, which was unnerving. Even Aubrey looked away from the chandelier for a moment. I wondered if he saw white spots in front of my image.

I waited for my father to come at me—verbally, at least.

He never did.

He dug back into his prime rib. Literally, viciously, as if the meat had caused all this trouble. Whatever the trouble was.

My brother Joseph's gaze flickered up to me one more time. He had a look in his eyes as if he were staring up at me from the bottom of a very deep well. I'd say it was desperate, except desperation usually means you're trying to save yourself. Joseph was not trying to save himself. He had accepted his fate.

Whatever it was.

———

It was my job to do the dinner dishes—not because we didn't have the staff to cover such tasks, but because my father had strong opinions about instilling a work ethic in children. And I adored doing the dishes. That may sound strange, but picture this: At dinner, we were all forced together at the table. Then I was freed by a word from my dad, and I headed straight for the kitchen, had the whole room to myself, and then life was good again.

When I washed the dishes, I could always feel the stress rolling off me like chlorinated water when I jumped out of the pool.

Oh, I suppose I could have gone to my room and gotten the same silence there. But I didn't, because I couldn't, because it was my job to do dishes. And I guess the dishes had gotten all mixed up in my mind with the rolling-off of stress, so they were my friends, those soapy dishes.

After a while, Joseph came into the kitchen and leaned on the counter between the toaster and the espresso machine. His elbow was maybe five inches from mine, but he didn't look at me. He looked over the sink and out the kitchen window, and I couldn't tell whether he wanted to be with me or just didn't want to be with the rest of them.

I stopped washing. Moving. For a minute, I had to remind myself to breathe.

"Hey, Duck," he said.

I looked at the blond hair on his arm. It was hard to look at his face, his head, because it was so weird to see his hair military-short. Some people can pull off that look, but this was my brother Joseph. It made him look like some alien had come down to Earth as a

Joseph impersonator. Not only would he never voluntarily do that to his hair, it was hard to imagine he would ever go someplace where anyone would force it on him.

At least, the Joseph I'd always known.

I wanted to ask him, *What the hell happened?* Because there was a hole in the room the size and shape of that unbelievably obvious question, and I couldn't bear to leave it gaping open another second. But that would have been something like direct communication. I didn't have a lot of talent in that field at the time, probably because I had no experience and no real role models.

So what I said was, "Why did you take a cab? From the . . . I don't know. Airport or bus. Or train or whatever. Why a cab?"

He still didn't look at me. He said, to the window, "Uh . . . to get home?"

"Why not call Mom?"

"I did."

"She wouldn't come?"

"She was in the middle of her book group. The ladies who lunch were here."

"But this . . . I mean . . . it just seems kind of big."

"It was her turn to host. You know how she feels about social responsibility."

That was a private joke between us. When most people use that term, they mean some kind of progressive societal awareness. Joseph used it with our mom as a way of suggesting that her number-one priority is looking good in front of the ladies in her social circle.

"Still," I said, unsure how to finish making my point, and also vaguely aware that I shouldn't need to.

"Duck," he said, "it's Janet."

He'd been calling our mom "Janet" since he was eighteen. He'd been calling me "Duck" since I was a baby, and nobody remembered where it came from. Lots of people have nicknames that they earned somehow as babies, but there's always a family story about why. So I think it says a lot that nobody bothered to remember, like our family history was never worth recording.

"Joseph, what happened?" I asked, surprising myself. Surprising us both, I think.

A long pause.

"Something not very cut-and-dried," he said. Then he paused again. "Something people won't quite be sure what to make of. And so now you'll get to watch people turn themselves inside out to try to make it into something very simple. Very black and white."

I wanted to ask him what that meant. Also why people would do that. But my first question seemed a little nosy, even to me. He'd obviously already told me as much as he wanted to tell.

People think if somebody's in your blood family, then you know them well enough to ask anything, but some families know each other better than others. We were mostly boundaries, with not a lot of permission to cross. Approaches were always handled with great caution, and the applications to do so took an abnormally long time to process.

As to the second question, well . . . it's one thing to know what you think people will do next. It's another to know why anybody does anything. It's always easier to know the "what" than the "why."

"I missed you, Duck," Joseph said.

It was such a rare blast of affection from anyone in the house that it left me unable to speak.

———

The thing I'll always remember best about that time is not how quickly our family fell apart. The memorable bit was when I first looked back at how we'd convinced ourselves we'd ever been together in the first place.

Chapter Two: Aubrey

———————

I always broke the stereotype of an astronomer, I think. Even as a boy wannabe. Actually, I guess it would be more accurate to say that's what everybody else thinks. Somehow astronomers have been typecast as mild mannered. Usually wearing those thoughtful-looking half glasses. But I never thought of having a hot temper and being fascinated by space as mutually exclusive. I think people watch too many movies.

I'm not meaning to stray off track. My temper is relevant. Because the day Joseph came home happened to have been a day I was sent home from school early for fighting.

Fighting is an exaggeration.

Actually, so is home. Because, although I left school with a note for my parents, I didn't go home. At least, not for many hours. I skulked around town, keeping a low profile, burning with shame, the note a presence in my pocket I could psychically feel. It was hot and heavy and irritating. It meant my father would disapprove of me even more than he already did. And rather than dismiss it as unrealistic expectations on his part, I would have to admit he had a point.

Not that I would have put it in those words at the time. But it all seems quite obvious, looking back.

All I did was push Greg Butterfield. Well, hard. Well. What I did exactly, in detail, was to hit him in the chest with the heels of both my hands, hard enough that he stumbled backward and slammed into a handful of other people in the crowded hall.

What will forever be lost in the telling is what he'd done to incite it.

He had been taunting me. And taunting me. And taunting me. Because I was small, and because my name is Aubrey. But of course he called me "Audrey."

To this very day, I wonder why, when a man wants to insult another man, he calls him a woman or a girl. Now that I'm grown, I notice that these are guys with wives and girlfriends and daughters. Don't they see what they're saying?

I'm getting off track again.

Greg had raised the taunting right up to my boiling point. He must have known where that was, too. Because his timing was flawless. At that boiling moment, he reached out and grabbed a big piece of the skin at my waist. Right through my T-shirt. And pinched and twisted.

Adding a sudden and unexpected stab of pain to my rage at that boil-over moment was too much. I couldn't be responsible for my actions after that. It was wrong for anybody to expect me to try.

Once I was watching a football game with my father, and he told me that the referee will always catch the second bit of unsportsmanlike conduct. You know. When the play is over, and one guy takes a swing at another. And the guy swings back. The ref always sees the second infraction.

This little story I just recounted is amazing not so much because I actually learned something from my father that proved useful. Although that, too. But more because we were sitting watching a football game together. Like a regular bonded father and son.

I must have been very little, is all I can say. Either that or I'm remembering wrong. Maybe I was hanging in a doorway, listening to him yell at the screen. Maybe I was only wishing I was sitting and sharing the moment with him.

Yeah. That's a much better fit with everything else in my young life, isn't it? What was I thinking with that other '50s sitcom thing?

———

When I finally slunk through the door, I saw that Joseph was home. Sitting on the couch between Brad and Janet. Nobody noticed me for a long time.

My jaw went down. My heart rate went up. Took off like my heart wanted to fly away.

It didn't stay up long, though.

The story of my family: Everything that takes flight will be shot down. You need only soar to draw antiaircraft fire. It was the law.

———

After dinner, once the evening had worn on, Joseph was bedded down in the basement. The rollaway bed was rolled away, and sheets and blankets put down. It wasn't exactly a dungeon in the basement. More like a rec room. Probably nicer than some people's apartments. But it had a dungeonlike feel to it. You know. Being banished to "below." Like a judgment call between heaven and hell.

Not that upstairs was heaven by any means.

The excuse was that Joseph's bedroom had been turned into a reading room/den/library for our dad. Well, Ruth's and my dad, Brad. Brad wasn't Joseph's dad, which might have been part of the problem. There was so much complexity to the problems, though. It's really hard to look back and say.

The funny part of Brad in a reading room is that Brad didn't read. Legal briefs, maybe. But I expect he farmed even those off to subordinates. What Brad did was smoke. Not cigarettes, but cigars and pipes. And Janet couldn't stand the smell of it. Never could. So the reading room was really a smoking room with an overly noble misnomer of a label. But whatever you called it, no way Brad was giving it up.

Especially not for a soldier who had no business being home.

It wasn't until years later that I realized we had a guest room that Joseph could have used. Not that I forgot we had it. I just never realized it would have solved everything. As far as I know, there was never any talk of letting Joseph use it. So maybe there was more to the Dungeon of Hell theory than I first thought.

Before bed, I wandered down to the basement. Well, maybe "wandered" is not the right word. Crept? I instinctively knew I didn't want to get caught. I was only going down to talk to my big brother, who'd been away fighting a war. Why it should have been a crime . . . Well. I didn't know any of the details then. I just knew I'd get yelled at, even swatted. Joseph was at the very least in purgatory. The last thing my parents wanted was a messenger of love to his quarters.

He'd moved the Ping-Pong table closer to the wall and folded out the big leather sleeper sofa. He was lying on its queen-size mattress. Propped up with pillows. Hands laced behind his head. Staring off into nothing.

Then he heard the light shush of the legs of my jeans rubbing against each other as I came down the stairs. He looked up at me and smiled. It was a genuine smile. It spread out in my gut like a hot drink on a snowy day. It glowed inside my chest and low belly. It was the polar opposite of being called "Audrey" and then pinched too hard.

"Mr. Universe," he said.

I hope there's no need to explain why he called me that. God knows it wasn't because I was huge and muscle-bound.

I walked over too carefully. As if the rec room were mined. I sat on the edge of the bed and tried to return the smile. I don't think it worked out.

"I'm so glad you're back," I said.

Joseph snorted a laugh. "That makes one of you," he said.

"Why are you back so soon, though?"

"I'm waiting to see what they—"

He never got the chance to finish his answer. I heard big heavy footsteps on the basement stairs. In a rush of panic, I dove under the bed.

I curled there, a little shaky, for what felt like too long a time. Nothing moved. Nobody spoke.

Then I heard Joseph, right over my left ear. He said, "Say what you came to say, Brad."

I winced, expecting the same bluster we'd heard from my dad at dinner. Instead, he spoke in a voice that was barely over a whisper. "I just want you to know that you haven't only shamed yourself, you've cast a shadow on this entire family. You've shamed us all. I just thought you should think about that."

Then I heard him clomp back up the stairs.

I waited under there far too long. Not daring to stick my head out again.

"He's gone," Joseph said.

I wiggled out and pulled up into a sit.

"Thanks for coming down here," he said.

"I better go to bed now."

I jumped up and scrambled for the stairs. Like a coward. Like exactly what I hate the most. What I try hardest never to be.

Before I could get out of that rec room, Joseph said, "I missed you, Mr. Universe."

I stopped dead. Frozen. I wanted to say, "I missed you, too, Joseph." I opened my mouth. I swear I thought that's what would come out. I was surprised when all I said was, "You did?"

"Yeah," he said.

"Thanks," I said, and ran for the stairs again.

As I made my way back to my room, I wondered if it was true that Joseph had shamed all of us. I didn't figure it was. Because I didn't feel shamed.

I didn't know how short that reprieve would be.

That's when I remembered I had a note from the principal. And I hadn't shown it to my parents. And I damn well wasn't going to. Not that night, anyway.

These were extenuating circumstances, whether the powers that be at school understood or not.

———

I woke up at about eleven p.m. with Joseph in my room. Which was not something that had ever happened before. So I responded with fear. An icy, cutting little ball of it wedged into my gut. Though there was no real reason why I should have been afraid of my brother.

Maybe I was afraid of what he'd come to say.

I sat partway up in bed, holding the blankets against my chest with one arm. I'm not sure why.

He was leaning his forearms on my dresser, spinning the little planets on the mobile solar system that lived there. It spun around on a base. Well, not spun all on its own. It waited for someone like Joseph to come along and spin it.

It wasn't the only solar system in the room. There was a much more elaborate system overhead. So I guess it was redundant. But I was definitely into more space-related stuff than necessary. My view on life in general, I think, was that anything would have been better than not enough.

Now that I think about it, that might have been my approach to all of life. It might still be.

"Joseph," I said.

He glanced over his shoulder at me and said nothing.

It was dark, of course. But not too dark to see him. My room was on the second floor. And we were the only two-story house on the block, so no one could look in. So I never kept my curtains drawn. I left them open to look up at the stars. At least, those few that could overpower the light pollution of the Orange County suburbs. The moon was three days waning. Its light seeped through the window. Enough that I could see my brother turn his face to me. Not enough that I could make out his expression or the look in his eyes.

"Why are you in my room?" I asked him.

He didn't answer for several beats. Then he said, "Is it not okay?"

"I'm not saying you can't. Just . . . you know. You never did before."

Another painfully long silence.

I was tempted to fill it. I didn't give in to that temptation.

"I . . . ," he began. Then he stalled again, for many seconds. "I know you heard what Brad said. I felt bad about it. You know. You all huddled under the bed listening to him say a thing like that. Not that it's very surprising coming from Brad. But I just wanted to make sure . . ." Another brief stall. " . . . that you didn't feel the same. Like he obviously does. Like I shamed you. I don't want you to be ashamed of what I did."

"I don't even know what you did."

Joseph sighed. The sigh seemed to collapse part of him. The area around his chest and shoulders. The part that should have held air, or at least been supported by a couple of lungfuls of it.

He pulled away from the dresser. Came and sat on the edge of my bed.

"I refused to go out on a raid," he said.

"Oh," I said. When he didn't go on, I asked, "Can you do that?"

"No," he said. "You can't." Then he laughed. But not the way people laugh when something's genuinely funny. "Well, of course you *can*. I mean, nobody can stop you from doing what you're going to do. But it's highly discouraged. And that's putting it . . . Well. That's understating the case so much it's almost funny. They make sure there's a high price to pay for not obeying a direct order. But if you're willing to pay it . . . I guess I was willing to pay it. I guess whatever legal action they had in store for me suddenly seemed like the less bad thing. Of two very bad things."

I held the blanket even tighter to my chest. Felt the cold blades of fear slice my gut more deeply.

"So they're going to discharge you?"

"Yeah."

"But you got to come home. So that doesn't seem so bad."

"Except it won't be an honorable discharge. Obviously."

"But if that's all they can do to you . . ."

But the minute I said it, I had a bad feeling it wasn't.

"It isn't. They can also court-martial me."

"Are they going to?"

"Not sure. There's an investigation going on. Depends on what turns that takes. What kind of stuff comes out."

"And if they do . . . Then what? What could they do to you?"

"Let's cross that bridge when we come to it," he said. "*If* we come to it."

We both sat for a moment, not saying anything. Over and behind my brother's head, I could see my miniature patch of the universe. It looked like a view of actual space travel in the dark. Which was the point. I tried to look at it the way I usually did. Like I was an astronaut flying out into infinity. Feeling tiny in comparison to the cosmos around me. I thought it would make the problem in front of me seem fleeting and small.

It didn't.

"Why didn't you go out on the raid?"

"Because I didn't think it was the right thing to do. Going into people's homes in the middle of the night. Hauling families out into their front yards at gunpoint. I won't go into a lot of detail, but if you can imagine a bunch of soldiers breaking through our door right now and doing the same to us . . . Let's just say it was a very bad experience for everybody."

"But they did something wrong, right? What did the people do?"

"Sometimes nothing. We were looking for insurgents."

"Insurgents?"

"Rebels. People who wanted to fight us back. But part of the time, nobody in the house had done anything wrong at all. Anyway, it was a lot more complicated than just that. And I'm not going to dump it all on you, because I want you to get back to sleep. But I wanted you to know that I did what I did for a reason. I did what I thought was right. I don't want you to be ashamed of me."

"I'm not," I said.

He sat a minute. Maybe taking that in. Then he rose to his feet.

"I'm glad," he said. And moved toward my bedroom door. "I know you look up to me." Then he seemed to scramble to verbally walk back a statement that hadn't come out right the first time. "I'm not saying you *should* or anything. I know I'm no hero. But me being ten years older and everything. I guess it's kind of inevitable."

"You're only nine years older."

"Aren't you twelve?"

"No. I'm thirteen."

"Oh. I missed a birthday while I was gone, huh?"

"Yeah."

"Sorry. I should have called."

"It's okay," I said. Which was, at least on an emotional level, a lie. "You were busy."

"Even if I'd remembered, I still would have thought it was your twelfth."

I had no idea what to say to that. So I said nothing.

He moved toward the door again. Put his hand on the knob.

"Joseph," I said. And he turned back. Waiting for it. "If you thought it was wrong, what they asked you to do, then I think it was wrong, too."

"You don't know the whole story yet."

"I know *you*, though."

He paused for a time with his hand on the knob.

Then he said, "Thanks. Now go back to sleep."

And with that he was gone.

I didn't go back to sleep. At least, not until nearly morning.

———

At school the next day, I got an early glimpse of what would follow. What our lives would be like in the foreseeable future. It was small. It wasn't dramatic. But if I had been looking for clues, it would have been a good one.

I walked into the principal's office to explain why I hadn't given my parents the note.

She looked up from her desk. From a sheaf of papers she was scribbling on—writing in the margins, in blue pencil. Her eyes changed when she saw me. I can't describe exactly how.

I held up the note.

"I didn't show them this," I said.

"Don't worry about it," she said.

I thought I must have heard her wrong.

"I'm sorry?"

"Don't worry about it. I heard about . . . what your family's dealing with. It's a hard time over at your house. So I'll overlook the acting out. This time. And this time only."

With a tipping of her head she indicated the wastepaper basket beside her desk.

I put the note in it. Gently. As though it were fragile.

Then I walked out.

Of course, I hadn't known anything about Joseph coming home when I "acted out."

But what kind of fool would bring that up when he could just walk out of trouble? Just walk away.

Chapter Three: Ruth

The day after Joseph came home, I walked through our gate to find a stranger sitting in the sun on our blindingly white porch swing. He was wearing khaki pants and a khaki bag—like a messenger bag—slung across his chest. He was staring at an electronic device in his hands, some kind of Blackberry, I think.

Suddenly I wished Aubrey had gotten home first instead of me. I was all the way up on the porch boards before he looked up.

He wasn't too old. I mean, over thirty, but not old like my parents. But his hairline was already receding sharply above both temples, and you could tell he would be one of those guys with nothing but a ring of hair over his ears by and by.

He narrowed his eyes when he looked at me. I told myself it was just the sun making him squint, but to this very day I'm not sure that's true.

"Hello," I said, awkwardly, because he wasn't saying anything, awkwardly or otherwise.

"Are you related to Joseph Stellkellner?"

"I'm his sister."

"Are either of your parents home?"

"I doubt it."

"You should get him to talk to me."

"Why should I get him to do that?"

"Because I'm going to run this story in the paper one way or the other. And if I have to print accusations like this and then say I contacted your brother and he had no comment, that's not going to look so good. He needs to get ahead of a thing like this, or it can get real ugly real fast."

I sighed hard, brushed my bangs out of my eyes, and put on a prickly, irritated attitude, but it was all a big fake. Really I was scared.

"I just got home from school," I said, in an attempt to deflect him. "I don't know why you're telling me all this stuff like I know the beginning of this . . . whatever this is. What story? What accusations?"

He flipped his head in the direction of the house. "Your brother knows," he said.

That feeling of fear intensified. This time it felt like cold water running down the insides of my thighs. I think I was silent too long. I think I tipped my hand on the fear.

"Have you got a card?" I asked him at last. "I can talk to him, but I can't make him do anything he doesn't want to do. If I can get him to change his mind, or if he changes his mind on his own, he can always call you."

He rummaged around in his khaki bag for what seemed like a long time. I gathered that things weren't too organized in there. In time he brought out a card case that looked like sterling silver, which did not match him and his bag and his khaki pants and his faded polo shirt at all. He opened it and handed me a card.

I stared at it for a long time, but I'm not sure where my mind was, because thirty seconds later I couldn't have told you the guy's name. I could have told you the paper was the *Register*, but we only had the one around here. I mean, one *real* paper. We had that giveaway tabloid-size one that my dad said was left-wing propaganda, and some other lesser things, but only one actual newspaper that somebody would throw at the end of your driveway in the morning.

When I looked up, the reporter was on his feet, his chest not five inches from my left shoulder. I felt intimidated because he leaned in so close. Probably that was the point.

"You tell your brother he definitely wants to take this opportunity to tell his side of the story."

Then he stepped off my porch and headed down the walkway to the gate. I didn't turn around, but he was wearing big boots with heavy heels, and I could hear every step of his retreat.

I exhaled a breath I didn't know I'd been holding.

———

I didn't find Joseph in the basement, so I kept looking.

Finally I found him in my dad's reading room. He was sitting in the big leather chair by the window, looking out over the street. It was my dad's special chair, which nobody else was allowed to sit in, and the fact that he always kept it pulled over to the window should have been everybody's clue that he spent more time staring out into space than reading.

Joseph was smoking a cigarette, which made me deeply uneasy, because it seemed against the laws of the house itself.

He had his knees drawn up to his chest, his sock feet tucked up against his butt on the leather seat of the chair. The hand that held the cigarette was gently exploring his head, mostly around one temple, barely touching skin, as if he desperately needed to touch his own head but couldn't bring himself to do it.

"You okay?" I asked him.

He looked up at me, and his eyes seemed hollow. Almost not alive. His left eye twitched repeatedly, which made my own eyes water for reasons I couldn't quite find my way around in.

"Migraine," he said. "I need a little space. No offense, Duck."

"I'm not sure Dad—"

"Is this where you tell me there's no tobacco smoke allowed in this room? That's a joke, don't you think?"

"But when he does it himself, that's different."

"Used to be my room, don't forget. So he talked to you, too."

"Dad?"

"You know what I mean."

I hadn't, but I caught up fast.

"Oh. That reporter. Yeah. I have his card. You know. In case you change your mind and want to talk to him."

"I don't."

"But if you change your mind."

"I won't."

"He says he's going to run the story one way or the other, and that it's better for you to tell your side. He says you have to get in front of a thing like this or it gets really ugly really fast. But he didn't say what kind of a thing it is. He just said, 'Your brother knows.'"

A long enough silence that I thought the conversation might be over, that I might just have to slink out and leave him alone. Which, come to think, he'd asked of me the minute I walked into the room.

Then he said, "Let's hope he's bluffing."

"What story?" I asked, even though part of me knew better, knew he didn't want me to.

"Please, Duck. I'm begging you here."

I quietly let myself out of the room.

That was the beginning, right in that moment, of the chronic heartburn and other digestive problems that would plague me for years. It felt unfamiliar at the time. Within days it would feel like my most steadfast companion.

Not two minutes later, I heard the front door softly open and close. I'm not sure how I knew it was something out of the ordinary, but I did. Maybe just because everything was, everything had been, since Joseph came home.

I went downstairs to see who was around. No one. So it must not have been anyone coming in—it must have been Joseph going out.

It would be the last I saw of my brother for longer than I could possibly have imagined at the time.

———

In the morning, after my mom dropped me at school, I waited until she drove away and then walked to the corner and bought a morning paper, a *Register*, out of one of those automated racks. I plowed through it on the way back to school, then spread it out on the concrete steps and kept plowing.

The bell rang, making me late, but I explored every page, even the sports section and the movie listings. There was no story about my brother.

I threw the newspaper in the trash on my way inside, with a deep conviction that the threat had passed, that there was no story, only a bluff, that Joseph had dodged a bullet, though it felt more like I'd dodged one myself.

There's an art to not taking these things personally. I still haven't perfected it. I hadn't even scratched the surface at age fifteen.

Waiting outside that conviction was the sure knowledge that not every story makes it into the paper the very next day after the reporter stands on your porch. I knew it was there but I refused to acknowledge its existence.

I think I was peripherally aware of exactly what I was doing.

I was buying myself one more day.

———

The following morning I showed up in homeroom, the fourth or fifth person to arrive. Mrs. Blankenship looked up immediately and met my eyes with a look I couldn't possibly understand. I can only say that nobody had ever looked at me with that exact set of emotions showing in their eyes before. I can only describe it by saying she seemed to view me as an unstable nuclear weapon, but one she felt deeply sorry for.

She silently called me up to the front of the room with the motion of one bent index finger.

My blood froze, and I almost couldn't feel myself making the walk. The desks on either side of me registered in my peripheral vision as I moved by them, but they looked blurred. My whole life suddenly suffered from too much depth of field.

I stood in front of her desk with my textbooks held in front of my gut like a shield.

"You okay today?" she asked.

"Sure," I said. "Why wouldn't I be?"

I watched through her eyes as she backed out of the whole moment in her brain, like watching one of those big construction trucks try to take all that bulk into reverse gear. All that was missing was the irritating beeping noise.

"No reason," she said. "No reason at all."

"Okay then," I said.

I walked back to my desk again, feeling numb. Everything tingled slightly. You know how your foot feels when you cut off the circulation to it by sitting the wrong way? Numb and dead but tingling at the same time? Like that. My whole body—my whole self—had gone to sleep.

I sat at my desk for a minute, or it might have been a second, or it might have been ten minutes. I wasn't looking at the clock and it was hard to tell.

Then I walked back up to Mrs. Blankenship's desk.

"Do you still have the newspaper?" I asked.

"No," she said quietly. "I mean, not right here with me I don't. I left it out in my car."

"Maybe you can just tell me the gist of it. Because now I really feel like I need to get this over with."

She looked past me to the kids filling up the room. I'd forgotten they were still coming in while I hadn't been able to notice. I looked around, too, and saw that we were standing in a crowd now. Thirty-five students or so.

The bell rang.

Mrs. Blankenship tossed her head in the direction of the hall, so I walked out into it. For a minute or two she didn't, and I wondered if I'd been wrong to expect that she would. I also wondered what I was supposed to do next.

Then she was there, closing the classroom door behind her.

She never once met my eyes.

"I hate to be the one to have to tell you," she said.

I want to report that I had a reaction to those words, but the truth is that I was fresh out of reactions. I was at the bottom of the reaction well, with no more options beneath me.

"But you just have to, though," I said, "because when you know something is that bad, it's torture to have to wait."

She raised her eyes to my face and smiled sadly, but I couldn't help noting that her gaze landed more or less on my nose.

"I understand," she said.

But then she didn't say anything for a torturous length of time. I think at the time I might truly have believed she was trying to torture me. Now I look back and see that it was hard for her, too.

"Could you please . . ."

"Somebody who fought in the war with your brother is saying some things anonymously. Somebody got in touch with the reporter. With a lot of people, I guess. Anyone who'll listen. He says your brother didn't just fail to show up for duty one night. He's saying Joseph talked several other soldiers out of going. So he thinks Joseph should be charged with mutiny."

I'm not sure if there was a silence while the word "mutiny" rang in my head, or if I simply missed something else she was saying. I tried to think what I knew about the word. It made me picture men on a ship dueling with their captain, swords drawn, but I knew I would have to find out what it meant in real modern life.

"They had to go out on a raid four men short," she added. "And two men in their unit were killed."

I found a new level at the bottom of the reaction well.

"How does he know they wouldn't have been anyway?"

"That's a good question," she said. "An important question. I guess we don't know, and maybe we never really will. But he's saying that when a unit loses men it's hard on morale, and it throws off the whole way they've been trained to operate. So he's making a strong case for the two things being related. But he can't prove it all by himself. It's something the army will have to investigate. They'll decide if one was a direct result of the other. And outside the army, well . . . people are going to have to decide for themselves, I guess."

"Oh," I said. "Okay. Well. People will see that it could have happened anyway, right? I mean, they'll look at both sides." I waited for her to assure me. She must not have known how desperately I needed that worldview confirmed. "People will be fair, right?"

More silence.

Then she said, "Some will. I'm sorry to have to have been the one to tell you. Also I hate to tell you it's time to go in and sit down now, but you know it is."

"No," I said. "I'm going home."

"You need to go to the office and get permission."

"No," I said again. "I'm just going."

"If you're not feeling well—"

"I'm not."

"You have to go to the nurse first."

"No. I'm just leaving."

And I did. I walked down the hall without looking back. Down two flights of stairs and out into a cold and bright morning that felt unfairly unchanged. I was outraged at how unaffected the world seemed to be, and with seemingly no sense of apology, either.

I knew no one would stop me, and no one did. I knew I would never be taken to task later for the desertion, and I was right.

At the very bottom of human experience comes a set of certain privileges, a special zone where the rules apply to everyone else except you. It was good of the world to build itself that way, and include that tiny consolation prize for those who have nothing else to recommend their lives in that moment.

The trick, I've found as the years go by, is not to get addicted to that feeling. It would be easy enough to do. It can be used like a Get Out of Jail Free card, because the universe has just skewered us right through our core and put us over the coals to roast, so it's unthinkable for anyone to expect anything from us in that moment.

Anything that lifts responsibility for our actions is addictive, I've found.

So really, looking back, I'd have to say that was not the hard moment. The tough bit is always later, when you're held responsible for yourself again, and your life is expected to go on.

Chapter Four: Aubrey

I'll say one thing in favor of the other thirteen-year-old boys I went to school with. It may be the only positive thing I have. They didn't read the morning paper. So I went through first period and half of second not knowing anything was wrong.

Then my science teacher's phone rang. Not his personal phone. Not his cell. The one on the wall. The one that links the office to the various classrooms.

He stepped away from the board, answered it. A second or two later, he looked straight at me.

Does it go without saying that this is never a good sign?

He nodded, but not to me. Which seemed weird. Who nods into a phone? Then he hung up, and looked right at me again.

"Aubrey," he said. "You're wanted in the office."

A murmur of low noise from the other kids. A reaction to the trouble I must be in. There's a special noise kids make, like the word "ooh," but with more inflection. More attitude. It sounds like taunting. Only in recent years have I decided they might just have been letting off tension. You know. From that moment when they didn't know for sure the trouble wasn't theirs.

"What'd *I* do?" I yelled out.

It was reflexive. Instinctual.

I'd been in trouble so recently, but the principal had let me off the hook. Was she allowed to put me right back on?

"Nothing," he said. "It's not like that. Your mom's coming to pick you up. She needs to take you out of school early."

I must have risen to my feet. Or partway there, anyway. Because I was surprised when my thighs hit the bottom of the desk. I guess I wasn't clear on what my body was doing.

"Why?"

"She didn't say. Just go down there and find out, okay?"

On the way to the office, I busied myself thinking up reasons why my mom might take me out of school in the middle of the day. Which, of course, she never had before.

Dad had had a heart attack. One of our distant relatives had died. Ruth was sick, though I'm not sure what that would have to do with me finishing out the school day. They'd found out about something I'd done, and now I was in trouble. There had been a bomb threat or a gun at school, but why would she be the first to know?

Farther down, in the part of my gut that's better left alone, I think I knew it probably had something to do with Joseph. Everything did in those days.

———

"What do you *mean* you don't know where my daughter is?"

My mom was in the office, at the counter, yelling at the staff. I was in the corner, on the farthest possible bench. Trying to disappear.

Those who haven't been in school for years may have forgotten the piercing and utter humiliation of almost anything your mother does there. Even if it's marginally acceptable by adult standards. I haven't been in school for years. University and graduate school not counting. And yet I remember.

I couldn't hear the answer, because the only one yelling was my mom.

"So you're saying you misplaced her."

Inaudible answer.

"Well, isn't it your job to know?"

Inaudible answer.

"This is completely unacceptable."

Then she stormed out of the office and into the hall. I swear I thought she'd forgotten all about me.

A few seconds later, she stuck her head back in.

"Aubrey!" she barked.

And yet I was the one who followed like a dog.

————

We drove for three or four blocks in absolute silence.

Then I said, "Are you *ever* going to tell me what's going on?"

"There was an article in the paper."

"So? There are articles in the paper every day."

"Not about our family, there aren't."

"What did it say about us?" I noticed I didn't sound scared. Not at all. Which is interesting. Because I was.

"It was about your brother. And it was very critical."

"That doesn't make sense."

"Why doesn't it?"

"Why do I get to leave school just because someone criticized Joseph?"

"You'll see when we get home. There are newspeople. Reporters."

"At the house?"

"Yes, Aubrey. Where else?"

"Then isn't that the last place we want to be?"

She sighed. Obviously quite taxed to have to talk to me. To be fair to her, she was having a horrible day. To be fair to me, so was I.

"Our house is private property. They can't step over our property line. Your dad made that very clear. So that's safer. We didn't want those vultures surrounding you or Ruth on the way home from school."

"Dad's home?"

"He *was*."

"Why was he not at the office?"

"Oh good heavens, Aubrey, must you ask so many questions? At least stick to the ones you can't figure out on your own. Please. Obviously he was home because of this—"

I was waiting anxiously to hear what "this" entailed. But I never got to find out. I mean, only later. When I got to find out the hard way.

"*There's* your sister!" she practically shouted.

I looked where our mom was pointing and saw Ruth walking along the sidewalk, her back to us. Looking dark and mad. Yeah, I know. I couldn't see her face. But it radiated from her body language. It hung over her like a cloud. Like that messy kid from the cartoons whose dirt surrounds him in the air every place he goes.

Mom pulled the car over to the curb and powered down the passenger window, bumping my elbow away. It had been leaning on the glass.

"Ruth! Where on earth are you going?"

"Home," Ruth said. Without stopping. Without turning around.

"Get in! Now!"

Ruth stopped. Sighed deeply. I could see her shoulders lift up with the sigh, then collapse.

She got into the front, right beside me. Forcing me over closer to Mom on the bench seat of our big Mercedes. I wished she'd gotten in the back. Not that I had anything against my sister. But that's a lot of people in a small space.

Ruth slammed the door much too hard.

"I have no idea how you knew I wanted you home," our mom said, "but fine."

A few silent blocks. Then we pulled around the corner and our house came into view.

There was a news van parked out front. The kind with the satellite receiver on top and the name of the station painted on the side. It was the local NBC affiliate. Don't ask me why that stuck in my mind. Another three or four cars sat near the curb, all unfamiliar. Nobody ever parked on the street in our neighborhood. We had garages. Big garages. Our parents would have been humiliated to have a garage too small for their multiple vehicles.

About half a dozen people milled around on the sidewalk in front of our gate. One man had a big video camera on his shoulder. A woman in a jewel-tone violet suit held a microphone.

I was stunned by what felt like a lot of news traffic. Three or four days later, I would look back at that day and view it as so close to silence and peace that I would feel nostalgia for the moment.

All six people surrounded us as my mom turned into the driveway. They stood much too close, considering the car was still moving. The man with the camera filmed us pulling in. I couldn't understand why anyone would want video footage of us arriving home. The others hovered close to our windows as she slowed down to make the turn. They asked questions I couldn't make out because they were all talking at once.

My mom powered down her driver's window and was rewarded with a microphone in her face.

"I will run you down," my mom said. Her voice was so calm, so even. It was genuinely scary. "I swear. You stay twenty or thirty feet back from this car or I swear I'll run you over. I'll say it was an accident. That there were so many of you I couldn't avoid hitting at least one. Got that? Don't test me."

Six people backed up fast.

The garage door powered up, and we pulled in. My mom hit the remote to roll the door back down. The world went dark.

"Wait," my mom said, and turned off the engine. Then the world went silent as well. "Don't move yet."

We didn't.

"I don't want you to say even a word to those snakes. If they have the nerve to get close to you, you say 'No comment.' That's *all* you say. You don't tell them what jackals you think they are. You don't defend your brother. You say 'No comment.' That's all. Whatever you say, they'll use it against you."

"Like if you threaten to run them down with your car?" Ruth asked. "They might use that against you?"

She was mad, my sister. And when Ruth was mad, she ran to sarcasm.

"Exactly. That's exactly what I'm trying to tell you, Ruth. Don't make the mistake I just made. Now I'll probably be on the news tonight, threatening them. And we'll just look like a horrible family."

"So you're telling us to do as you say, not as you do."

"I'm telling you to learn from my mistake."

And with that, even my sister, Ruth, shut up.

———

I looked for Joseph everywhere. In every room of the house. He hadn't been at dinner the night before. In fact, I hadn't seen him since I found him in my room in the middle of that first night. And yet it never occurred to me he might be gone for good.

Not only did I not find him, but the basement was free of any Joseph belongings. His big duffel bag, his hanging shirts. Gone. Even the little bathroom off the rec room was cleared. No toothbrush. No shaving cream. No comb.

I found my mom upstairs, in the kitchen. Drinking coffee. Looking out at the intruders on the sidewalk through the filmy curtain. As if she could keep herself safe by watching their every move.

"Where is he?" I asked.

"Your dad? I think he finally went into the office."

"No. Joseph."

"Oh. Joseph. He's gone."

"Gone where?"

"I wouldn't know, Aubrey. Your father went downstairs to tell him to pack up and get out, but he already had."

"When's he coming back?"

"He's not. Not if your father has anything to say about it. And he does."

"Well, how am I supposed to talk to him if I don't know where he is?"

"You're *not*. You're *not* supposed to talk to him. Your father would have a coronary if he thought you were in touch with your brother. He's no longer part of this family."

I tried to answer that. Nothing happened. No words came.

I stomped out into the backyard. Bent down and picked up the biggest pieces of gravel in the trim around the flower beds and hurled them one by one at the trunk of the giant oak tree.

After ten or twelve good hits, it came to me. What I wanted to say.

I stomped back inside. My mother hadn't moved. Hadn't so much as changed position or expression.

"If I do something you don't like, am I out of the family, too?"

"Don't be ridiculous, Aubrey."

"Why is it ridiculous?"

"Because you're a minor. A child. Joseph is a grown man."

"So? We're still his family. And he didn't do anything bad enough to get kicked out."

My mother took her gaze off the street for the first time. Leveled it on me. Then I immediately wished I'd never started with her.

"Didn't he? Getting two of his fellow soldiers killed with his selfishness? You don't think that's such a bad thing?"

As she finished the last sentence, I was vaguely aware that I was backing up. Then I hit the big stainless steel fridge with my shoulder blades. I turned and ran up the carpeted stairs two at a time.

———

I opened the door to Ruth's room. She was on her bed. Staring at the ceiling.

"Knock, will you?" she said.

"Sorry. Did Joseph do what Mom says he did?"

"Did she say he got two guys killed?"

"Yeah."

"Well, that's what they're saying, anyway. That's what it says in the paper. I don't know if it's true."

I stood still a moment. Unsure what to do next. Then I walked closer to her. Sat on the edge of her bed.

"What are you doing?" she asked.

"I don't know what we're supposed to do."

"Nothing, I guess. What *can* we do? Nothing we do will make any difference, anyway."

"Joseph's gone. I guess he ran away. But even if he hadn't, Dad would've thrown him out. So how will we find out if it's true?"

"I guess we won't."

"But I have to *know*, Ruth. I have to."

"I don't know what to tell you," she said.

I wanted to ask her more questions. Dozens more. I wanted someone to tell me not only what the paper was saying happened, but what really happened. So I could judge for myself if they were treating us fairly. I wanted to know if the fact that my parents no longer considered Joseph their son meant that I could no longer have him for a brother. And, if so, what I was going to do without him.

I didn't ask anything. Because it struck me, in a sudden wave of helplessness, that my sister had nothing for me. Or even for herself. She was as lost as I was.

I let myself out of her room. Shut the door behind me. I decided I would find the morning paper.

I looked everywhere except the kitchen. I really wanted to avoid the kitchen.

———

"What are you doing out there, Aubrey?" my mom called out after a time.

"Looking for the paper."

"Don't bother. Your father burned it in the fireplace."

"Can I walk to the store and get one?" Later, I would realize that the paper could have been accessed online. But it hadn't been available that way for long. And before this incident I could not have cared less about accessing the paper in any medium. So at the time it didn't even occur to me.

"Is that a joke?"

"No. Why would that be funny?"

I stuck my head into the kitchen to better gauge her mood. She was leaning her forehead into one hand. When she lifted her head to look at me, her mascara was running. It jolted me. I had never seen my mom cry. It had never even occurred to me that she did. Ever.

"How are you going to get past that gang of vultures, Aubrey? Use your head."

"Oh. Right."

I ran back upstairs to my room. I turned on the TV that hung on a raised platform on the wall over my bed. Thinking I could get lost in something. I had a bunch of good shows digitally recorded.

An hour later, I couldn't have told you a line from any of them. I couldn't even have told you what show I'd just watched.

———

Later, I watched the news. I was relieved when there was no footage of my mom threatening to run anybody over with her car. Nothing about our family at all. I knew it wouldn't last. I felt better all the same.

———

Dinner was pizza. We never ordered pizza. That's when I realized that Isabella wasn't around. And that in all the confusion, I hadn't even noticed. I hadn't even thought to miss her.

We were encouraged to take our slices to our rooms to eat. Actually, "encouraged" is the wrong word. Ordered.

Under normal circumstances, we'd have faced a firing squad for eating in our rooms.

Not only did Ruth and I do exactly as we were told, we didn't even point out the irony.

To the best of my knowledge, my dad never came home.

———

Sometime in the night, I was wakened by voices. Male strangers' voices. Quiet voices, so I'm not really sure why they woke me. But they did.

Maybe it was because my window looked out over the front yard. Because I was close to where they stood. Which, from the sound of it, was right up against the front of the house. Maybe it was their energy that woke me. Or the fact that the danger felt and sounded so close.

First I thought the reporters were back. Then I thought maybe someone was going to set our house on fire. Or bomb it. Or just throw a brick through our window. That would have been bad enough.

Or a Molotov cocktail.

But all I could hear were their quiet voices. And a slight hissing noise I couldn't identify.

I crossed quietly to the window. First I saw nothing. Then I saw two dark figures running away. They didn't even open the gate. Just vaulted over our low picket fence.

I ran to my parents' bedroom to get my dad. To tell him there might be a bomb, or the beginning of a fire. He had to go see. I opened the door to their room quietly. He wasn't there. Just my mom, fast asleep.

I took a big deep breath and decided it would have to be me. My family needed saving. And if my dad wasn't home, I figured I was next in line.

A bit of patriarchal thinking, I suppose. But what do you want? I was young.

I tiptoed downstairs and found the big, powerful lantern flashlight in the kitchen pantry. Carried it to the front door.

I stood longer than necessary with my hand on the knob. I knew somebody could still be out there. I knew something could explode or burn me when I stepped outside. But I had to step outside. I needed saving, and so did my whole family. What else could I do?

I think I was scared but happy in that moment. Because suddenly the harm that faced my household was tangible. It could be bravely faced. Fought. I could save us from this, because it had a form. When I opened the door, I at least would know what it was.

I turned on the powerful beam of flashlight and threw the door wide. Every muscle taut, I stepped out onto the welcome mat. The bristles of it poked into my bare feet, hurting me. I swept the beam of the flashlight around, but saw nothing out of the ordinary.

I stepped off the mat and took a dozen steps down our paved walkway, hopping slightly from the cold. Then I realized the some-one or something dangerous was probably behind me now. So I swung around fast, shining the light toward the house.

On the left-hand side of the house, ending at the porch, some-one had spray-painted three enormous letters. They stretched from almost down to the dirt to up as high as a tall person could raise his hand. Seven feet or more. Uneven, dripping black spray paint on our neat blue house.

COW

"Cow?" I asked out loud. It made no sense, and yet it fright-ened me. I could feel the chill run through my gut. Someone had come to our house to slay us with a word. To insult us in a way the entire world could see. To mark us.

But . . . cow?

It took me several breaths to realize there might be more. I swung the flashlight to the right. Lit up the house on the other side of the porch.

ARD

I turned off the flashlight and ran back inside. I could feel my face flushing, angry and hot.

I didn't wake up my mom. I didn't tell her.

And I knew I wouldn't tell her in the morning, either.

I used my last-ditch strategy: I pretended I hadn't even seen it. I simply acted as though what was bothering me, the thing I couldn't do anything to fix anyway, had never happened at all.

Needless to say, I never got back to sleep.

Chapter Five: Ruth

When I woke up the next morning, I knew it was bizarrely late. I could tell by the way the sun blasted through the curtains. Every weekday morning, my mom came in at six thirty and coldly rousted Aubrey and me out of bed for school. Except this morning.

I just lay there for a few moments, wincing into the light. I was still half-asleep and trying to remember why everything was different. When it came back, it hit me as something heavy and cold in my stomach, hard-edged like steel. I wondered for a minute where Joseph had gone and if he was okay. Then I began to focus on the noise that had wakened me.

It sounded like a generator in the front yard, irritating and loud. My guess was that it had something to do with the news crews—maybe they used a generator to run some of their heavy equipment. But my room looked out over the side yard, not the front, so I got up and crossed the room to my bedroom door. I checked out in the hall to see if anyone was around. Nothing. I slithered down the hall to my father's reading room. The door was open, and I looked carefully to be sure no one was hiding in there, seeking refuge from the action out front. But there was nothing in there except a lingering stench of old smoke.

I'm ashamed to say I ran to the bathroom and washed my face and brushed my teeth and hair before I did anything else. I had this unfortunate mental image that involved sticking my head out the window and becoming a picture for the front page of the next morning's paper, or footage that I'd see on that night's local evening news—that *everybody* would see. Even as I was washing and brushing, I knew I probably wasn't important enough to warrant all that attention. Still, the thing with Joseph was still new and unexplored, and it was almost impossible to know where the property lines fell. In fact, I had a strong sense that they had not yet been fully drawn, that they could re-form at any time, and without warning.

When I thought I'd made myself halfway presentable, I stuck my head out the window of the reading room. Two house painters in Jackson Pollock–like splattered overalls looked up. The generator in question was more like a big air compressor for a professional paint sprayer. They had apparently already done a weird, loopy, complex stretch of the bottom of the front of our house in gray primer, by hand from the look of it. Now they were covering it with an even coat of paint the color of the rest of the house, only not quite—just a little too fresh and shiny looking, a little too blue. At least, that's what I gathered from that admittedly difficult angle.

One of the men raised a hand to wave to me, and I pulled my head back inside, humiliated for reasons I couldn't quite sort out.

Aubrey's bedroom door was closed, so I wandered down to the kitchen, vaguely aware that I was hungry.

My mom was talking on the phone. Well, *complaining* on the phone would be a more accurate description.

"No, it's not that they didn't bother to match it properly," she said in a voice she only ever used against my dad. So I figured that's who it was, but it was only a guess. Just because something had never been true before didn't mean it couldn't be so now—I knew that instinctively. All the rules were suddenly undependable at best. "I gave it to them straight out of the garage." Pause. "Yes, we had it left over from last time we had the house painted, don't you remember? Three gallons, and you were all mad because it was over thirty dollars a gallon. I said we'll use it for touch-ups, or next time we have them come paint, but still, you grumbled." Yeah. My dad, all right. "Do I really need to tell you that the sun fades paint? It's been six years, Brad. The stuff they're putting on just looks too new, that's all." Another brief silence. "Yes, you can see what it covers. I mean, not make out the letters or anything, because they painted between them, but it's just this blotch. Any idiot could see it's patched over something. And if you want them to do the whole front, they'll have to mask all the windows and buy a lot more paint."

In a brief silence, I watched her pull a pack of cigarettes out of her skirt pocket and slide one out of the pack, grabbing it with her lips. I was shocked. My mom had never smoked as far as I knew. To my further amazement, she lit one of the front gas burners on the stove and leaned over, drawing on the cigarette until the first little clouds of smoke began to fill the kitchen. My head spun with all the changes to my formerly solid world order.

"Yes, I know it's a big headache, Brad, but you're at the office and I'm here having to cope with it, so it's *my* headache. And yet here you are complaining in my ear. Would you like me to wave a magic wand and make all the inconvenient things disappear, your highness?"

That's when she looked up and saw me standing there. I could see it register, but not in any way she intended for me to see. More like workmen were moving lumber and accidentally slammed a two-by-four into her belly, but she didn't want to let on that it hurt.

She covered the receiver of the phone with her cigarette-holding hand.

"This is a private conversation," she said to me. "Scoot."

"But I'm hungry."

"Cereal in the cupboard next to the fridge."

But she just stared at me, conversation on hold, while I rummaged in the cupboard, so I skipped the milk and grabbed some Fruity-O's and took the box toward the stairs with me.

"You don't want milk?" I heard her call after me.

"Not particularly," I called back.

I stuck my hand in the box on my way up the spiral stairs and shoved a handful into my mouth, but it tasted much too sweet and made my stomach turn. Well, something made my stomach turn, and I guess the cereal wasn't helping.

I closed myself back into my room and turned on my laptop.

In a fit of uncharacteristic bravery, I did an Internet search on my brother's name. "Joseph Stellkellner," in quotes. Fortunately, we had an unusually distinctive name—at least, I thought it was fortunate for a very brief moment that morning. It was never destined to feel like an advantage again.

I got five hundred and eighty-seven hits. Five. Hundred. Eighty. Seven.

I lost my appetite for the cereal.

I narrowed the search by choosing "News." It returned sixty-seven stories from papers and news websites across the country, and some national—and, because they were sorted with the newest first, none seemed to be the original story. These were dozens of versions of a more recent update. They all had similar titles, and the titles were all about my brother's mental health history.

I just froze there a moment, trying to think whether my brother Joseph had a mental health history, but nothing came to mind. He'd always been just like everyone else, as far as I knew. At least, as much as any of us were.

I clicked on one of the articles. Actually, over the next few minutes, I clicked on four of the articles. I was so wrapped up in my shock—almost literally from the feel of it, like being mummified in Bubble Wrap or cotton batting—that it took me four articles to realize they were all the same. Something a bunch of papers had picked up from the Associated Press or something.

They said Joseph had been institutionalized when he was twelve and that once upon a time that would have caused the army to reject him, or at least probably it would have been a deterrent to his making it into the army. But now, the papers said, it was wartime, and there was no draft the way there had been during Vietnam, and so the armed forces had lowered their standards to get new recruits, because who wants to volunteer when they know they'll be shipped over to Kuwait or Baghdad pretty much straight away? I'm paraphrasing, of course. They worded it much more politely.

"Maybe somebody who wants to get away from Brad and Janet," I said out loud, but quietly.

Then I read some more.

I had wildly mixed feelings about what I was reading. On the one hand, the rush to hold someone sickeningly responsible came through loud and clear. But now this new revelation seemed to take a tiny bit of the heat off my brother and direct it toward the army itself, for the crime of letting him join. And yet that was its own mortal insult: the idea that my brother Joseph was so deeply defective that they should have known better than to even consider letting him serve.

And there was another wild card thrown in: apparently, the army was also investigating the commanding officer to see why he sent soldiers out on a mission that was clearly undermanned.

It wasn't much in the way of relief—still, it was a lifting that I could feel. They were saying that something bigger and totally outside our family was really to blame, and that helped me breathe a little more easily.

I heard the paint sprayer shut down out front, and I wondered if they had actually succeeded in covering whatever shame had been placed there, or if my mother had simply told them to give up and stop trying.

Then I finished the fourth article—or at least the fourth repetition of the same one—and made the mistake of reading down into the comment thread.

Now, any fool knows you never read the comments on an Internet article. It's like one of the three modern rules for living a decent life, although I'd be hard-pressed to say what the other two are. Maybe "don't feed the trolls," but then I run out of ideas. But in this case, it felt inevitable, unavoidable. They were there, they already existed, and I couldn't look away. I had to see what they said.

I sat reading for a few minutes with my mouth open, each new well-aimed statement a knife stabbing into my already bleeding gut.

One person was kind to my brother Joseph and suggested we wait and gather more information on what happened before rushing to judgment. One. The rest just piled on Joseph, and then, when the one nice person defended him, they all piled on that commenter.

I'm not going to detail what they said. I want to pretend I no longer remember specifics, but some of the things I saw are burned in, seared into my brain like the chandelier lights burning a pattern into the corneas of Aubrey's and my eyes. But I won't repeat them word for word, because they were ugly, and I feel like I'd only be helping to keep them alive.

I'll just generally say that, according to their vitriol, Joseph had killed more than just two fellow soldiers. He had killed us all. He had emboldened the enemy, showing the weak underbelly of America, which wouldn't be weak in the first place without the Josephs of America, thus signing all of our death warrants.

More than a few said he was a traitor to his country and should be put to death for his crime.

I'm sorry to say I'm not exaggerating.

Some not only took the blame and threw it back on my brother, but even on his family—which, I realized in my well-knifed abdomen, was me. People were saying things about what kind of family we were—*our family*—people who had never met us, never laid eyes on us.

All I could think was how I could correct them, every one of them. I felt like I had to fix everyone's perceptions of us and argue back with everybody until they saw the light.

I sat another minute, half aware that my mouth was still hanging open, wondering what I should write to set the record straight. It would have to be something like the one kind commenter had written. I'd have to say they didn't know Joseph, so they didn't really know what they were saying, and they had no right to judge a person they'd never met, especially so soon, when all the facts hadn't even had time to come out.

Then I went back and read the abuse that one person had taken for arguing against a rush to judgment.

The decision as to whether I was brave enough to jump into that fray made my head spin, quite literally. It made me dizzy, and when the knock came on my bedroom door, even though it was a soft knock, it made me jump.

"Who is it?"

"It's Aubrey," Aubrey said, sounding unusually cowed. He was normally a confident little brat. "Can I come in?"

"Um. I guess so."

He came in and closed the door behind him. Then he walked over and sat on the edge of my bed, but he didn't speak, at least not at first. He just gazed around my room as though this was the first he'd ever seen of it. He looked as though he hadn't slept in a week.

"What?" I said, finally. I didn't mean to sound harsh, but I might have anyway, accidentally.

"Was Joseph ever in a mental hospital?"

I wanted to say, *So you've been reading them, too.* I guess I could have, but I didn't.

"Not that I remember. I've been trying to think. It said he was twelve. Which means I would have been five. So, I don't know. It's pretty hard to remember what happened when you were five, you know? I do remember he was gone a lot. Like all summer, every summer, and I don't really remember where they told us he was going, or even if they did. But he couldn't have been spending every summer in a mental hospital."

"Why not?"

"Because they just don't work like that, Aubrey." Of course I had no way to know how mental hospitals worked, but, being the teenager I was, I spoke with absolute authority. "They're not summer camp. If you have to go, then they just send you. Right then. Whether school's out or not. And they keep you till they're done with you."

"Oh," he said. And looked around my room some more. "So what's the thing about that guy?"

"What guy?"

"That guy who they say was like another father to him."

"I didn't read anything about a guy who was like another father to him."

"Oh," he said again.

I decided to fight against this new development—maybe any new developments. If there was one thing we had too much of already in our new world, it was developments.

"You must've made a mistake," I said. "If Joseph had some guy who was like another father to him, don't you think we'd know it?"

"I don't know," he said, which I thought was a bad answer. "Anyway, I'm not wrong. They said his name, but I don't remember it now. But it's Scottish. It was a first name most men don't have. American men, I mean. At least, the ones I know about."

"I read everything I could find," I said, which was not entirely true. I had read the news portion of the thing, as much as I'd had time to read before Aubrey came knocking. "And I didn't see anything about a guy like that."

"It's not in the news stories," he said. "Maybe it will be. You know, later. After they go talk to him. Right now it's just something people are saying on the blogs."

"I don't believe you," I said. Which was not only a slightly mean thing to say, it was pathetic on my part. It was obvious he was not making any of this up, and I couldn't think of any reason why he would have wanted to. A more honest statement might have gone something like "I desperately want not to believe you." Or "If I believe you, this whole thing will cross the line into too much for me to hold up," because, believe me, my toes were right on that line as it was.

He got up and shuffled to my door, as if he barely had the energy to lift his feet off the carpet. His shoulders looked rounded in a way I wasn't used to seeing.

"Aubrey," I said, and he stopped. I didn't know what else I wanted to say, I just knew that I wanted to say something that would be kinder than I'd already been.

But then I got stuck on what that would be.

"Don't read the comments," I said.

He actually smiled, but it was a tragic-looking thing. "Too late," he said, and then he quietly let himself out.

———

I called Sean's cell phone seven times and left messages each time, but he didn't call me back. It was something that felt wrong, even as I was doing it, because I didn't really know Sean all that well. We had a date for Friday night, but it was going to be our first. So he wasn't exactly my boyfriend—more like a boyfriend-to-be. But in that moment, I desperately needed a connection to someone, so I tried to speed up our process. That was the part I knew felt wrong, but it was less of a want and more of a need, and I felt utterly helpless and just along for the ride.

I'd really never had an honest-to-goodness boyfriend. I'd had a few brushes with boys, but nothing that carried that genuine sense of connection. There'd been that boy, Jacob, who was the older brother of one of Aubrey's friends. It was clear that he'd liked me, but he was so shy—pathologically shy—and so we never even held hands. And there had been two boys who wanted to go very far with me very fast, but I didn't trust them and I wasn't ready, so they moved on in short order. There was not a boy in that pack that I could have talked to about all this, even if he hadn't been long gone.

I started to think our date was off. That *we* were off. Maybe he'd read some of the things I'd read, or heard about them from somebody who did, and maybe that was just that. Who would want to walk into a firestorm like this if they didn't have to?

I spent a big part of the day trying to decide what I would do if the tables were turned. It was scary to think about, but I decided I'd be strong and march into the fray for him, because I was just a solid person like that, and loyalty was the most important thing.

But maybe it's easy to tell yourself stuff like that when you know you won't be put to the test for real.

While I was thinking, I saw a piece of paper slide under my door, silently, and with no words or knocks to go with it. I walked over and picked it up, but all the movements felt less than real. Or more than real, I'm not sure which.

It was a blog post that Aubrey had apparently printed off the Internet. A paragraph was highlighted in yellow, too sloppily I thought, not really following the lines of text, as if he'd been too busy or too upset to do it right.

And it didn't seem like a very professional or well-written blog to me, but maybe I was just anxious to find fault.

The paragraph said this:

Now it's beginning to come out that Stellkellner told some of his fellow soldiers that he spent every summer, starting at age twelve, with Hamish MacCallum, the man who had this article written about him last year.

The words "this article written about him" were clearly a text link, underlined and in a different color, but of course you can't click on the paper of a printout.

MacCallum, who emigrated from Scotland decades ago, lives in a house high on a bluff in Northern California, which he purchased because in Scotland he had also lived at the edge of a cliff over the sea, and had become accustomed to inviting potential jumpers into his house for a meal. It's unclear whether Stellkellner met MacCallum in an aborted suicide attempt, but Stellkellner did tell his fellow soldiers that he met MacCallum when he was twelve, which would place the incident right around the time the press is saying he was institutionalized. Stellkellner reportedly told his former friends in Baghdad that MacCallum was "more of a father to him than his own late biological father or his adopted father."

Then the yellow highlighting ran out, and the article went on to say that this was unconfirmed, plus it wasn't clear whether there was any connection between this information and the controversy at hand, and then I stopped reading.

I folded the sheet of paper in half, and on the blank back of it I wrote, "I'll believe this if and when I see it in the real papers."

I slid it under Aubrey's door.

Even as I did, I think I knew it was less of an "if" and more of a "when."

———

Sean called my cell phone about four p.m., around the time he would have been getting home from school.

"Hey," I said, my gut flooding with relief.

"Sorry I didn't call you back. I was looking at my phone in math class to see who called, and old Mr. Bertram noticed and confiscated it. I still don't have it back from him."

"Oh," I said. "That's okay." Then I added, "Sorry. I'm sorry I got your phone taken away."

"Whatever. Not your fault. I should have waited and called you back in the hall between classes."

He sounded okay, as if he hadn't yet decided to treat me like the contagious disease I probably was, but I still needed to approach it as a tenuous reprieve.

"So," I said. "Is this all crazy, or what?"

"I know," he said. "Huh?"

Then the conversation just died. And, in a small way, so did I.

"So . . . ," he began. "What did you want?"

I felt my face turn hot, and probably red, and felt a sudden surge of the heartburn that had become the constant accompaniment to my life, like background music in a movie. I froze in silence for an embarrassing length of time.

I couldn't bring myself to tell him that I'd needed to talk to someone, and still did, and worse yet that there was no one in my house—not even anyone in my more extended world—who could fill that void for me. That I'd had to turn to a boy who'd just asked me out for the first time and rush him into the role of confidant.

It was all just so wrong now.

"I was wondering if we were still on for Friday," I said.

"Well, sure," he said, as if nothing could be more obvious. "Why wouldn't we be?"

But it was a question I couldn't answer, so it froze me again.

"Wait," he said. "You didn't think I was going to drop you just because people are mad at your brother, did you?"

"Um," I said. I wanted to say no, unequivocally no. Instead I said, "Maybe. I don't know."

"You're not your brother," he said.

And he may have said more. I'm sure he did, in fact. I could vaguely hear him talking in the background, but not a single word came through, because that was the moment I heard the big knock at our front door.

I didn't know how to tell Sean to stop talking, so I just stopped listening.

I ran with the phone to the smoking room—I mean the reading room—and looked out the window again. The painters were gone. Standing on the porch were two very official-looking soldiers in uniform, their faces grim, as if the gravity of their mission was weighing them down.

"Sean," I said, cutting him off in the middle of a sentence, but a sentence about what I'll never know. "I'm going to have to call you back."

Chapter Six: Aubrey

I ran past Ruth's room. Down the stairs two at a time. Because I heard my mom arguing with somebody at the door. Well. Arguing *at* somebody. I never heard any other voice argue back.

I didn't talk to myself on the way down. So I wasn't clear on what I was expecting. But when I skidded up behind my mom and saw the two uniformed soldiers, then I knew. I knew in retrospect what I'd been hoping for.

I'd hoped maybe Joseph had come back. I could tell. Because I could feel the loss of it. I could feel it being ripped away.

"I will tell you one more time," my mom said, as if there was nothing the tiniest bit scary about them. "He was here barely twenty-four hours. My husband went downstairs to tell him to leave, but he already had. We don't know where he is, and we don't want to know. As far as we're concerned, he's no longer a part of this family."

She wound down. Turned around. Saw me there. Her face darkened further, if such a thing were possible.

"This doesn't concern you," she said.

She turned me back toward the stairs and sent me on my way with a swat on the butt. Like you do with your four-year-old.

My face burned. But I just ran. Ran up to my room.

I remember thinking in a vague way, *A couple of army soldiers are here to arrest my brother. What could possibly concern me more than that?*

———

At dinner that night, I could tell Isabella was back. Or had been back, anyway. Even though I hadn't seen her with my own eyes. Because the food was great again. A perfectly seasoned chicken-and-rice casserole. My mom couldn't have approached it on her best day in a kitchen.

I could hear voices. Motors. No more and no less than I'd been hearing all day, but still. The circus on the other side of our gate was becoming a constant.

I stared at the chandelier while my dad announced that the following day we would go back to school.

"Don't be ridiculous," my mother said.

"It's not ridiculous," he said. "Not at all. What's ridiculous is thinking we can hide them away from all this. How many days of school do you think they can miss?"

"I can get some homework from their teachers, just the same as if they were sick."

"For how long, Janet?"

His voice had hardened in that way it did sometimes. I glanced over at my sister, Ruth. She looked a little green around the gills.

My father continued to lecture. "We thought this would blow over. One, two days of lost school for them and that would be that. It didn't play out that way, Janet. Face it. That was back when we thought Joseph just refused duty. Before this whole . . . mutiny mess. Now we've got four times the media clowns out front. And now we're headed for a military court-martial. With the whole country watching. Assuming they catch him. And if they don't, that's an ongoing story, too. This could go on for months. Years. This is our new normal, and everybody's just going to have to learn to deal with it."

Absolute silence. I was trying to imagine what it would feel like to live this way for months. Or years. I figured everybody else was, too.

"No, we can't shield them from this anymore," he said. "They're just going to have to find their own way through."

As was usually the case in our family, no one bothered to offer us a pat on the back, a cheerful thought, a boxed lunch, or an instruction manual. We were just thrown out into the harshest corners of the world to figure things out for ourselves.

———

The following morning, I raided my piggy bank. This is not as childish an act as it may sound. I didn't have pennies and quarters in there. I had hundred-dollar bills. Thirteen of them.

Every year on my birthday, ever since I was one, my Aunt Clara had given me a hundred-dollar bill. The first one had come with—in—the piggy bank. Or so I'd been told. Because I was always swimming in presents anyway, I was taught to tuck the bills away in the piggy. Save for the future.

It wasn't one of those banks with the rubber plug in the bottom. It was a deposit-only model. If you wanted what was in there, you had to smash it.

I smashed it. With my math textbook.

I had a savings account at the bank, too. Which didn't require the smashing of anything. It did, however, require a second signature from one of my parents. So that was out.

I quietly wrapped the pieces in some old newspaper—a sports section I'd rescued from my dad's smoking room. I snuck them downstairs. Out the kitchen door. I saw no one on the way to the outdoor trash shed.

Until I got there.

Then I was startled to see a total stranger going through our recycling.

He wasn't a homeless guy. Not down on his luck or anything like that. He was wearing a camel-hair coat that probably cost a grand or more. Wing-tip shoes.

He ran like a thief when he saw me coming.

I stood staring after him for a moment. Then I wedged the piggy-bank shards deep in the trash.

When I got back upstairs, I stuffed the money in my jeans pocket. Already feeling vulnerable. Like muggers and thieves would just sense all that money. Smash me with their own math textbooks the minute I stepped out the door.

I did a little research online. Wrote down an address and phone number. Then I marched out the front door as though headed for school.

My mom walked ahead of us. Ruth and me. Walked us through the crowd. I swear it was a genuine crowd by then. Probably forty people or more. News vans—three or four. Spectators who may have had nothing to do with the media. Women anchors or correspondents talking into microphones, right into the cameras, with our house as the background.

My mom didn't say one word to them. She just accomplished it all with a look. Plus, in retrospect, I'm thinking the incident where she threatened to run them over with her car might have passed from ear to ear.

They parted like the Red Sea for Moses, and we walked through. In relative silence. Just one news lady in a bright-red pantsuit kept talking.

Nobody had the nerve to follow us to the bus stop.

———

I was going to wait for the bus with Ruth. Get off at school. Walk away from there and move on.

But I got impatient.

"I'm not going to school," I told her.

"Oh," she said. Then, a bit later, "Where are you going?"

"Can I not tell you?"

"Sure," she said. "Whatever."

"Thanks."

My idea had been to take the bus to this Marshall Kendrick's office. But I started getting uneasy with that plan. Like I'd get lost. Like it would be too confusing. Too much. I think I could have bitten it off easily enough on most other days. Since losing Joseph again, everything felt overwhelming.

I asked Ruth if I could borrow her phone.

"What happened to yours?"

"I forgot it at home."

"Whatever," she said. "But you owe me the minutes if I run out."

"This'll be quick."

I called directory assistance for the number of the cab company.

"That's two dollars extra," Ruth said when she heard what I was doing. "Dad'll demand it from my allowance. You owe me."

Then I let the automated service autodial for the cab.

It arrived in just a matter of minutes. Two or three. It beat the bus.

Ruth gave me the strangest look. But she said nothing.

I decided I loved her for that.

———

I had no choice but to pay the cab driver with a hundred-dollar bill. He gave me back mostly ones and fives. A ridiculous stack. I gave him a tip which he must not have liked. It must not have been enough. Because he frowned at it.

I wanted to say, *What do you expect? I'm thirteen. How am I supposed to know how to tip a cabbie? Who ever taught me stuff like that?*

I said nothing.

I climbed out of the cab. Stuffed the ridiculous wad of bills into my jeans pocket. It made me three or four times more sure that everyone would know. Everyone would see. Everyone would be willing to hurt me for that money.

I followed the street numbers.

Marshall Kendrick had an office that, on first glance, was just a glass door. It sat between a furniture store and a dry cleaner. Through the glass I could see stairs. Nothing more.

I tried the door. It was open.

I marched up the stairs and through another door. This one said "Marshall Kendrick" in neatly stenciled paint. And, under that, "Private Investigations." It opened into a sort of front office. The kind with a desk for a receptionist. But it was tiny, and there was no receptionist. I could hear him talking to someone behind the closed office door.

I sat. Waited. For what, I wasn't sure. If there was someone in there with him, they'd come out. Eventually. If he was just on the phone, he might never come to the door.

I'd guess I waited about ten minutes, my knee bouncing up and down. It exhausted me, because it reminded me how much tension I had to vent. But I couldn't stop.

Then the office door swung open. An old couple walked out. Walked through the outer office where I sat. They looked sad. They looked the way I felt.

Kendrick came to the door to walk them out, and he seemed surprised to see me. Startled, in fact. Then again, I hadn't bothered to tell him I was coming.

"May I help you?" he asked as the old couple made their way through.

"I need to see you about a . . . what you do."

His face twisted in a way I couldn't quite make out. But I didn't like it. One eyebrow was slightly up. Like he was asking me with his face if I was for real. Like maybe my very existence was only a joke.

"How old are you?"

"Fifteen."

The eyebrow inched up higher.

"Okay, thirteen. But I have money. I have thirteen hundred dollars. Well. Minus the cab fare. I have about twelve hundred and eighty-five. Four."

Kendrick sighed. Dropped his head and shook it.

"I guess there's no law against hearing you out," he said. "You're lucky I have a fifteen-minute break before my next appointment."

I walked into his office feeling numb. Sat on the edge of a wooden folding chair in front of his desk, which was piled with books and files and papers. He walked around and sat in a chair much more comfortable than mine. Leather, and the kind you can lean back in. With arms. The window behind his head looked as though it hadn't been cleaned for years.

"I want you to find my brother," I said.

I took all the money out of my pocket. Spread it on the only blank space on his desk. He just watched me, looking halfway amused. At my expense, apparently. I thought better of giving it all to him and took back twenty. For a cab back to school.

Then I just looked up at him. Waiting.

"That's not quite how it works," he said.

"Oh. How does it work?"

"Put your money back in your pocket and I'll tell you."

I scooped it all up and stuffed the ridiculous lump back into my jeans pocket again.

"I'm not so sure about working for a kid," he said.

"I could just pay you cash. Who would even need to know?"

"This's not the movies, kid."

"Please don't call me 'kid,'" I said. Which took some courage. I could feel it. What it required. What it drained out of me.

But all he said was, "You haven't bothered to tell me your name yet."

"Aubrey."

"Aubrey what?"

"Stellkellner."

I watched his face change into something entirely different. He didn't say anything for a minute. I didn't, either.

"Is this a joke?" he asked in time.

"No. Why would I joke about that?"

"You want me to find your brother. That would be *Joseph* Stellkellner?"

"That's right."

"Well, that's a joke, kid. Aubrey. Whether you meant it to be one or not." He held up a section of the morning paper, but not long enough for me to see much of what it said. "I wouldn't be the only one looking for him. Would I? The military is looking for him, too. He's going to be court-martialed if they find him. Though why they didn't just keep him while they had him, I'll never know."

"They didn't think they would at first," I said. "Court-martial him. At first they just wanted the whole thing to go away. They were just going to discharge him. But he said they could change their mind after the investigation. And they did."

"Still don't know why they let him off base, though."

"They didn't know about the mutiny thing when they let him off base. Not that it really was mutiny. But they didn't know the extra stuff. You know. How he maybe talked to other guys about maybe not going out on duty."

Telling the story now, looking back, it strikes me that it's possible the army never did say Joseph could leave base. I only know he was briefly there, at our house. I don't know that he had permission to be. At the time, that didn't occur to me. I was taking everything at face value.

"Yeah, that sounds about right. That stunt he pulled . . . that idea about how you get to say no after joining the army . . . encourage other guys to say no . . . that's not one of those things they want to catch on. They wouldn't want anybody else getting similar notions. Look. Kid. I don't think you see what you're asking me to stick my nose into here. Your brother is a fugitive from justice. How am I supposed to find him if he's hiding himself so well that the long arm of military law can't find him? And another thing. How many reporters have you got camped in front of your house right now?"

"A few," I said, hoping he wouldn't push for a more exact number.

"I hope you don't think I want them here instead. Or in addition. Because I don't."

"So you won't do it?"

"I think it would be a waste of your money."

"I'd be willing to try it. Even if there's only, like, one chance in a hundred you could find him. I'd still like to try."

He sat back. Rocked his chair back with him. Steepled his fingers that way grown-ups do when they want to look thoughtful.

"To what end?" he asked.

"I don't know what that means."

"It means *why.*"

"Then why didn't you just ask why?"

Silence in the office. I wondered how many minutes were left of my fifteen.

I wondered why.

I knew on a feeling level in my gut. But I hadn't talked it out extensively with myself in my head.

I wanted to create a pact with Joseph. A secret bond. I would know where he was. He would contact me, and no one would have to know. I would never have to feel cut off from him again.

Maybe I could even save him. Hook him up with some money. Or a lawyer. Or a place to hide. Or feed him the information he needed. I could come to his rescue.

That's heady stuff, to be your hero's hero. That's the stuff of dreams right there.

Looking back, it was quite the naïve fantasy. But I never claimed to have been any more mature or realistic than the average thirteen-year-old.

I had lost something I couldn't afford to lose. It really wasn't much more complicated than that.

"Do I really need to tell you?" I asked him.

"Not sure," he said.

"When grown-ups come in to hire you, do you ask them why?"

"I do," he said. "The end use of the information is the most important factor in whether I say yes or no." Another uncomfortable silence. Then he said, "Okay. Off the books. Just between you and me. I can do for you what I call a smell test. Two hours. That's a hundred and eighty dollars. I stick my nose in. See how hard I think this is going to be. Then I can advise you whether I think you're crazy to spend another cent on this. That sound okay?"

"Sure," I said. "Thanks."

Because he had given me the one commodity I needed so badly right then. The ability to walk out of there without having lost my last shred of hope.

I counted out the one hundred and eighty dollars. Gave him my cell phone number. Then we heard his next client come in.

I was all the way down on the street before I realized I'd have to walk around until I found a pay phone. And get change to use it. Also that I'd have to break another hundred to pay another cab driver for my ride back to school.

———

It was after ten when I got to school. I didn't think I'd have to answer to anyone for being late. And I was right.

I was walking through a wholly changed world.

I ducked into science class halfway through. Which was good. It gave me time to decompress. It gave nobody a chance to talk to me.

When the bell rang, I was stunned. It felt like only a minute or two could have passed. I couldn't remember a single thing the teacher had said.

I stumbled out into the hall the way I sometimes stumbled out of bed after being wakened from too little sleep.

The first thing I ran into was the brick wall of Kevin Connolly. And brick wall is not a bad way to describe Kevin.

"I wouldn't be you for all the money in the world," he said.

I put my head down and tried to walk around him.

"If that was my brother, I would be so ashamed."

When I was six, I broke my arm and sprained my ankle trying to fly. I jumped out of the tree house in the giant oak, sure I could do it. I'd accepted later that day that I'd been wrong. Boys don't fly.

But on this day, I turned that outcome back around again. I flew. There's just no other way to describe it. I didn't walk the steps between myself and Kevin. I didn't run them. I lifted off and landed on him. It was all one giant birdlike movement.

Next thing I remember was a teacher hauling me off Kevin with one big arm around my waist. It hurt my ribs—that arm—because I struggled so hard against it. I continued to struggle all the way down to the principal's office. I could feel the knuckles of my right hand. They felt bruised and achy. But I couldn't remember hitting anybody.

When the arm let me go, I looked up into the principal's face.

The owner of the arm, who turned out to be my science teacher, Mr. Nesbit, leaned over and said a few quiet words into her ear. Then he left us alone.

She looked into my face and sighed deeply.

"I'm not without empathy for your situation, Aubrey," she said. Her words had that speechlike quality. Rehearsed sounding. "But I told you last time. I gave you one pass. I know everything must be very difficult and confusing for you right now. But this won't do. I have to suspend you for fighting. I don't have a choice about that. But I'm going to call your parents and talk to them about pairing you up with a counselor. Maybe a school counselor and a private one for your off hours, both. You obviously need some support to get through this."

I said, "Yes, ma'am."

Because they hold all the cards. Because there's really nothing else you can say.

————

The following morning at nine o'clock, I got a call from Kendrick. My heart leapt again, the way it had when I saw Joseph had come home. Then I felt myself draw in. Guard that feeling. Because the antiaircraft fire could not have been far behind.

I was learning.

He called on my cell, of course. Because that was the only number I'd given him. So I was able to talk in private, up in my room. Where I was trapped in suspension exile.

"We need to meet," he said.

"Did you find out something?"

He gave a snorting laugh. "In a manner of speaking," he said.

I wasn't sure what that meant. What difference did it make how you said it? I didn't ask.

"I'm not supposed to leave the house," I said. "But I might be able to sneak out for a few minutes." I'd get in trouble if I got caught. But I really didn't care. I cared whether meeting him could be prevented. Not whether it would be punished. "I couldn't get all the way down to your office."

"You want to meet near your house? Give me your address."

"Don't come here, though," I said. "It's a circus. You'd end up on the news."

"Where should I meet you?"

"You know that Starbucks on Wilson?"

"Yeah. All right. I'll be there in ten minutes. Fifteen tops."

"Can't you just tell me now? On the phone?"

"I need to give you your money back," he said.

Which I knew was not a good sign.

———

There was something very adult about the way he was waiting for me. Like a real meeting. The kind a real grown-up would have.

At any other time, I would have been elated by it. But there was no space left inside me for elation.

I sat down across from him, and he laid my hundred and eighty dollars on the table. I grabbed it up fast and stuck it deep down in the front pocket of my jeans.

"So you don't know where he is."

"Oh, no," he said. "I do."

"You do? Where is he?"

"Back with the army. In pretrial confinement."

I felt myself sinking. It felt like falling down the shaft of a well. One I thought I'd already been lying at the bottom of for a long time.

"They caught him?"

"He turned himself in."

I wasn't sure what I thought about that. I didn't know if I thought it was stupid or brave, honorable or unimaginable. I just knew I wished like hell it wasn't the case.

"Do you know where they're holding him?"

"No. But it won't be all that hard to find out. You're family. You can do that without me."

"Why are you not charging me for finding all this out?"

He held up the morning paper, which I hadn't seen. Hadn't known he had with him. Apparently, it had been folded on his lap.

"Not really fair to charge you for what I read in the paper over my morning coffee," he said.

———

When I got home, I wasn't in any trouble. Nobody had noticed I was gone.

I should have been relieved. I wasn't. I was insulted and disappointed that nobody even cared enough to enforce my punishment.

I felt as if I didn't exist in anybody's world at all.

Chapter Seven: Ruth

I wasn't surprised when one of the other girls started in on me, and I wasn't surprised that it was Stacey Bingham. I was more surprised that it was between second and third periods, and nobody had so much as ruffled my feathers all morning. It almost felt good to get it over with.

She stood in the hall in front of me with her hands on her hips, her forehead all knitted up as though she could be fierce, with her anorexic body and her breasts that never got smaller no matter how much weight she lost. I always figured there had to be a surgeon involved in an equation like that, but the boys loved it, no questions asked.

I didn't want any part of it, whatever "it" was, so I turned and walked back the other way, toward my locker. But that's a bad strategy. It only draws them in, like when you back away from a mean dog. It only makes him feel more powerful and reminds him he's winning.

A moment later, she was hovering near my locker with backup. Three of the girls in her group had materialized out of thin air to stand behind her and frown. These were the girls who had always treated me like I was nothing, after making it clear that I would never be welcome to join them, not anytime in this life or anywhere on this planet. So my sense of shame was on full alert before Stacey even opened her mouth.

There were many things she could have said that would have rolled right off me, and I was prepared for all of them. Any insult or negative judgment would have been tolerable or at least survivable, but I was not prepared to be told that she knew something I didn't.

"Your brother is *where he belongs*." She leaned forward and spat out the words near my ear like food she found inedible and refused to swallow.

"My brother is . . . where? How do you even know where he is?"

She laughed, which was the other girls' cue to laugh, and they walked away, enjoying that nice laugh at my bruised and broken family's expense.

I ran—literally ran—down to the principal's office. I rarely showed up there voluntarily, but it was the only place in school where I figured I could demand information.

"I need to know where my brother is," I panted, all breathless and scared, to the woman who worked behind the counter doing attendance.

"Your brother? He's home. He got suspended."

"No, not that brother. My other brother." I was still oxygen-depleted, so much so that I could barely be understood.

"Your brother Joseph," I heard another woman's voice say.

I looked over to see the principal standing in her office doorway.

"Somebody just said to me, 'Your brother is where he belongs,'" I told the principal. "But how would she know where he is? *I* don't even know where he is, and he's my brother. Was there something in the paper this morning?"

She nodded—gravely, I thought.

"Do you have a paper?" I asked her.

"No. But I read it."

"Where is he? Please tell me right now."

"The military is holding him in confinement. Because he's a flight risk."

I stood a moment, catching up on my breathing. Then I realized that fear had been the only thing holding me up, and I was now in danger of collapsing. I could feel the core of me, normally rigid, go floppy and unsupported.

I reached out for the nearest hard wooden bench, leaned wildly in its direction, and landed on it with a clunk. A moment later, the principal was sitting next to me, which was too bad, because I really wanted everybody to stay far away.

"What were you thinking that had you so scared?" she asked me.

Oddly, it was a question I hadn't even considered, but when she asked, I found the answer was right there at my disposal, and not even very far under the surface at that.

"I figured everybody thinks he deserves to be in his grave," I said.

"Not everybody thinks that," she said, putting a hand on my shoulder.

My shoulder instinctively retreated.

"I want to go home," I said. "Can I go home?"

A pause, during which my life was in someone else's hands entirely, which more or less sums up the experience of being under eighteen.

"Yes," she said, "you may go home. I'll write up the absence so it makes sense."

———

When I walked out of the office I felt my phone buzz once, so I pulled it out of my pocket and looked. It was a voice mail, and I could tell by the number that it was from Sean. It was also the second message from him in just the last few minutes. I guess I'd been too busy to feel the buzz of the first.

Before I could even listen to it, my phone went off again, but this time in that pattern it buzzes when someone is calling. I looked up to see Sean at the end of the hall, his cell phone to his ear, his back to me.

I waved, but he didn't see me.

He wasn't the most handsome guy in school, Sean, but the more I looked at him, the more I liked looking. His skin wasn't perfect, to put it mildly, but he had intense gray eyes and shaggy hair that always looked like he'd meant every individual hair to be exactly in that wild and spontaneous place.

He was already starting to feel like someone I knew.

I walked up behind him and tapped him on the shoulder, and he jumped.

"You calling me?" I asked him.

"Oh. Yeah, I was."

"I'm right here. Hang up."

He seemed off balance, and his face was a little too flushed, so I should have known I was in trouble.

"I left you two messages," he said.

"I know."

"Have you listened to them?"

"Not yet."

"So . . . listen to them."

"Sean . . ."

"What?"

"I'm standing right in front of you. Just tell me."

"Oh. Just tell you. Right." But for an awkward moment, he didn't. Then he did, and that was awkward, too. "I have to cancel Friday."

"Oh," I said. "Okay." A lot was going on in me, but none of it was good, so I worked hard to keep it inside where it belonged. "Well. Another time, then."

"Um . . . ," he said. And then he trailed off, and I knew. I knew everything. A brick wall didn't have to fall on me.

"You said you wouldn't do this." I was already fighting back tears. They were old tears, I realized as I fought them. They'd been trying to get out for days. "You said I'm not my brother and you wouldn't drop me just because everybody's mad at him."

"I *wouldn't*," he said. The bell rang, but we just stood there, ignoring it, alone in the hall together. Except it didn't feel very together all of a sudden—it felt more like we were on two opposite sides of a dark and remote planet. "I swear, *I* wouldn't. It isn't me. It's . . . They found out. That we're friends. I mean . . . I don't know if we're friends, or . . . I don't know yet what we are, but they found out."

"They?"

"You know."

"Sean. If I knew, I wouldn't be standing here with this stupid look on my face."

"The . . . you know . . . reporters."

A long silence while I breathed that in.

"How did they find out?"

"I have no idea. But they're on me now wherever I go. They want to know all about your family. Anything I know. I keep telling them I don't know anything. But then they started coming around the house and trying to get to me through my parents. And now my mom says I can't ever see you or talk to you again. I'm really sorry, Ruth."

He stood there for a few seconds, probably waiting for me to say something. But I had no idea what to say.

"I'm really sorry," he said again, over his shoulder as he walked away.

I erased the messages on my phone and then walked home, crying.

———

I got microphones stuck in my face on the last block, our block, because my mother wasn't there to defend me, but I just ignored them and kept walking, and kept crying.

I heard a lot of questions, but I couldn't really separate out the voices and I didn't try. I just noticed the word "brother" seemed to appear in every sentence.

Of course it occurred to me that I might end up on the evening news, crying like a baby, but there wasn't much I could do to change that, and besides, by that time I really couldn't find a place in me that cared.

You can only save face for just so long before you wake up and realize you have nothing left worth saving.

———

My father was home.

Really, I just can't tell you how out of the ordinary that is. I had to figure if it's daylight, and my father is home, this must be *The Twilight Zone*. It wasn't even lunchtime yet, and there he was, sitting on the couch drinking a large glass of something brown and quite obviously alcoholic, his face an impenetrable mask of nothingness.

He looked up at me as though I was no one he'd ever met.

"What are you doing home?" he asked. He wasn't even looking at me anymore when he asked.

"I was just about to ask you the same question."

I waited, but he never said more.

I looked in the kitchen, in case my mom was in there. She'd been hanging out in the kitchen a lot lately, which was unlike her, but it was a good spot from which to supervise the jackals out on the street—or the snakes, or vultures, or whatever disgusting animal she wanted to compare them to on any given day.

She wasn't there, but Isabella was, cooking something that smelled absolutely wonderful. She looked up at me and her face morphed into a perfect look of utter maternal pity.

"Oh, honey," she said. "You okay?"

I shook my head, and she held out her arms and I ran into them. She was a big woman, Isabella, which made her soft and comforting when she held me. It made her a full-fledged sanctuary of a person. That and the fact that she had a heart.

"Poor missy. Poor missy. Very hard time for your family."

She rocked me back and forth for a time while I cried.

Then I pulled back out of her embrace and tried to cobble myself together. A fresh new pink tissue emerged from the pocket of her big apron as if by magic, and I took it and nodded and wiped my eyes.

"Thanks. Where's my mom?"

"Out. She didn't say where."

"Why is my dad home?"

"His clients canceled."

"He has clients cancel all the time. He never comes home in between."

"All the time he has *one* client cancel. Today your mom say *three* clients canceled."

I had no idea what to say to that. Inside, I'm ashamed to report, I thought mostly of myself.

What if he couldn't make a living as a lawyer anymore? How would he pay the bills? He was always complaining about how close to the line we were on this gigantic mortgage and how much pressure it put on him to have to come up with all that money every month. Except he called it "making the monthly nut." What happened to the monthly nut if you all of a sudden couldn't make it? What could the nut do to punish you if you failed?

"Is Aubrey upstairs?"

"In his room, yes," Isabella said.

In a rare act of sibling bonding, I decided to go upstairs and commiserate with my little brother.

———

"I need to go see Joseph," he said. And then when the conversation lagged he said it again. And then again. Every time we ran out the thread of a topic and every time I allowed too long a gap between sentences, Aubrey said, "I need to go see Joseph."

Behind his head, planets hung silently in space as he spoke.

"We don't even know where he is, though," I said after the third time.

"We can find out, though. Because we're family."

"How do you know that?"

"I just know."

"How?"

"I just do, okay? Don't ask. Please."

I sighed and looked up through the Milky Way with unfocused eyes.

"So let's say you find out where he is," I said, "and he can have visitors. It could be three or four states away from here, this place where they're holding him. They could have him anywhere in the country. How will you get there? You're not even old enough to ride a bus or a train by yourself."

"You could come with me."

I snorted. "Yeah. Some big help that would be. I'm a whole two years older. I'm just barely old enough to ride a bus or a train by myself if I can prove there's a grown-up waiting to pick me up at the station. No, if you're going to pull off a thing like that, you'll need a lot more than just me."

We looked out into space for a minute more, then at each other. Aubrey had a look on his face I wasn't used to seeing, as if he were doing calculus in his head.

"Aunt Sheila," he said.

"Oh, I don't know about that."

"Aunt Sheila is great for things like this."

"*Things like this,*" I repeated. "Aubrey. There are no *things like this.* Nothing in our lives has ever been remotely like this and you know it."

"But she always helps us get around Dad."

"She likes to be a thorn in his side, yeah. That doesn't mean she'll be willing to wade into a stink pile like this one."

"I'm calling her," he said, and reached for his backpack, where I'm guessing his phone had been hiding since he got suspended. Aubrey didn't have much of a circle of friends, to put it mildly. Then again, look who's talking.

"It's the middle of the day," I said. He just looked blank, like he was barely listening hard enough to understand, so I added, "She'll be at school. You know. Teaching."

"Oh. Right. Well, later, then, I'm calling her. I'll come get you so you'll know what she says."

But I couldn't help noticing I felt less obsessed about the situation than my little brother seemed to feel. I didn't say so. It would have been cruel, so I didn't say anything.

"How do I find out where he is?" he asked. He pulled his PowerBook onto his lap and opened the cover, as if the info were right there on the Internet just waiting for him to come up with good search terms.

"I have no idea," I said. "But I'm not sure you're going to find it on the web."

"I was going to look for something more like info for families of military prisoners. You know. Instructions for how to contact the military to find out where your family member's being held. They have that somewhere, right?"

"I don't know," I said. "Maybe. Or maybe . . ." But then I just trailed off—not because I didn't know where I was going, but because I wasn't anxious to get there.

"What?" he asked.

"I just think maybe it's a problem most army families don't have. Because maybe they just wait for their relative to contact them and *tell* them where they're being held."

"Oh," he said, and closed the cover of his laptop. He sat a minute, looking a little queasy and like he was downshifting his gears inside—from fifth gear on the highway down to neutral. Idling isn't always easy. Then he said, "What would you do if you were me?"

"Um. Probably wait a few days and see if they print where he is in the paper."

"Oh," he said. "Right." Then he looked straight into my face for the first time. Or, at least, for the first time it seemed he was actually seeing me. "Why were you crying?" he asked, his head tilted slightly like a dog who wants to understand but doesn't.

"Why would you think I was crying?"

"You can tell. Your eyes are all puffy."

"I don't really want to talk about it."

"I just—"

"Look," I said. "Remember when you asked me to please not ask you any questions? Well, it works both ways."

"Got it," he said. "Sorry."

Then I decided that was more than enough commiseration, and I headed back to my own room.

———

About four thirty that afternoon, Aubrey came and got me by rapping on my bedroom door. When I opened it, he pointed to the cell phone in his hand in absolute silence. Then he gave me a hand signal for "follow me."

I followed him through the house. As far as I could tell, nobody was around except Isabella, who was making a pie from scratch in the kitchen. She only smiled and asked no questions.

I followed Aubrey through the backyard and out the gate in our back fence.

"Where are we going?" I asked when I knew we were too far from the house to be heard.

"Down by the creek."

Calling it a creek was really elevating its status, I have to say in retrospect. Only city kids who hadn't spent much time in nature, like we were back then, would even see it as a natural body of water. It was more of a culvert carrying water down through the canyon from the fancier yards of the still fancier houses up on the hill. It ran open for a few flat stretches, then disappeared through concrete pipes again. But it was flowing water, and it had a few trees on either side, and the closer we got to it, the less I could hear voices and engines and car doors slamming and mic checks on the street in front of our house. It was a relief, a lifting of a great weight I'd forgotten was compressing me.

Aubrey stopped by the flowing water, looked around three hundred and sixty-five degrees, then held the phone to his ear.

"Sorry, Aunt Sheila," he said. "Sorry to keep you waiting."

I was surprised, of course. I thought he'd dragged me down there just to try dialing her house.

"So, okay, maybe when school gets out for the summer. Because, like you said, it would be a little weird to tell Mom and Dad we want to go stay with you during school. I'm suspended, but only for the rest of this week. And Ruth has to go to school."

I watched his forehead knit as he listened, and watched the sunlight flash in and out between the leaves of the blowing trees overhead, and listened to the water gurgle.

Then he said, "I don't know yet, but I can call as soon as we find out."

His forehead scrunched down even more tightly.

"Really? Why there? Why so far away?"

Another long silence during which I had no idea what was going on. I started to wonder why he'd dragged me down here with him. Three people can't really talk on a cell phone, and he could just as easily have told me later what she said.

A second later, he held the phone inches from my face. "She wants to talk to you."

I took the phone, which was warm—more like hot, really—from Aubrey's anxious ear.

"Hi, Aunt Sheila."

"Ruth. Honey. How *are* you? How *is* everything over there?"

I was struck with a rush of having missed her. I hadn't ever thought about missing Aunt Sheila when I didn't see her, but it was unmistakable in that moment.

"Fine, Aunt Sheila," I said.

"Really?"

Then I lost control of the tears again and had to swipe them away with the back of first one hand and then the other.

"No. Of course not. I don't know why I even said that. The street in front of our house is packed with reporters and we can't get through them without Mom guarding us like a pit bull and my new sort-of boyfriend just dumped me because his family said he had to, because the reporters wouldn't leave them alone. And Dad's home in the middle of the day because he's losing clients over this . . ."

"Uh-oh," Aunt Sheila said.

"Uh-oh which part?"

"Well, all of it, really. But especially the part about Brad losing clients. He's not as rich as everybody thinks. More like comically overextended. Only, at a time like this it's not so funny. But let's not get into that now. Hopefully it'll blow over. I'm not sure about what Aubrey's asking me, kiddo. I mean, you're welcome to come here for the summer, both of you. And it goes without saying that you can do all kinds of stuff here you can't do at home. But I told Aubrey they might hold Joseph someplace like Leavenworth."

"Leavenworth?" I asked, and I noticed Aubrey winced at the word.

"It's in Kansas."

"Kansas! Why so far away?"

"Look, I'm just guessing, kiddo. I'm guessing Leavenworth because it's sort of a big central place for federal prisoners. But it could be anywhere. Once you're in the federal system, I don't know if they care much what part of the country you hail from, you know? And if I'm right, we can call him from here over the summer. If he can get calls. Or get him to call us or something. But you know kindergarten teachers aren't exactly made of money, right? So three people on a plane to Kansas . . ."

"We might be able to come up with the money," I said.

Aubrey bounced up and down. "I have money," he said, about four times. Even after I was trying to hear Aunt Sheila again.

"Great," she said into my ear. "Very nice. It's always a good feeling when your niece and nephew can buy you and sell you a couple of times over. Look. Kiddo. I'm worried about your brother."

"Which one?"

"The one I just talked to, although . . . both of them, now that you mention it. Aubrey sounds like he's about to come apart. So look after him, okay? See if there's anything you can do to help between now and summer. Without Joseph, he doesn't have much if he doesn't have you. I told him to start by writing a letter to Joseph and sending it to me. I'll figure out where to mail it to. That way Joseph can write back through me and Brad doesn't have to know. So encourage that, okay? Aubrey needs some kind of vent for all this. Otherwise he's going to go off like a bomb. You know how he adores his big brother."

The sun glared into my eyes off and on through the leaves as I listened, wondering why I wasn't getting credit for loving Joseph or needing a vent for all this myself. I'm sure Aunt Sheila meant well, and maybe she was just giving me credit for being older and better put-together, but it hurt. I didn't want credit for being together; I wanted help staying that way.

"Keep me posted," she said, and then we said quick good-byes and got off the phone, and that was that.

I looked at Aubrey and he looked at me, and then I handed him his phone back.

"What?" he asked me. "What did she say?"

"She wants you to write a letter to Joseph."

Out of all the information Aunt Sheila had just poured into my tender ear, that was the only part I dared repeat to my bomb of a little brother.

————

"Aubrey and I want to go to Aunt Sheila's for the summer."

I just said it straight out like that, over dinner. Aubrey never took his focus off the chandelier.

I watched my mom's eyes narrow suspiciously.

"Why? You never begged to go to Sheila's house before."

"I'm not begging," I said firmly, and with an unusual dose of poise. "We just think it would be a good idea. You know. Because of . . ." I tossed my head in the direction of the street.

She looked at my father, who nodded so slightly I almost didn't catch it.

"Okay," she said. "You're right. I envy you. Wish I could get out of this fishbowl. But don't get your hopes up for total peace and quiet. Because Sheila told your father she's been getting phone calls from the press."

Aubrey's eyes came down from the light and the prisms. We looked at each other in silence for a moment. I think we really had been assuming we would live out our summer in utter anonymity and peace.

"How do they even know she's related?" I asked my mom. It smacked of a complaint, like the world hadn't behaved properly, and I could fix it just by pointing it out. "She doesn't have the same last name."

My mom snorted in that way she did when she wanted to make the point that she knew the world and we didn't. "These things are not hard to find out," she said. She ate her lamb curry for a moment in silence, chewing thoughtfully. Or it looked thought-ful, anyway—like chewing and thinking couldn't be separated out. Then she added, "We'll call her and see what she says."

"She said yes," I said.

A dark silence fell, and I scrambled around in my mind, won-dering why I'd so thoughtlessly admitted we'd called Aunt Sheila behind their backs. Truthfully, it really hadn't occurred to me that we shouldn't. But the silence felt weird.

"Without asking us first?"

My mother was doing all the talking. My dad was lost in his food, and maybe other things as well. It struck me in that moment that he had turned the important job of calling us on our mistakes over to her, which was unheard of.

"Well," I said, keeping my voice casual. "What was the point of even bothering you with the idea if she was busy or said no for some reason?"

Another silence, and then she nodded and life went on, so I tried to breathe deeply without letting on that I was relieved.

I chewed a bite of lamb slowly, then said, "Wait a minute. How come *we're* not getting a bunch of phone calls?"

My mother laughed—actually laughed out loud, like I'd told a merry joke and she'd enjoyed it, if such a thing were possible in the Stellkellner family.

"Honey," she said. "We've had the ringer turned off on that phone since the day this hit the papers."

I swallowed hard and wondered who had to go through the voice mails, and how many there were every day, and what they said. Maybe that was why my dad looked as though he were lost on some distant planet. Maybe that was why he didn't say a word these days.

Chapter Eight: Aubrey

April 14, 2003
Dear Joseph,

Ruth and Aunt Sheila said to write to you. I haven't even thought of anything to say yet, and already I feel bad. Because I want to tell you a lot about how rotten everything is here. But then I think, that's nothing compared to the rottenness on your end. You're in jail.

And besides, I don't want you to feel like it's all your fault.

I have to be honest and say I really don't understand why you're in jail. I mean, I know what the charges are. I even know why people think it's such a big deal, what you did. I just don't know what you're doing in custody.

You were free. Nobody knew where you were. On the cop shows, they call that being in the wind.

Why did you turn yourself in?

I'm pretty sure if it happened to me, I'd still be in the wind. Especially if I were you. Because I just don't think they're going to be fair to you.

I don't think you should be able to put somebody in jail for doing what he thought was right. Not even if the people who are putting you on trial think it's wrong. I think you should be able to put somebody in jail for purposely hurting somebody else. Or stealing. Or something where you knew what you were doing was wrong and tried to get away with it. But not for this.

I have something I'm going to tell you that I haven't told anybody else. I'm still reading everything about you online. The news stories and the blogs and the websites for and against you. Except they're mostly against you. And then I read all the comments.

I can't stop.

I know I should stop. I think Ruth read them at least once. Because she told me, "Don't read the comments." But I do. Because they're there. Anybody can read them. I feel like I have to know what's out there for everybody to see.

Is that why you turned yourself in? Because people are saying such terrible things about you? And you wanted them to know you were honest? And maybe you even thought they'd know you're innocent if you turned yourself in? Because guilty people usually run? Which, well, now that I think about it, you did. At first. But maybe then you thought how that would just make you look guilty?

If so, this is just my opinion, but I think you shouldn't have. Because they will never give you a break. No matter what you do, it will never be good enough. They'll always be against you.

It's driving me crazy. And I can't tell anybody because I don't want them to send me to a shrink or something.

(Which I think they will, anyway.) But I can't sleep at night because I lie awake arguing with those people in my head. I feel like I need to find them all and beat them all up. Or maybe first try to change their minds and then only beat them up if I can't. And I feel like I can't rest or relax until I do.

But, you know. It's impossible. It's everybody.

As long as I live, I'm never going to do what they're doing. I made myself a promise. And now I'm making the promise to you. I'm never going to judge somebody I don't know. And if somebody is accused of something in the newspaper or on TV, I'm going to remember that maybe he did it or maybe he didn't. I wasn't there, so I don't know.

Why doesn't anybody do that? Why do they all think they know? They never even met you. They should be able to see how much they don't know.

Okay. That's enough of that, because I'm probably just making you feel worse. And it's their fault. Not yours.

Please write back to me, Joseph. I don't want to seem like I'm begging. Except I sort of am. It's so important to me. I need to feel like we're connected again. Lately I've been feeling like you belong to everybody else and not to me. Like those people who are screaming about you are acting like you're their brother, not mine. And I'm starting to feel like there's some kind of brick wall between us. And like I can't see you through it.

I guess I'm starting to feel like they're right.

So please write back as fast as you can so I can feel normal again. Then in June or sometime during the summer we'll fly out there and see you. Don't worry. Aunt Sheila is going to take us. And don't worry about Aunt Sheila spending all her money on planes, because I can pay for it.

*Maybe I can do something you need done. Do you need
a good lawyer? Well. I guess I don't have that much money.
But I still want you to tell me what you need. Better food?
Or maybe even something like cigarettes, either to smoke or
to trade for something else? Or is that only in the movies?*
   *Well. I'm going to leave you alone now. Write back.
Please. It's important.*

*Your brother,
Aubrey Stellkellner*

———

As soon as I finished writing it, I wanted to scratch out my last
name. Because Joseph knew my last name. It was the same as his,
even though we had different fathers. Because Ruth's and my dad
adopted him. So that was stupid, writing "Stellkellner." But I didn't
want to scratch it out, because then it would be messy. And it was
too long a letter to copy over.

I tried to put it out of my mind, how stupid it was.

I wrote a note to Aunt Sheila to put in the envelope with the
letter. It asked her to please call me the minute we heard back from
Joseph.

———

My mom woke me up at seven thirty in the morning. Banging on
my bedroom door. I saw a movie once where a mom woke her son
with a kiss on the forehead. I envied him so much I almost cried.
In front of people. I mean, I didn't. Of course. But still, that was a
close call.

"Up!" she yelled through the door.

"Take a hint!" I yelled back. "I'm suspended."

"Like I could forget."

"So why do I have to get up?"

"You have an eight-thirty appointment."

"What appointment? With who?"

No answer. I heard the scuff of her shoes on the thickly carpeted stairs.

I sat up. Looked around. I think I was still half-asleep.

Finally, I got up and pulled on jeans and a sweater. My favorite sweater. When I wore it, I always felt a little more secure.

I trotted downstairs and found my mom in the kitchen. She pointed to my breakfast, which was sitting waiting for me on the kitchen table. Bacon, eggs scrambled just the way I liked them, pancakes, orange juice.

Sounds like a scene from that movie with wake-up kisses. Except my mom hadn't made that breakfast. Isabella had made it. I could tell. Because it looked and smelled great. And because the eggs were scrambled just the way I liked them.

No, my mom's contribution to breakfast was to point at it. Nothing more.

"What appointment? With who?"

"You're seeing your new therapist today."

"I don't want to see a therapist."

"Really not optional," she said. "We promised your principal. Now eat your breakfast. Doesn't pay to get your head shrunk on an empty stomach."

I wondered if she was guessing. Or if she knew from personal experience.

———

We waited in the therapist's outer office. Yes, that's right. *We*. Me and my mommy. Can you imagine anything more humiliating for a thirteen-year-old boy?

"Why can't you just come back and pick me up in an hour?" I asked her.

"Because I don't trust you."

"To do what?"

"Oh, use your brain, Aubrey. You have a decent brain, you just keep it in mothballs all the time."

"You think I'm going to run off and get myself an ice-cream soda and then come back here just in time to be picked up and then tell you it went great."

"Bingo."

I sighed. It had never occurred to me to ditch the session, actually. But once we'd laid out the situation, I couldn't deny that it might have. The minute she left.

It was a moot point, though. Because she never left.

———

My new therapist's name was Luanne. I thought it didn't suit her. To me a Luanne was a fluffy type. A girly girl. This girl looked like she could take care of herself and then some. She was probably six feet tall. She had this gaze that I thought could turn steely. But it didn't, so I'm not sure why I thought so. Her face was no-nonsense. I don't think she wore any makeup. I also didn't think she needed any.

I think she was probably multiracial. She had light brown eyes and jet-black hair, and I figured she could have been African American. Or maybe not. Or maybe she was Mideastern or some other ethnicity.

I'm just reporting this. I didn't care. In fact, if anything, it might have been a point in her favor. In my neighborhood, you could get plenty tired of whiteness.

"Have a seat," she said.

And she smiled at me. And I liked her.

Which was a problem. I didn't want to like her.

It embarrassed me to look into her face, so I looked around her office.

I had never seen so many fish in one place in my entire life. Her office was decorated with seven aquariums. *Seven.* And they were huge. Like maybe a hundred gallons each. Though estimating the bulk of a small body of water was not my specialty at the time. Or now.

One was nothing but clown fish. Maybe fifty or more. Another housed fish that looked almost tiger striped, mixed with something bright orange with fanlike tails. Those tails never stopped waving. Here and there, a catfish or an eel came slashing up from the bottom of a tank, startling me. Some tanks had green water plants growing. Fish wound in and out between their tendrils. Tendrils that waved as if in a breeze, but I knew it was the push or pull of the filter. In one tank, the plants were less like plants and more like anemones that I was pretty sure waved under their own power. Some kind of bottom-feeder had its mouth attached to the glass of one tank. Cleaning off any stray algae. I could see what the inside of its mouth looked like. Which was eerie.

I don't mean to go on and on about the aquariums. But they really grabbed me and held on.

"You like the fish," she said. It wasn't a question.

"I can't stop watching them."

"I find them calming."

"Me, too," I said.

"Tell me about your life," she said.

"I can't answer a question like that."

"Why not?"

"It's not specific enough."

"Okay. Tell me about your life since your brother, Joseph, came home."

"It sucks," I said. "I hate it. But it's not Joseph's fault."

"Tell me what sucks about it."

I looked at her office door. "Not if she can hear me."

"She can't."

"Why should I take your word for that?"

"I'm not asking you to take my word. You were sitting in the outer office during the last few minutes of the session before yours. Did you hear anything that was said in here?"

"Oh. Right. No. I didn't." I paused. Wanting to get restarted, but lost in my brain. "What was the question again?"

"I was asking about life at your house since Joseph came home. What sucks about it?"

"Everything. The kids at school say terrible things. Like I should be ashamed of him. And every time I leave the house, people videotape me walking away. And if my mom doesn't come out and run interference for us, people stick microphones in our faces and try to get us to say things about Joseph. And in the newspapers and online, people say terrible things about him, and they never even met him and they were never in Baghdad and they don't know anything. But that never shuts them up. And I caught a guy going through our recycling. And somebody painted the word 'coward' on our house. He's not a coward. He was doing what he thought was right. And my father says I can't contact Joseph in any way."

I stopped. Ran out of gas, really. I watched two tall, flat yellow fish come together as if to kiss. Then one chased the other away.

"What's the worst part of everything you just told me?"

"My father says I can't contact Joseph in any way."

"And who can you talk to about things like this?"

"Nobody."

"Your parents aren't good listeners?"

I snorted. And I decided, just very suddenly like that, that I didn't like Luanne, after all.

"See? You don't know anything. You know nothing about my life. Or you wouldn't even ask a question like that. You don't know me. *Or* my family."

"Aubrey . . . ," she said.

"What?"

She glanced at her watch, which she wore with the face on the inside of her wrist. "You've been in my office for two and a half minutes."

"So?"

"I accept the fact that I don't magically know all about your situation. We're here so I can find out. You have to tell me. Then I'll know. Then maybe I can help."

"You can't help me."

"How do you know that?"

"Can you get Joseph out of prison and back home?"

"No."

"Can you get people to shut up about him and keep their opinions to themselves?"

"No, I can't."

"Then you can't help me."

"I hope you're not saying you're a helpless victim of your own life."

"What? No! I didn't say that."

"Sounded like you did. You said the only way I can help you is to get everything back the way you want it. In other words, the only way to fix your misery is to have everything in order in your life. All your ducks in a row. You're not even allowing for the possibility that the world could stay a mess, but you could be less miserable about it."

"I can't do that."

"Why can't you?"

"I just can't. I never could."

"The fact that you never did doesn't mean you never will."

"I can't relax about things. I don't know how."

"Ah. Now *that* I can accept. You don't know how."

"Right."

"Do you know how to play the piano?"

"No."

"But you could take lessons. Right?"

"I don't like music."

"You're missing the point."

I looked from the anemone tank to her face. I felt a little bit ashamed. Usually I had a good mind. But she was trying to tell me something. And I was being thick.

"I'm sorry. Tell me again, then."

"This thing you say you don't know how to do—keeping yourself a little more together while everything around you is falling apart—that's what you're here to learn. These are your lessons. You don't take lessons only in things you already know how to do. You don't refuse to take piano lessons because you don't already know how to play the piano."

"Oh," I said. And my eyes drifted back to the clown-fish tank again. "I get it. Yeah."

"So tell me more about what it's been like at your house since Joseph came home."

And, in a move that surprised even me, I did.

———

"What about this other man Joseph was so close to?" she asked, much later in the session. I could not have been more stunned. "This Hamish MacCallum. Is he somebody you can talk to?"

I made a strange snorting sound.

"I don't even know who he is. I've never met the guy in my life. I never even heard his name until I read it in the paper. How do you even know about him?"

"I read it in the paper," she said.

A long silence while I watched the fish swim. It wasn't always peaceful. Sometimes it was jerky and chaotic. But it was nice not to talk for a minute.

"I thought Joseph spent every summer with him," she said.

"You know as much about it as I do."

"Is it not true?"

"I have no idea. I'm just his brother. I'm just his flesh and blood. It's not like I have a right to know what's going on or anything."

She ignored the sarcasm and asked, "Was Joseph home during the summer?"

"No."

"And you never asked where he would go?"

"I guess Ruth and I thought he was in some kind of summer camp or something. You have to know how it is in my family. You don't ask a lot of questions. You just don't. Nobody says straight-out that you don't. You just figure that out after a while."

I saw her writing notes down on her pad at that point.

"Tell me something about Joseph."

"Isn't that what I've been doing all along?"

"Not about the mess he's in right now. About *him*. Before all this happened. Tell me something you remember about him. When things were better."

"Oh," I said.

Then I watched the fish for a while. Let my mind drift over a short lifetime with my brother. Although I don't think it seemed short at the time. When you're thirteen, thirteen years is a lot.

"Nothing?" she asked a minute later.

"No. Everything. There are just so many things. I can't even figure out how to pick one. And now for some reason they all seem just the same amount of important. *Very.* They all seem *very* important. I think before this happened, I would have picked an obvious one. Like the time he saved my cat when my dad wouldn't pay for his surgery. Or when he scared this kid who was bullying me, and the kid never came near me again. Or how patient he was with our grandmother when she didn't know she'd already asked you the same question six times. I used to think those were most important. But now it *all* is. Like, every minute he ever spent with me."

"That was my error," she said. "I thought this would be a quick exercise. I'm sorry to say our time's up for today."

I thought that went fast. But I didn't say so. Because that would have let on that I was getting along fine with the therapy so far.

Chapter Nine: Ruth

When I woke up the next morning, the unfairness of things came down on me like a fog that suddenly drops low enough to obscure everything but itself.

Aubrey was still fast asleep in his room, which made being suspended seem like quite the treat. To make matters worse, he'd been to see a therapist the previous day, which I figured he probably hated, but to me it sounded great: lie on a couch and have somebody focus on what hurts you and ask you all about it and treat you like you're fragile and need lots of help and attention.

But I didn't get all that, because I hadn't pummeled anybody with my fists.

My dad was sitting in the living room, all dressed up in a three-piece suit and a tie, like he was on his way to court, but he wasn't on his way to anywhere. He was drinking a glass of something brown at seven o'clock in the morning and staring off into space.

I stepped into the kitchen and asked, of nobody in particular, "Where do we keep the antacid? We do have antacid, right?"

My mom was pacing around the kitchen, tending to things that didn't need tending. First she put away the big, tall wooden salt and pepper shakers, but they had never gotten put away before. They lived on the counter at all times. She saw a mug on the table and grabbed it and hung it back up on the mug hooks in the cupboard, as if it offended her sense of order by being out of place. She paced the other way, then suddenly stopped and turned back.

"Oh, wait. I was going to bring your father some coffee," she said, and got the mug back down.

"I think he has a different kind of drink on his mind," I said, settling at the table.

There was a fabulous breakfast laid out in front of me. Huevos rancheros, with two poached eggs, refried black beans, and what I knew by smell to be Isabella's homemade ranchero sauce.

"Hush," my mom said, pouring the mug full of coffee.

Then she did something that seemed bizarre, to put it mildly. She came rushing at me—and it alarmed me, I couldn't help it. I felt like I was being charged—assaulted, almost. But when she got to me, she only threw her arms around me and held me, very tightly and for a very long time.

My face was smashed against her shoulder, so I couldn't have talked even if I'd wanted to or had any idea what to say. I tried to relax my muscles, to relax into her embrace, but it didn't work at all. Not even a little bit.

She kissed me hard on the top of my head, right where my hair parted, and then just as fast as she'd grabbed me, she let me go. I wanted to say something, but I didn't know what it should be, and she had grabbed up my father's coffee again and was back into that frenetic motion. And meanwhile, I didn't have words for what had just happened.

As she hurried off into the living room with the mug, my eyes snagged on Isabella's eyes. She was standing in the far corner of the kitchen, looking for something in the pantry. I hadn't realized until that moment that she was still in the room, but that was Isabella for you—for a big woman, she sure had a way of not taking up much figurative space.

"Good morning, missy," she said.

"Hi. This smells good. Thank you."

"At least you can have a good breakfast. Even if nothing else is so good."

"Why didn't *you* get coffee for my dad? Oh, I'm sorry. I didn't mean it like—I didn't mean you're not doing your job. You always do. Just usually . . ."

"I know what you mean," she said. "She needs more to do with her hands. So she's doing lots of stuff I should be doing, and I'm not saying nothing. I'm just staying out of her way."

"Oh," I said, and took a bite of breakfast. It was fabulous. She was right—it was almost enough to make up for the fact that nothing else was okay. "Why's my dad all dressed up but not going anywhere?"

"He's hoping the partners will call him in. You know. Maybe need some help with something. Anything for some billable hours. But he's got no appointments of his own today. So maybe just wishful thinking?"

My stomach turned slightly, but I took another bite of the food anyway. A moment later, a bottle of liquid antacid appeared beside my plate with a sterling-silver tablespoon beside it. I looked up into Isabella's loving face, and she smiled back down at me, a little sadly I thought.

"You don't feel so good, missy?"

"No. I don't. I'm sick. I don't think I'm going to go to school."

I wasn't sick—my gut was just in a twist, as it had been for days—but once the idea of staying home sick popped into my head, it seemed to be the solution for everything. It eased that nagging feeling that everyone got to go belly-up except me. If they could give up on life and just drift, so could I.

"Poor missy," she said, and stroked the hair off my forehead, holding one warm palm there for a moment to check my temperature. I knew the sensation of the warmth of her palm was not a good thing. When you have a fever, the hand checking your fever should feel cool in comparison, and I knew she was feeling the same thing. "You want a different breakfast? Not so *picante*?"

"No. Thanks. I like this. This is good."

It made no difference to my heartburn if the food I ate was spicy or bland, because it wasn't food that was causing the issues.

My mom hurried back in. "What's wrong with her?" she asked Isabella, as if I didn't exist, or couldn't speak for myself.

Isabella peeled away, off into the dining room without answering, which I appreciated. I think she knew it was important to me that she not say the wrong thing.

"I feel like I'm coming down with something. I think I should stay home."

Then I turned my attention down to my plate and began shoveling in as much of the food as I could. It was good, and it was making me feel more grounded, and I honestly didn't see until a moment later that it was hurting my case for the sick day.

My mom picked up the antacid bottle.

"You don't get to stay home from school for heartburn," she said. "If you could stop the world because you have heartburn, I wouldn't have done a damn thing for the past twenty years."

"It's not just that," I said, my mouth full of tortilla and egg. "I think I'm getting the flu."

"Based on what?"

"My muscles are all achy, and I'm sick to my stomach."

She looked down at my plate, and so did I. I had eaten almost three-quarters of my spicy food—scarfed it down, really.

"But you felt like a big breakfast."

"I thought my stomach might feel better if I could hold down some food."

She held a hand to my forehead the way Isabella had done, only not quite. Isabella's gesture had felt caring, a question. An investigation on my behalf. My mom's hand felt rough and hurried, and the only question in that touch was how quickly she could dismiss my complaints.

"Nice try," she said. "Now eat up and I'll drive you."

———

When I got to school, I didn't talk to anyone and no one talked to me, which was not unusual. In fact, I felt like I could clear a space in the hall just by walking through a crowd. I felt like the wrong end of a magnet.

When I got to my locker, I spun the combination lock and opened the door. There were two notes in there, and neither were anything I'd seen, and neither had been there the day before when I'd opened my locker. One was just a torn scrap of yellow lined paper, and the other was actually tucked into an envelope with my name on it. Someone—well, two someones—had pushed them through the vents on my locker door.

I picked up the scrap of yellow paper first.

In handwriting I didn't recognize, it said, *I hope you didn't shake hands with your brother before he went off to jail. Be a shame to get all that blood on your hands, too.*

I stepped back and dropped the note.

Then I picked it up fast, so no one else could see it. I grabbed up the other one, the one in the envelope, even though I knew I'd never read it. I tore them both into tiny shreds as I walked, then dropped the shreds into the trash can in the corner of the hall. A path opened up for me as I walked—everyone jumped out of my way, and as they noticed me they stopped talking, so I created a ribbon of not only space but eerie silence wherever I walked.

I walked into my first-period class and right up to my English teacher, Mrs. Mallory.

"I'm not feeling good," I said. "And I need to go see the nurse."

Her brow furrowed—maybe because she didn't believe me, or maybe because she felt bad for me, though if I'd been a betting woman, I'd have put money on some combination of the two.

"Wait, let me give you a hall pass," she said.

———

I had a transformative experience lying on a cot in the nurse's office. Seriously, my life changed in that moment. Not by magic, though—by me. *I* changed it.

We'd made a deal, the nurse and I, that I'd lie down through first period and then decide whether or not to go home.

But when all was said and done, I decided a lot more than just that.

I sat up suddenly when I realized it, and she didn't notice at first.

All this falling apart was stupid. No, more than stupid—it was pathetic. My father was pathetic for drinking at seven in the morning and my brother was pathetic for beating up everybody who looked at him wrong and sitting in a shrink's office, and I was pathetic for pretending to be sick—for trying to imitate the way they were solving things, when it was obvious their way was no solution at all.

I decided I would be strong, not because I had to be, not because they had used up all the weakness, but because strong was what I wanted for myself.

"I feel better," I said to the nurse. "I'm going back to class."

She was surprised, I think, and so was I. I'd only been lying on that cot for three or four minutes, but it doesn't take long to change your life—at least, not when you finally get around to it.

I've never gone back on the decision to be strong, not to this very day.

———

Aubrey came to my bedroom with a soft knock about an hour before dinner.

"You can come in," I said when he stuck his head through the partly opened door.

I'd been spending the bulk of the day feeling contemptuous toward him, but when I finally saw him, he just looked small and weighted down and sad, and I felt sorry for the poor guy.

So I asked him, "How was your appointment with your new therapist?"

He made a face that looked as though he was still busy deciding. Then he came and sat on the edge of my bed.

"I don't know," he said. "It was . . . I don't know."

"It's okay. You don't have to talk about that if you don't want."

"No, I don't mind. I just can't decide. I sort of like her. And then, in another way, I sort of don't. Like, I feel like she's being nice, but I also feel like she could be scary. Like any minute I could be scared of her. But mostly I'm not. Does that make sense?"

"I think so," I said.

Then we both went silent for a long time, and I realized I'd had more actual conversations with my brother Aubrey since Joseph came home than in the two or three years before that all put together.

"Is that what you came in here to talk to me about?" I asked after a time.

"No."

"I didn't think so."

"I've been looking online all day."

"I told you not to read that stuff."

"No. Not that stuff. Well. That stuff, too. But that's not what I want to talk about. Because why talk about it? What's the point? You know how bad it is, and it's all the same. I was online reading about court-martials. Only turns out that's saying it wrong. You're supposed to say 'courts-martial.' Which sounds weird. But it's right. Technically. But I still don't think I'd say it that way, because people would think it was wrong. Even though it isn't."

"You want to jump to the part that got you in here?"

"Right. Sorry. I read that they can give a soldier the death penalty."

Silence for a moment while we both listened to the phantom thump of that information landing on my bedroom carpet.

"Not for this they wouldn't, though. Right?"

"I don't know," he said. "It was that kind of legal writing, mostly, and it was hard to tell."

"I think that's for when a guy does something really bad on purpose, like gives secrets away to the enemy. You know, like a spy, a betrayer. And he gets other soldiers killed by betraying."

"But everybody's *saying* Joseph's a betrayer who got two guys killed."

"But they can't prove that those two guys wouldn't have gotten killed anyway."

"That never stopped anybody else," he said, and I had to admit—at least silently, to myself—that he had a point about that. "Some of the people who leave comments are even saying now that Joseph should get the death penalty for what he did."

"Aubrey . . ."

"What?"

"I told you not to read the comments."

"Yeah. You did. You just forgot to tell me how to stop."

I sighed. I almost laughed, but I knew it would come out wrong, and Aubrey would misunderstand it, because everything was so very unfunny in his world. Well, in all of our worlds.

"Things will be better when we get to Aunt Sheila's for the summer," I said.

"Why will they be better?"

"Because even if there's a reporter or two calling, most people who live around there won't know who we are. So when we go places, we don't have to go around telling everybody our last name, and we'll just be her niece and nephew visiting. And then we'll go see Joseph, and he'll tell you for himself that they don't give out the death penalty just for talking to a few guys about not going out on duty. And then you'll believe it, and things will be better."

"That does sound better," he said.

And he even got to his feet, like what I'd given him was enough.

"Thing is," he said, "it's only May. Till June is a long time to wait."

Strong as I was, and expert as I'd suddenly become at calming things to say to my little brother, I had nothing in my bag of tricks to help either one of us through the seemingly endless maze of the days we'd have to wait.

Part Two

Before You Jump,

a Hearty Breakfast

Remembering Summer 2003

Chapter Ten: Aubrey

I had to ride in the back. It was a two-door. So Ruth had to stand there holding the passenger seat forward so I could get in.

Aunt Sheila's car was an old Nissan. Not old like from another generation. Just old like ten or twelve years. It was a foreign concept to me. If my parents kept a car for three years instead of two, they were deeply ashamed by how ancient it was. Unless it was one of my dad's "classics."

The Nissan was yellow and had rust on its hood.

I wasn't ashamed to be riding in it. And I wasn't trying to judge it. I just couldn't focus off it. Not only the age but the fact that it was cheap and light. The doors made more of a ping when you closed them. Less of a thunk.

Looking back, I'm a little ashamed. Of myself. But I just couldn't help it at the time.

At least I had the back of the car to myself.

I turned on my CD player and stuck the earbuds in place. Then I cranked it up high. I don't remember the band or the song. I remember the mood. Pounding and loud. It was the kind of music that can make everything else go away. Because it *drives* it away. It forces everything that isn't itself to leave.

I waved at the reporters and cameramen as we pulled away from the curb. Not because I liked them. Because I was happy to be saying good-bye. It was meant to be more like a taunting wave. *Going where you can't get to me. Bye.*

Maybe. I hope.

Nobody waved back.

———

My sister threw an empty plastic water bottle at me, and it bounced off my forehead.

"Ow," I said, pulling one earbud out. The left one. Letting it dangle. "What?"

"Aunt Sheila is trying to talk to you. Are you deaf?"

"I was listening to my music."

"Well, listen to me," Aunt Sheila said. "For a minute at least. We're not going all the way to Texas to see Joseph until I can talk to him first."

Joseph had landed in Texas, not Kansas. That much I knew. Only the subtext of Aunt Sheila's caution was unfamiliar to me.

It set something off in my stomach. I didn't know what it was yet. I still had the thumping music in my right ear. But, just my luck, it coexisted with this new feeling. It couldn't drive the new stuff out. It didn't even feel as though it was trying.

"Why not?"

"Because it's too far to go if we're not going to get to see him."

"Why wouldn't we see him?"

"I don't know, Aubrey. I don't know what's going on. I just know you've sent him three letters and he hasn't written back."

"He didn't get them," I said. With some strength. To preempt whatever might come back around to me. Maybe even to over-power it.

"You don't know what he did or didn't get. You just know there's been no word from him."

"If he got them, he would have written back to me."

"In the past, maybe. But maybe things are different now."

I felt myself starting to get mad. The kind of mad that nor-mally landed me in the principal's office. "*Things* may be different," I said. "But *Joseph's* not."

"A thing like this can change someone," she said.

"He didn't change!" I shouted. I hadn't meant to shout it. And part of me almost felt like I hadn't. More like it had shouted itself. "Why would he change into someone who wouldn't even answer me? That's stupid. That could never happen."

"I can think of a lot of reasons," she said. As if I hadn't just called her stupid.

I watched the back of her head at an angle. Hoping she wouldn't tell me any of them. She had her hair up, but loosely. She had a big head and face. Huge glasses. She looked nothing like Dad. They didn't look like they could even have been related. Didn't act like it, either.

And she was older than Dad. More like fiftysomething to his late forties.

"He might just be trying to keep this whole mess away from you," she said.

I heard my sister snort a little.

"Too late for that," I said. I guess I said it *for* Ruth. For both of us.

"But he might not know that. Or maybe Brad told him not to get in touch with you. Or the letters might be censored going out and he might be worried what they'd sound like after the censors got through with them. Or a dozen other reasons we don't know about because we're not in there with him. I'm not going to waste the trip if he's not going to come out and see us."

"He'll come out and see us," I said, trying to keep my voice calm. Failing. I wanted to scream at Aunt Sheila. Throw something. Put tape on her mouth. Anything to keep her from talking. "Besides, it's my money that would be wasted. Not yours."

"But it's a big deal, a long trip like that. Especially when you consider the risk I'm taking, doing this behind your parents' backs. If they find out, I'll never hear the end of it. Which is a risk I'm willing to take if we can see him. But it's too much risk to take if it turns out to all be for nothing. I'm only going if it's going to do any good. So I'll call when we get home. I can't call Joseph. But I'll call and get a message to him, or get him to call back collect. Or at least I need to get a message back from him that he'll see us if we come."

"That's the stupidest thing I ever heard in my life!" I shouted. Completely losing the battle to disguise my panic. "He's going to *see* us!"

I saw Ruth and Aunt Sheila exchange a look with each other. Aunt Sheila's look seemed to say, *Has he been like this all along?* and Ruth's seemed to say, *Oh yeah.*

"Humor me," Aunt Sheila said. "I want to hear it with my own ears."

I put my earbuds back in and steamed and fumed all the way back to Aunt Sheila's house.

I looked out the window. I don't remember what I saw. If I even saw it in the first place at all.

———

My new room for the summer was the basement. I thought that was ironic. I mean, after the way Joseph had been banished to the basement and all. When he came home. Brief as that turned out to be.

I didn't feel punished, though. I didn't mind at all. It made me feel closer to him. Like the world had given us one more thing to share in common.

Aunt Sheila had brought down a little foldable cot. It sat in one corner, with sheets and a pillow and a pillow slip and a coarse blanket all folded neatly on one end.

One concrete wall of the basement was covered with shelves. Floor to nearly ceiling, wood shelves. But the only thing they stored was Aunt Sheila's bottle collection. All the bottles were empty. I got the feeling that every one meant something to her, though I couldn't imagine what. Only about one in ten had anything to do with alcohol. Sure, there was the odd champagne bottle here or there. I tried to imagine that one was left over from when her now-grown daughter was born. Or some other huge life milestone like that. There was the occasional brown bottle from some rare imported beer. But there were also Coke bottles. Root beer bottles. Sparkling water bottles. I couldn't imagine why they all had meaning to her.

After a few minutes, I realized it was giving me a headache to try. And I didn't want to wonder or care anymore.

I walked over to the high windows. There were two kids kicking a soccer ball around in the yard next door. All I could see were their legs through the chain-link fence.

Last time we'd been here, there had been no kids next door. Just an old couple. I wondered if they'd died. Or maybe they just had grandkids I hadn't seen yet.

I watched their legs and wondered what it felt like to be them. Not to have to hide from reporters every day. Or write to your brother in federal prison and wonder why he never wrote back. Never once wake up to find the word COWARD painted on your house. Or still not be sure your brother wasn't going to get the death penalty. And have no idea who to ask or how to find out.

I'd been them just a couple of months ago. But I swear I couldn't remember how it felt.

In more normal circumstances, I might have wanted to go over and kick a soccer ball around with them. But these were not normal circumstances. And now nothing could possibly have seemed more pointless.

It was like suddenly I wasn't a kid anymore.

After a while, I realized I had to go to the bathroom. I looked around, but there was nothing down in the basement. It wasn't a converted rec room, like our basement. It was just exactly what it was. A water heater and a washer and dryer on one end. A bottle collection and me on the other.

I padded up the basement stairs to the kitchen.

Well. Not quite.

The kitchen had been my goal. But I didn't go all the way *to* it. Because Ruth and Aunt Sheila were talking in the kitchen. And when I heard what they were saying, I stopped cold—in more ways than one—and just listened.

"I didn't actually talk to Joseph," I heard Aunt Sheila say. "You can't just ring up an inmate. But I called. I had to call three times, actually. It's a very complicated process. They bounce your call from person to person. And you're on hold for what feels like hours. But I finally got a real person. And he told me Joseph definitely got the letters."

"What if this person was wrong?" Ruth asked.

"I don't think he was. He looked into it and then called me back. He talked to a guard on Joseph's block. The guard said he goes by there a dozen times a day, and all three letters are sitting opened out flat on his bed, next to his pillow, all the time. The envelopes are gone. But the letters have been opened. And he must have read them. Maybe even more than once if he keeps them on his bed."

"But he never answered."

"No."

"What if he answered and the prison system lost what he wrote?"

A short silence. I wondered if Aunt Sheila was nodding or shaking her head. Or if they were just giving each other a look. Or God forbid maybe they were saying the most important stuff too quietly for me to hear.

I wanted all of the conversation. Every facial expression. Every glance. But there was nothing I could do.

"The same guard goes around every day collecting outgoing mail from all the inmates on that block. He says Joseph never handed him anything. Nothing could have gotten lost because there was nothing to lose."

Another maddening silence.

Then I heard Ruth ask, "So that's why you're worried about whether he'll see us?"

"It does make you wonder," Aunt Sheila said.

"When did you find this out?"

"A couple of weeks ago."

"Why didn't you tell Aubrey in the car?"

"Oh, kiddo. So many reasons. I wasn't sure he'd believe me. I thought he might freak out. There's a *way* to tell him. Something that's more like the right way. But I'll be damned if I can figure out what it is."

I swallowed hard. Just for a moment, I felt bad for Aunt Sheila. In a few minutes, I would feel bad for me, and the feeling would last for a very long time. Years. More than a decade. But in that moment, I felt sorry for her. Because she had to figure out a way to tell me a thing like that.

And I didn't know what the right way would have been, either.

I just knew I'd found out. And the way I'd found out sure wasn't it.

I needed to go pretty badly by then, so I made my footsteps loud on the stairs. And they shut right up.

I got past them without incident. I mean, without further incident.

———

Lunch was tuna-fish sandwiches and lemonade. I liked tuna okay, but it was another reminder of what I'd be missing this summer. Too bad we couldn't take Isabella on the road with us.

The last thing I ever wanted was to see myself as spoiled. But it's a funny thing, spoiled. It sneaks up on you.

"I'm going to try to call the prison right after lunch," Aunt Sheila said.

The interesting thing is that she waited until I'd shoved the last bite of sandwich into my mouth to say it. Like she was smart enough to know it would make me lose my appetite. And she was right. It did.

See, my parents would never have thought to wait. And I don't think they were any less smart. I think they just didn't pay attention to stuff like that. They either didn't care, or didn't see anything outside themselves. Or some other explanation I might not have guessed. Because I was me, not them.

I chewed fast and swallowed, even though my stomach didn't really want the last bite anymore.

"You mean to see if we can visit?" I asked her.

"Right."

Ruth spoke up, startling me. I'm not sure why.

"Why didn't you find out before we got here?" she asked.

Aunt Sheila looked a little hurt. I tried to remember if she ever had before. Nothing my dad said ever made a dent in her. But she'd had decades of experience with him. Maybe it was different with us.

"I was hoping you'd want to come visit me either way," she said.

"Oh, we do!" Ruth said, too fast and too loud.

But I was busy wondering if I did. If we couldn't go see Joseph, and if the reporters might know we were here, maybe I'd rather be home. For a strange reason, I realized. Because then I wouldn't have to give up my weekly sessions with Luanne.

"It might take a while to find out," Aunt Sheila said. "I'll have to get somebody on the line. And then maybe Joseph can call me back collect. I mean, if this is a day or a time he even can. Or if he gets to make outgoing calls at all. I don't know. And if he . . . you know . . . will. Or maybe somebody will have to ask him if he's willing to have visitors, and then call me back. Or I can call back and hear his answer. I just want to warn you that it's not always quick or easy getting through to the prison."

"I'm going for a run," I said.

I trotted down to the basement. Changed into my shorts and track shoes. Fast. Before I could hear even a single word Aunt Sheila said into the phone.

———

Aunt Sheila lived only a few blocks from the beach. So it wasn't too hot. Hot, but not scorching. I wouldn't have cared if it had been a hundred and twenty degrees. The sidewalks rolled up and down easy hills. I wouldn't have cared if they had gone straight up the sides of brick walls.

I just ran.

I ran past tiny homes on tiny lots with peeling paint and overgrown weeds. And others with tended roses and freshly painted fences. I ran past schools and churches and libraries and frozenyogurt shops. I ran past playgrounds with basketball courts, and kids on Big Wheels, and old ladies walking their dogs.

I ran until my chest ached and sweat poured off me and dripped into the breeze. Until I could feel the heat radiating out of my face. And then instead of backing off, I pushed harder. Sped up. I could feel how much I'd needed a vent for all this anger and frustration. All the not knowing, but pretty much knowing I wouldn't like what was there to know once I knew it.

I felt like if I ran until I collapsed and couldn't move a muscle, that might almost be enough.

I looked down at my watch and saw I'd been running for twenty-five minutes. Which I didn't figure would be long enough.

Besides. I was completely lost, I realized. I had no idea where I was, or where Aunt Sheila's house was in relation to that.

I slowed to a jog. Turned down every street, in every direction I could think of.

It took me nearly an hour to find my way back.

———

When I stepped through the doorway, I knew. Aunt Sheila was sitting at the kitchen table with a mug of coffee between her hands. Frowning down into it. Ruth was staring out the window.

I knew they knew I was there. But for a minute, there was no sound except the gasp of my breathing.

Then Ruth said, "Joseph says no."

My whole body felt tingly. That was all I could feel. For the moment.

"He said that himself?"

"Aunt Sheila asked an administrator to find out if he'd take visitors. And he said no."

"He probably meant visitors in general. Not us."

Ruth shook her head. "He knew which visitors," she said.

Aunt Sheila never once met my eyes.

Something started to change inside me in that moment. At the time, I couldn't have told you what it was. It felt like milk going sour or soft bread turning rock hard. Inedible. Except it was happening inside me somewhere. And it was part of *me* that was turning unusable.

"I'll be in the basement," I said.

I ran down the stairs two at a time. Next thing I knew, I was standing next to the bottle collection, my hand raised to scrape off a whole shelf. I could almost hear the shattering glass. So satisfying. I saw it so clearly. It was in my head as if it really happened.

But then I was sitting on the cot. Hunched over my own gut.

Nothing was broken. Not outside me.

For the first time in thirteen years of life, I didn't react to pain with rage. Sounds like good news. It wasn't. This had moved me beyond that somehow.

I curled up on my side on the cot. Stayed that way until bedtime.

Aunt Sheila came down and asked if I wanted dinner. I said no.

She came down one more time to see if there was anything I needed.

A few hours before, I would have said I needed Joseph. But now I didn't. Now there was nothing left to reach for. Even if I'd still wanted to save myself, there was no saving option. At least, not that I could think of at the time.

Chapter Eleven: Ruth

The three of us were sitting at the table eating breakfast, which was really just cereal, which made me miss Isabella. Aubrey hadn't said a word yet, and Aunt Sheila looked like she was still half-asleep.

I knew what I wanted to say, but I wasn't saying it. I couldn't think of a thing that was wrong with it or a single reason why I should be afraid to say it, but I was.

Maybe I was afraid to say anything that day.

"I had an idea," I said, because I knew if I could just spit that much out I'd have to keep going.

"Let's hear it," Aunt Sheila said, sounding more awake than she looked.

"Since we can't go see Joseph, maybe we could go see Hamish MacCallum."

I expected her to ask me who that was, but I should have known better. Everybody who knew Joseph's situation knew who Hamish MacCallum was, and everybody knew Joseph's situation.

We both looked at Aubrey, but he might as well have been in a room by himself for all he seemed to register anything.

"That's an interesting idea," she said. "But I'm not really sure how we'd find him."

"It's a pretty small town. And he's been in the paper a bunch of times. So people around there will know him. I might even be able to find his house just by the description of how it sits on the cliff. And it has a fence, a chain link fence with a big slash cut into it, and there's a reason he never gets it fixed, but now I don't remember what the reason is."

I think Aunt Sheila and I were both surprised when Aubrey the zombie spoke.

"Because then people would just go somewhere else to jump," he said, staring into his cereal and stirring it. "And then maybe nobody would notice. He'd rather they try to get through there, so he'll notice."

"Right," I said. "Anyway, if I'm wrong, and I can't find it, I bet we can find somebody to tell us where he lives. But I can't guarantee it, and I can't guarantee he'll be willing to let us in and talk to us, so maybe it's just another one of those things that you won't want to try if it might not do any good."

"Oh, hell, I'll drive three or four hours up the coast on guesswork," she said. "That's a far cry from Texas. And your parents never insisted that you don't see Hamish MacCallum. Which I guess is the downside for them of forgetting to mention to you kids that he existed at all." We both looked at Aubrey, whose face showed nothing. "We have to do *something*," Aunt Sheila added. "It's only the second day of your visit. First full day. And already this summer is in the toilet. Total disasterland. I'll try anything at this point."

"I don't want to go see Hamish MacCallum," Aubrey said.

"It'll be an adventure, Aubrey," I said. "It'll be the next-best thing to seeing Joseph."

"I don't want the next-best thing to seeing Joseph. I don't even want to see Joseph. Not anymore. As far as I'm concerned, there is no Joseph. He might just as well be dead. He doesn't exist to me. At all. And I definitely don't want to go talk to somebody who knows him. I don't care anymore."

"I don't believe that," I said.

"You can believe whatever you want, Ruth. But it's true. I don't care."

"Well, I do," I said.

"Fine," he said. "Go. Leave me here."

"No way," Aunt Sheila said. "You're thirteen. We didn't get you out here for the summer just to leave you unattended."

"I'm old enough to stay alone!"

"Debatable. But I won't debate it. You're going. For the ride at least."

"Fine. I'll just wait in the car."

I didn't think he would. I thought once we found the place, his curiosity would get the better of him and he'd go in. I also thought he was lying about Joseph not existing to him, and that he would get over that proclamation quickly enough.

I was wrong a lot that day.

———

"I don't even want to be here," Aubrey said from the backseat of Aunt Sheila's car. "And I don't just mean here on this drive. I mean here at all for the summer. Now I just want to go home. And I'm sorry if that hurts your feelings, Aunt Sheila. I don't mean it to. It has nothing to do with you. I just want to go home so I can go back to seeing Luanne."

"Who's Luanne?" Aunt Sheila and I both asked at almost exactly the same time.

"My new therapist."

"Oh," Aunt Sheila said. "Well, I really don't think that's an option, kiddo. Your folks planned on having you away for the summer, and they're not going to like having the plan changed on short notice. Maybe you could do some phone sessions with her. Do you have her phone number with you?"

"Yeah," he said. "She gave me her card."

Seconds later he was dialing.

"Luanne?" he said into his phone.

Then, "I didn't think you'd pick up. I thought I'd just get your voice mail. I thought you'd be in a session."

Then, after a pause. "Oh, right. Because the sessions are fifty minutes. I actually didn't even *know* it was five to anything. This just happens to be when I called."

Another brief pause.

"Everything totally sucks right now. And I was wondering if we could do a phone session."

Pause.

"You do? That would be great! Two o'clock would be great! Thanks!" he slid his phone back into his pocket. Then, to us, he said, "She had a cancellation."

"We won't be home by two," Aunt Sheila said. "Not even close."

"I know. But if you and Ruth are in talking to that guy, I'll call her from the car. If not, maybe you could go get something to eat or something. Because this is really important."

———

"How much you want to bet it's that one?" I said.

We'd been following the coastline through a pretty much uninhabited area. Just rocky cliffs and big drop-offs and not much else. There were no houses along this part of the coast, and then all of a sudden there was just one, sitting out on a jut of high cliff all by itself.

It wasn't fancy. It was on this huge, incredible lot, the kind of lot you'd build your dream home on, some thousands-of-square-feet mansion. But it was just a little cottage made of wood boards painted a dusty green. It almost didn't stand out from the untended vegetation around it.

Mom had a friend in her book group who was a real estate agent, and I remember hearing her say you're supposed to build a house that's four or five times the value of the lot. I figured that cliff was worth over a million dollars and the cottage maybe a hundred grand at best. But I knew just enough about real estate at my tender age to know he could sell the place for millions and the buyer would turn around and bulldoze the cabin and put up a McMansion in about ten weeks. Apparently, he wasn't selling.

On either side of the cottage, a high chain link fence stopped people from walking right up to the cliff—except on one side, it didn't. To the left of the house, somebody had cut a long vertical gash in the links, which now curled back at the bottom like some ancient scrolls of wisdom somebody would recover from the bottom of the sea after they'd been lost for generations.

"It does look promising," Aunt Sheila said.

"This is stupid," Aubrey said. "Why did we even come here? What do you think he's going to tell you that's going to help? It's not going to help."

Aunt Sheila only gave him a frowny look.

"Fine, so just sit here," I said. "Aunt Sheila and I are going to knock."

"Actually . . . ," Aunt Sheila said.

"You're not going in?" I gasped, immediately ashamed of the panic in my voice.

"I'm starting to think of this as your thing, Ruth. If you're brave enough to let it be. If you absolutely can't do it without the moral support, I'll go with you. At least to get you started. But what would be really terrific would be to watch you cowgirl up and bite off this project for yourself. It'll be good for you. It's a very grown-up thing to do."

My heart was doing an unusually thumpy dance as I reached for the car door latch.

"How much time do I have? I mean, if it works. If it's him, and he lets me in."

"No limit. However much time you need."

"But you don't want to sit out here for hours."

"I don't care," she said. "If Aubrey and I get hungry, we'll go find something to eat. If you come out and we're gone, just sit. We'll be back for you."

"I have my phone appointment at two!" Aubrey screeched, as if someone were already trying to wrestle it away from him.

Aunt Sheila asked, "Are you getting reception here?"

He stared at his phone for a second, then said, "Yeah, it's fine."

"Then what's the problem?"

"I'm not going to talk to her right here! *You're* here!"

"Then go *there*," she said, pointing to a stand of trees overlooking the ocean.

Aubrey didn't argue, so I figured everything was settled except the hard part, which was the part I was about to try to do.

I took a huge deep breath and stepped out of the car.

The way to the cottage was sharply uphill. It was hard to walk, and it took my breath away. Either that or I couldn't breathe because I was scared, but I figured it was probably both things at once, because that steep hill was definitely enough. I thought about what Aubrey said—that it wouldn't help, what I was about to try to do, and it felt like a prediction that might well be about to come true.

I stopped, puffed a little, and looked up at the cottage again, wondering if anybody saw me out the window and knew I was coming. Nothing moved inside the house that I could see. Then I wondered if it would turn out that nobody was home, or even that he'd moved away from here or died. That would be the biggest letdown of all, to come all this way and knock on the door and never get any answer and never know why.

I moved uphill again, looking at that big gash in the fence. It gave me the shivers, thinking of people walking through it and right off the cliff to the rocks below. I wondered if he'd stopped them all, or if some of them got by him unnoticed. I wondered how bad your life had to be before you started thinking that was the best plan for you. My life had gotten pretty bad since Joseph came home, but I sure had no intention of leaping off any cliffs.

Of course, the most important question—to me, anyway—about the people who walked through that fence was whether my brother Joseph had been one of them.

Then I was close enough to almost reach out and touch that opening in the chain link, and it gave me the shivers. I stopped, as if the broken fence still had some power to keep me out. Then I ducked down and stuck my head through and kept going. I knew I was trespassing on private property, and it scared me to do it, but something kept pulling me forward.

The ground evened out as I came through the fence, and turned into a level pad that somebody had flattened out to build the cottage. It took only a couple dozen steps to get close enough to the edge to see over—barely see over. I wanted to look straight down, but I didn't dare get so close to the cliff. A good strong wind had come up, and even though it was not wild enough to knock me off my perch, I felt like some unseen force might—a rogue gust, or maybe the ground would crumble under my feet, or I'd get dizzy.

The roar of the ocean beneath me sounded far away, but it rose like an echo. The drop from cliff to sea was probably three hundred feet. That's just a guess, but it's a decent guess, I think. I could see the waves turn to white foam around the rocks below.

A voice startled me so much I swear I almost went over. Or it felt that way, anyway—one of those false feelings, because really I could have fallen onto my face and still been on solid ground.

"Mind if I ask when you last ate, young lady?"

I spun around to see him. Finally, to see him.

He was walking in my direction from the house, bent over a cane. I'd had no idea he would be so old—maybe in his eighties, from the look of him. I expected somebody that looked like a father to Joseph, but this guy looked like he could be Joseph's great-grandfather. He had only a ring of disheveled hair left over his ears, and it wasn't a color much different from his skin, which was a weathered gray. All in all, he didn't look like a perfect specimen of health, to put it mildly, but he was walking.

"I wasn't going to jump," I said. "Honest."

He stopped and straightened up as best he could. He had a curvature to his spine. He could lift himself up if he needed to, I guess, but it looked like a lot of work, and I imagined he wouldn't want to do it all day long. He looked right into my face and cocked his head, and in his eyes I saw a twinkle of humor.

I wondered where he was able to find humor in the subject of people throwing themselves off cliffs. I figured if you could find it there, it was available to you everywhere, and I wanted to beg him to teach me how to do that. But I was frozen, of course, and didn't speak.

"You'd be surprised how many people tell me that," he said.

I knew it was him, because he had that rolling, nearly magical accent that could only be Scottish. Not so thick that I couldn't understand him, but every word was wrapped in that lyrical blanket. It was unlike talking to anybody else I had met.

"Really, though. I'm telling the truth. I didn't come here to jump. I came here to see you."

He cocked his head again, like a curious dog.

"Do I know you?"

"No, sir. You don't. But you know my brother."

Much to my alarm, he took several steps closer. With a toothy smile blooming on his face, he reached a hand out and touched my cheek. I was more than wary, but I didn't move a muscle.

"So you must be Ruthie, then," he said.

My mouth dropped open. I could feel it, and he could, too, in addition to seeing it with his own eyes, because he still had one warm, ancient palm on my face.

"How did you know that?"

"First off, Joe's told me so much about you and Aubrey, I feel like I know you both for my own self." He dropped the hand, as if his old arm could no longer hold it up. "But that's not really the whole story, if I'm being honest. Truth is, lots more people have been by here in the last couple o' months, and they all come here to talk about Joe."

"Joe?" I asked, as if we were talking about two different people. I started to feel like he couldn't know Joseph the way everyone said he did, or he would have known that nobody, and I mean *nobody*, called him Joe.

"Joe Stellkellner. That *is* the brother in question, right?"

"Yes, sir."

"Then back to the original question. When did you last eat?"

"Oh. Let me think. I had cereal for breakfast. But it was a long drive. And it's pretty much lunchtime by now, I'm thinking."

"So come inside and I'll make you my signature breakfast. You'll have breakfast for lunch. It's really the only thing I know how to make worth a darn, anyway. But it's quite famous, because it's saved more than a few lives. Whatever time o' day it is, I always make 'em breakfast. And it never seems to fail to help people."

He turned back toward the house and began to make his way along a gravel path to the patio door, hunched over his cane.

I followed.

I was thinking about a breakfast that saves people's lives, and even though I had never been about to jump off a cliff, I felt as though I needed rescuing, and I desperately wished for him to be proven right—that the breakfast would be magic, and that it would have the power to save me.

———

There wasn't much separating Hamish MacCallum's kitchen from his living room—really just a partition on one side—so I looked around the place without feeling like I was being rude and leaving him alone to cook for me.

"I hope you're not going to all this trouble just for me," I said. "Did you have your lunch yet?"

"No, I haven't, Ruthie, so it's for both of us. And I have to say, I'm a bit glad you dropped by . . . well, for a number of reasons, but on the small end because all I was going to fix for myself was a frozen dinner. I'm happy for the excuse to make a nice big breakfast instead."

Halfway through the word "breakfast," I saw the photos. He had a huge stone mantelpiece—flat shale-type stones all cobbled together around a wood fireplace—and on it were seven framed photos. They sat up on their own, obviously the kind with easels on the back of the photo frame to hold the thing in place, and the people all looked like they could be no possible relation to each other. None of them looked like Hamish, and nobody looked like anybody else.

One of them was my brother Joseph.

"Who are all these people on the mantel?" I asked. "I mean, if you don't mind my asking."

"Well, you know who one o' them is," he said, punctuated by the sound of two cast-iron skillets hitting the stove burners, one after the other. "The rest are some other friends o' mine who I got to know over a breakfast like the one I'm about to make for us right now."

I walked back toward him and leaned my shoulder on the partition.

"So those are all the people you saved from jumping?"

"No, not all of them. Just the ones kept in touch. There've been five more than that over the years, but I never heard anything from them afterwards. Maybe they went through with it somewhere else, or some other way, but I like to think not. I think some just don't keep in touch because they feel embarrassed. Ashamed, even. You see, the magic of their coming here's more than just the breakfast, though that's not insignificant, let me tell you. People don't eat when they're upset, and they let their blood sugar get quite low, and their brain has nothing to power on, and then everything looks so dark. And they're always so astonished at how they feel after filling up on bacon and eggs and home-fried potatoes. They need some protein, and they need to feel solid again. And then after they eat, they always tell me nothing has changed, but *everything* has changed. The whole world is the same, and they can still see it clearly, but now, all of a sudden, it doesn't feel like more than they can bear anymore. But the breakfast is only part of it, and you're a smart girl, so I'm sure you know that. It's the fact that I made it for them. It means they've been seen. And it's a funny thing, this being seen. Everybody's looking for it, and nobody would go through that fence if they hadn't given up on finding it. But once they get it . . . well, it seems to go one o' two ways. They either grab onto it like a life preserver and never want to let it go . . . and that's those in the photos, the ones that went on to be a part of our lives. Well, my life, now. They were part o' my wife's life, too, but she passed on year before last."

"I'm sorry," I said.

"That makes two of us, Ruthie. That makes two." He laid strips of bacon in the bigger cast-iron skillet, four for each of us. The pan must have been preheated, because each strip set up sizzling the moment it touched. "But then there's the other kind. They're not used to being seen. They want it but they don't want it. It's like bright sunlight. You live in the dark all your life, you want nothing more than to step out into that warm sun. But then it hurts your eyes because it's too bright. It burns you. So the others, when they know they've been seen, they go away from the seer from that point on. Whether that means they were helped or not, I really can't say. But I never thought I could save the whole world. I can save what I can save and that's that."

"I'm sure some must have gotten by you in the night," I said, but I don't know why I said it.

"I wouldn't be so sure," he said. "There's a motion sensor."

I watched him in silence for a moment as he cut onions and briefly microwaved potatoes before it hit me that my one big question had already been answered.

"So Joseph did come here to jump off a cliff."

Hamish MacCallum's hands stopped moving, but his eyes began to move instead, and they drifted far away.

"I never really was sure what to think about Joe. He showed up not too long after the first article about me got printed in the paper. The San Francisco paper, I think it was, but then it hit the Associated Press and I was everywhere. And then there's this boy in my yard. This child. That shook me up a bit. Twelve years old, he was. I couldn't figure how he'd even got anywhere on his own. They'd always been full-grown adults showing up here, both before and since. And he came at dawn. Nobody comes at dawn. Everybody comes in the night if they mean business. When they think nobody'll see. But he came in the light, and just around time for breakfast. So to this day, I'm not sure he came because he heard it was a good place to jump off a cliff. I think maybe he came because he heard it was a good place to get saved from it."

"That sounds right," I said. "Well, maybe I shouldn't say that. I don't know what's right, because I wasn't there, but it sounds good. It sounds like what I want it to be, and I believe it."

"Well, your folks were of another mind. In fact, they pretty well lost their minds when they heard. Hustled him off to a mental hospital, and to this very day I think it did him more harm than good."

"Did you tell them?"

"No, I told Joe to go home and come clean with 'em. Your parents are the heart o' the problem, you know, and how could he solve the problem if he couldn't even talk to them? Except in another way they're not the problem, at least not the start of it and not on purpose, because they likely grew up the same. They didn't get what they needed from their folks, so now they can't give you kids what they don't have. They're the victims and the perpetrators, both, and the cycle just keeps going around and around. And I don't know what to do to stop it any more than anybody else does, except I just know bacon and eggs and potatoes. It doesn't fix everything, but it makes a dent, and anyway, like I said before, I can only do what I can do and no more."

I wandered over to the kitchen table and sat, because I felt heavy and needed to get off my feet. I played with the salt and pepper shakers that were made of porcelain in the shape of Mr. and Mrs. Santa Claus. Here it was, June, and he still had the Christmas salt and pepper shakers out.

"So if I have kids," I said, "I'll mess them up the same way?"

"You're not required to, and I don't recommend it. It's not mandatory. You can heal your own self first, but most people never do. Maybe because you have to start by admitting you're broken."

"I could do that."

"I'm not surprised," he said. "So could Joe."

I felt my head shake when I hadn't meant to shake it. "I don't get something. Nobody calls my brother Joseph 'Joe.'"

"Wrong," he said, not missing a beat. "One person does, and that's me." He indicated his chest with one withered thumb.

"Didn't he mind?"

"Did and still does. But it never mattered. I had a reason for it, and I told him the reason, and I told him to just try and stop me. And that was the end of that."

By this time, both the bacon and the potatoes sizzled in the pan, and we had to raise our voices to be heard over their enthusiasm.

The smell was making me hungry. Desperately hungry. I could feel what he'd been trying to tell me—how life starts to feel unmanageable and we don't realize that at least part of it is just a simple message that we need food.

"What's the reason?"

"Because you can't go through life treating everybody like a stranger. 'Joseph' is what you call somebody you don't know. It's their whole, full name. It's formal. Nicknames are about more than just making a name shorter, you know. Think about me calling you Ruthie. It *adds* a syllable. It's not about the syllables. It's about the familiarity. It makes a name more familiar, and that makes the *person* more familiar. It's something you grow into as a way to show you know somebody. It's how you open the door and let him in. Going by 'Joseph' your whole life is just a way of showing the world that nobody gets in. It's like those hospitals and repair shops that have the doors that say 'authorized personnel only.' Well, somebody has to be authorized personnel, don't they? Or what's the point of the room behind the door?"

"What do people call you?"

"Ham. Or Hammy. My wife called me Hammy. And it's a bit of a laugh, you know? Because what could suit me better?"

He turned his face away from the stove and to me, and it was there in his eyes again, that flash of humor—only this time it wasn't hard to imagine where he found humor in the moment in front of us.

———

I might be embellishing as a result of the years, but I don't think so: I really think the breakfast was magic.

It was huge. Three small, perfectly poached eggs all crowded onto a single piece of whole-wheat toast, four strips of bacon, a mountain of crispy fried potatoes and onions. I thought I'd never eat it all, but the more I ate, the more I couldn't imagine stopping. It felt as though I'd been a dried husk, about to blow away in the wind, and now I was forming an anchor with the earth—and furthermore, I felt like the earth would never hurt me, and I'd be safe.

Hamish MacCallum seemed satisfied to eat in silence if need be, but I was still full of questions, and the walls that normally held my inner thoughts in check were crumbling fast.

"Why didn't we know about you?"

He shrugged. "I would've thought your parents would have told you where he was all summer, but I can't speak for anybody else. You'll have to ask *them* about that."

"What do you think about what happened?"

"You mean over in Baghdad?"

"Yeah."

"I don't go by what I *think* about things like that. What it was to Joe is what it was. My impression of events is irrelevant. I've never even been to the Middle East, and I've never fought in a war."

I remember desperately wishing everybody in the world had taken that attitude, but I couldn't bring myself to say so. It was too much of a tragedy that they hadn't, and I wasn't ready to drag it out onto the table just as I was beginning to feel better.

"So have you talked to him about it?"

"I have, yes."

"What did he say?"

"He said what he wanted me to hear, and maybe not what he wanted anybody else to hear. And I could be wrong about that, but I always err on the side of not repeating what's been told to me. You're his sister. Ask him. He'll tell you what you need to know."

"Not really," I said. "He won't talk to us now."

"I'll be darned," he said, his eyes coming up to mine. It was the first time I'd seen him look even remotely surprised.

"Aubrey's been writing to him, but he won't write back, and we were going to go and visit him, but he said he wouldn't see any visitors. Not even us."

"Seems unlike him," he said. "But still, he was home for a short spell. You must have asked him what happened."

"I did. He just said it wasn't anything very cut-and-dried, but that I was about to watch people try to make it that way. To make it very simple."

"Amen to that," he said.

"You don't think it's simple?"

"Nothing in this life is simple," he said. "And all the troubles o' the world come in because people can't abide that. They have to try to make things black and white, but nothing ever will be. It's where all the bad stuff gets its start."

"*All* the bad stuff?"

"Well. Maybe not hurricanes and droughts. There's the trouble people make by trying to shape the world to suit them and failing, and then everything else I'd say is more weather related."

Chapter Twelve: Aubrey

_____

"There's something I want to do while we're waiting," I said to Aunt Sheila.

I'd moved to the front seat. Because it was weird after Ruth left. Like Aunt Sheila was my chauffeur. In that car, yet. And because I was sick of Ruth always calling shotgun. Well. Not even calling it. Just getting it. Like it was never up for grabs in the first place.

"I'm listening," she said.

"Are you willing to drive us back to that last big town we went through?"

"I was already thinking about it. I'm getting hungry."

She turned the ignition key. That tiny, noisy engine jumped back to life.

"Okay," I said. "Good. Now we just have to figure out if they have a pet store."

Aunt Sheila just sat a minute, looking through the windshield.

Then she said, "You don't even have a pet."

"I'm about to have pets, though."

"Pets? Plural? And you think you're going to try them out at my house? I don't think so, kiddo."

"It's just fish."

"Oh. Fish. What kind of fish?"

"Not sure. Any kind, I guess. Maybe just goldfish. I don't want to have to set up the whole tank thing at your house. Just something that can live in a little bowl. You know. Easy. No trouble."

Aunt Sheila sighed. "Well, they're quiet, they don't poop on the floor, and they don't shed, so let's go."

———

She said, "I really think you should eat the rest of your sandwich before your appointment."

I said, "I'm not hungry, though."

I didn't want to eat. I just wanted to sit there in the front seat and stare at my fish. There were five of them. In a plastic bag full of water. They were goldfish, but not the plain kind. The kind with the fancy long fins and tails.

We were back at the bottom of the big hill in front of Hamish MacCallum's house. And it bothered me a lot that it had been nearly two hours and Ruth still wasn't coming out. Like she'd found something in there. Which I'd told her she wouldn't. And it felt important that I be right.

I felt like I was losing.

Aunt Sheila held the open takeout container under my nose, and I smelled the bacon in the BLT. Normally smelling bacon made me hungry. This time, nothing. No reaction. I looked down at the sandwich. Only because I thought I was supposed to. It was only missing three bites.

"Maybe later," I said.

"You can still go in there, you know."

"Not you, too!"

"He's obviously willing to talk to Ruth, or she wouldn't have been gone so long."

"It's almost time for my appointment."

"You have nearly twenty minutes."

"I'm not going in. Period. I wish everybody would just get that."

Aunt Sheila sighed. But that's all she did. She didn't add the insult of any words.

———

I sat on the dirt with my knees at the edge of the cliff, my lower legs hanging over. Not *the* cliff. It wasn't super-high like up at the house. But it was a bluff over the ocean. Forty or fifty feet, maybe. And there was a horseshoe of beach under my dangling feet.

Only one side had trees, but they stood between me and the sun. If I leaned just right, I could see a starburst of sun in between branches. It radiated. While I dialed, I held the bag of fish up in front of it. To see them in a shinier setting.

"Luanne," I said when she answered. "You'll never guess what I'm doing."

"Okay," she said. "You're right; I probably won't. So go ahead and tell me."

"I'm sitting on a little cliff over the ocean, and I have fish to look at."

"You can look at the ocean and see the fish? Are you in Tahiti or something?"

"No. It's two different things. The fish are not in the ocean. They're in a plastic bag in my lap."

"Oh. That kind of fish. I thought you meant live fish."

"I do mean live fish. They're in a plastic bag of water. They're goldfish. I have five of them. Aunt Sheila took me to a pet store to buy them. I thought it would be better to talk to you if I had fish. I remembered all the times I came in to see you. And I always had your fish. And I thought the fish were important. They gave me someplace to look. I think that helps me."

"That's a good thing to know about yourself," she said. "So you're at your Aunt Sheila's house?"

"No. I told you. I'm on a bluff looking at the ocean."

"Right. But your aunt lives near the ocean, doesn't she?"

"I'm not there, though. We took a little road trip."

"Where are you?"

I clenched my jaw. Swallowed. I could feel my leg muscles tighten up. I looked up at the old green house. Then I looked at the fish. They didn't help. Not enough, anyway.

I didn't want to answer the question. But I'd backed myself into this corner. I couldn't just stay there for the rest of my life.

"My *stupid* sister . . . had this *stupid* idea. She wanted to meet that guy."

"What guy?"

"You know."

"Aubrey," she said. And my name was a mild warning, the way she said it. And I accepted that warning. "If I ever know the answer to a question already, I won't ask it."

"That guy you asked me about. Who Joseph was close to but we didn't even know about it."

"That's where you are? You went to see Hamish MacCallum?"

"Ruth did."

"And you found him."

"She did. Yeah."

"And she's in his house? Talking to him?"

"Well, she must be. She's been gone for hours."

"And you're sitting outside talking to *me*? Aubrey. Go in. Talk to him. Learn everything you can. I'll make another space for you at the end of the day."

I was silent for a time. A longish time. I wanted to say, *Not you, too, Luanne*. But I didn't talk that way to her.

"Aubrey?" she said after a time.

"I'm here."

I squinted my eyes and watched sea-gulls circling over the ocean. There were little dots of black birds, too. Hundreds of them. But not circling. They were sitting on the water. Bobbing there. Must have been something good to eat under that gray-green surface.

"Why aren't you going in?" she asked at last.

"Because I don't want to."

"I would think you'd love to talk to someone who knew your brother so well."

"Well, you would be wrong, Luanne. I don't want to talk about Joseph. I don't want to hear about Joseph. I don't want to think about Joseph. I wish he didn't exist. So in my head, he just doesn't. I hate Joseph."

"Okay," she said. "I obviously missed something. So fill me in."

"He got all three of my letters. He just didn't bother to write back. And we can't go see him. Because he won't see us. Aunt Sheila asked. And he said no. No visitors. Not even me."

A pause. Maybe she was taking that in. Maybe she was shocked and hurt and appalled, too. Or maybe she was just waiting to see if I was done.

"I can understand how that would upset you. But he may have a good reason."

"Wrong!" I said, and I was raising my voice now. Raising my voice to Luanne, and I didn't stop. And I didn't care. "Wrong! He *doesn't* have a good reason, because there *is* no good reason!"

"He might be ashamed to be seen that way. In custody."

"Not a good reason. I'm his brother. He should see me."

"You said your dad forbade you to get in touch with him. Maybe he insisted Joseph not see you or contact you."

"Don't care," I said. "He's done a million things my dad didn't want him to do. I'm his brother. I thought he loved me. There's no excuse."

"I still think you should go into this MacCallum guy's house. See what he has to say."

"I don't care what he has to say."

"But it might help you settle some of these feelings. It might make you feel better."

"I don't *want* to feel better!" I shouted. "I want to be *mad*!"

Another long silence on the line. I thought maybe it was over for me and Luanne. Maybe she'd just stamp my record with a big red "rejected." Tell my parents she tried, but there's no hope for me.

I held the goldfish up into a flicker of sunlight. Watched them swim circles around each other in that tiny space.

Then I wondered why I was doing that. If I didn't want to feel better.

"Here's the thing," she said. "All the work we're doing relies on the assumption that you want to feel better. On the other hand, I talked to you right before you left, and you didn't know any of these things about Joseph. You thought you were on your way to see him. So I know all this garbage got dumped on you pretty recently. And sometimes we need time to process things. Sometimes we need to sit in them for a while before we're ready to get up and get out. So I'm going to just let that statement of yours ride for now. But in the long run, you're seeing me because you want to help yourself. Otherwise it's not a very good use of time for either one of us. Are we agreed on that?"

"Yeah, I think so," I said. "I'm staring at the goldfish. And that's what I do to feel better. So I must want to feel better. Some part of me must. I think I want to feel better without talking about Joseph, though. I don't want any more Joseph in my life. I don't even want to hear Joseph's name. I hate Joseph."

"Hmm," she said.

"'Hmm' what? Are you, like, analyzing everything?"

"Aubrey, I think 'analyzing everything' is why your parents pay me the big bucks. I couldn't help noticing that you said his name four times. At almost exactly the same time you told me you never want to hear his name again."

"That doesn't mean anything," I said. "Not everything means something."

"I have a handicap," she said, "in the way I look at the world. I'm a psychologist. So I'm cursed with thinking everything means something."

A big wind came up and blew through the trees. The branches swayed. And the sunlight on the bag of fish sparkled on and off. Like a disco ball, but natural. One of the fish I already knew apart from the others. He was bigger and fatter. He had some silvery-white on him. A patch of it to offset the orange.

Just for a split second, I was going to name him Joseph. Then I erased the thought. Vehemently. If it had been a word on a piece of paper, I would have scratched through it so violently I would have shredded the page.

I was definitely not going to tell Luanne about that. She'd only think it meant something.

Hell, I barely told myself.

"Here's the problem with trying to solve this situation by hating your brother," she said. "Well, there are a number of them. It's really nothing *but* problems. First of all, you think you're taking back all the love you felt. But you're really just flipping it over. You cared a great deal about him in a positive way. Now you care a great deal about him in a negative way. It's not as different as you think. It still makes him a very important person in your world. It still puts a huge amount of your life energy into him, only in a destructive mode. The other problem is that I think you're trying to punish him for hurting you. I think you're trying to hurt him back by hating him. But he's in a cell in Texas, and he doesn't even know."

"I'll write him a letter and tell him I hate him."

"You're missing the point again, Aubrey."

"Oh. Sorry. What's the point?"

"The point is that it's you being destroyed by your hate. Not him. This is what the Buddha called picking up a hot coal to hurl at your enemy."

"Well, I would do that," I said. "If I got him a good shot. Hit him in the eye or something. And it hurt him. Then it would be worth burning my hand."

I thought I heard Luanne sigh. But I was never entirely sure.

"Let me put it another way, and this is also not original. Let's say there's a rat in your house. So you go out and get some rat poison. And you eat a bunch of it. And then you sit there, watching the rat. Waiting for it to die."

"Well, that would just be stupid," I said.

"Finally we agree on something."

"I'm not going to stop hating him."

"Are you willing to at least be open to the possibility that at some point in the future you'll want to leave your hatred behind?"

I breathed for a moment. The wind was tossing my hair into my eyes. I pulled it back away with one hand. Because I had the goldfish in the other. I held the phone between my shoulder and my ear. Hoping I didn't drop it fifty feet off a cliff.

The honest answer? Not a chance.

The answer I gave her?

"Sure. I'll try."

Because I thought she might be right on the edge of not wanting to see me anymore. And I felt like I needed her. Like I was an old steam boiler. I could explode at any moment. And she was the valve that let a little pressure off my lines.

So I just lied.

For the rest of the session she took me through a bunch of relaxation exercises. She wanted me to do them on my own. Every day. I didn't. I didn't even do them right then, in the session. I went through the motions with her. But I didn't relax. I didn't even try.

I didn't want to relax. I wanted to stoke my resentment into a glowing fire. Something had to keep me warm.

Chapter Thirteen: Ruth

"Is it after three?" I asked Hamish MacCallum, still halfway thinking about Aubrey and getting him in there. "Or even after ten to three?"

We were sitting out on his back patio, on his porch swing, facing the ocean, but it was nothing like our porch swing at home. It was hung from the patio roof with chains, not suspended from its own frame, and it wasn't freshly painted or blinding white, yet for some reason, I liked his better.

He peered closely at his watch, wrapped loosely on one age-spotted wrist.

"No. Only two thirty. Why? You have to go?"

The wind had come up stronger, and it kept blowing strands of hair into my eyes and mouth. I knew my hair was getting tangles, but I didn't care. I liked the wind. It made me feel alive. I loved the feeling of the fullness in my stomach. All of a sudden, it felt good to be me for a change, and it had been away so long, that feeling. Or maybe it had never felt good to be me. Not like that, anyway.

"I just wanted to see if I could get Aubrey in here."

"Aubrey's here?"

"Yeah, well, he didn't really get a choice. He had to come along for the ride. But he didn't want to come in. He doesn't want to talk about Joseph. He doesn't even want to talk to anybody who knows him. He's trying to pretend Joseph doesn't even exist."

"Since when?"

"Since he found out Joseph won't see us."

"Ah," he said. "I see. So why do you think you can only change his mind if it's ten to three?"

"He has a phone appointment with his therapist."

"I just hope it's a good one they've got him seeing. That can be a good thing if you do it right. But the people at that hospital where they sent Joseph . . . I think it can make things worse if done poorly."

"I think she's good. Because he seems to want to be there. I just wish he would've come in with me and met you and eaten. He needs that. We're all worried about him. I think he's the one who really needs saving."

"I think you both do," he said. "I think the only difference between you and Aubrey is that he needs saving at a louder volume, so's more people notice."

I looked at him, but he was looking off toward the sea. I looked past his face to watch gulls wheeling. They had that strange cry that sounded almost human. I wondered what they were calling for and what they wanted.

So this was what he meant about being seen. I'd told him Aubrey was worse off than me, and he didn't believe me. He looked right through those words. And he was right. I wondered if I'd be one of those people who latched onto being seen and wanted more, or the ones who get their eyes burned and run. Both, I decided. I'd come back and get burned again. I just knew it.

"Once my brother gets his mind stuck on something, he's really stubborn. But I just know he'd feel better if he met you. I just can't figure out how to change his mind."

"You can't."

"Right. I just said that."

"No, I don't mean you can't figure it out. I mean you can't change his mind. You can't change anybody's mind. No matter what you say to them. The sooner you figure that out, the happier your life will be."

"But you change people's minds all the time. They come here to jump, and you talk them out of it."

"No. I never tell them not to jump. I never tell anybody what to do. I just say, before you jump, how about a hearty breakfast?"

I laughed out loud, but I wasn't sure if he'd meant it as a joke or not. "But you don't think they're going to come in and have breakfast and then go back out and jump, do you?"

"Well, I hope not. And no one ever has. But I'm still not trying to talk them into or out of anything. I'm trying to give them an experience they need. They'll either change their own mind as a result of it or they won't."

"But it always works."

"So far. Because it's based on what people need. When people come here, everything in their life is bad, but that's not the problem. The problem is, they think it always will be. They can't see anything new and different down the road. People can bear almost any amount of pain if they think there's an end to it. So suddenly something happens that they never could have imagined: a daft old man invites them in for a nice hearty meal. It's not the man or the meal that convinces them. It's that they forgot how at any moment something can always happen that you never expected. Something better. Once they remember that, it's a whole new ball game."

I opened my mouth to answer, but I had no idea what I was about to say. My phone buzzed in my shirt pocket.

"I should see if that's my aunt," I said. "She might be saying we need to go."

I pulled the phone out of my pocket. It wasn't Aunt Sheila. It was Sean.

Seeing his number come up was like getting punched in the stomach by something icy cold.

I didn't answer.

"You look like you've seen a ghost," Hamish MacCallum said.

"Something like that. It's this guy who I thought was my boy-friend. Or was going to be my boyfriend. And then after this thing happened with Joseph, his parents said he could never see me or talk to me again."

"Well, then why's he calling?"

"Good question. I'll find out."

Just then I heard the tone telling me there was a new voice mail. I was glad Hamish MacCallum had asked the question, because it would have driven me crazy not to listen to the message. But I wouldn't have listened to it in front of him, because I would have considered it rude.

I played the message.

Sean's voice made my face feel red.

"Ruth," he said. "It's me. I still feel so bad about what hap-pened. I know I shouldn't be calling. I mean, my parents think I shouldn't. They'd kill me if they knew. But I want to talk to you. So call me on my cell, okay? I mean, if you're still speaking to me. You never answered that note I put in your locker. So I don't know. But I'm trying again. Give me another chance. Please. Nobody needs to know. Where are you? I asked a couple people and they said you went out of town. Call me. Just . . . you know . . . just so my parents don't find out."

I clicked the message off, saving it instead of erasing it, but I'm not really sure why, because I didn't like it well enough to listen to it again—it made my stomach feel funny, and not in a good way.

"He says he wants to talk to me but keep it a secret."

"Ah," Hamish MacCallum said. "Can't imagine you'd enjoy that."

"Right. I wouldn't." Then I wondered if I'd known I wouldn't. "Why wouldn't I again?"

"Well, I could be wrong. As I said before, I never try to talk anybody into or out of anything. But I wouldn't want to be anybody's little secret, so I figured you wouldn't, either. If he's a good young man, he'll stand up and tell his parents you're not your brother and you didn't do a thing wrong."

"It's not that, exactly. It's not that they think I'm guilty of anything. It's that the reporters wouldn't leave them alone."

"The reporters will get bored and wander off in time. And chances are so will the young man. But if he doesn't, then you'll know you've got something worth keeping there."

I took a big deep breath, and the wind stole the exhale and blew it away. It had never occurred to me that there was even a remote chance of Sean still in my future. And I liked Hamish MacCallum's plan, to wait and let time tell me if he deserved to be there. Somehow, when I was sitting next to that old man, I felt like everything was going to work out, which is an amazing talent when you think about it. No wonder nobody jumped.

I thought he knew everything, so I asked a big question.

"Do you think Joseph will get the death penalty?"

"Oh, I shouldn't think so," he said. "I certainly hope not. No, that I think would only be for doing purposeful harm to the war effort and then lying to cover up his tracks. There was no deception. There was no attempt to hurt anybody else. I don't think they'll let him off with a slap on the wrist, either, sorry to say. I think they'll make an example of him. Put him in jail for quite a time. But nothing as drastic as all that, I don't think."

And I believed him, because he was Hamish MacCallum, and he made you feel like everything was going to be all right.

———

I was holding the passenger door open and talking to my brother Aubrey, and he was still refusing to look at me. He had a bag full of water with a bunch of goldfish in it sitting on his lap, and all he was doing was staring at the fish. And the fact that he had them all of a sudden—when he hadn't had fish a few hours ago when I'd stepped out of the car—was so weird and out of place that I couldn't even stop to process it. I couldn't find room for that in my brain.

"Seriously, Aubrey," I said for about the third time. "You've got to meet this guy. He's amazing."

No answer.

I looked up to Aunt Sheila in the driver's seat and caught her eye. She shook her head.

"Everybody's tried," she said. "No go."

"Have you eaten?" I asked him.

Still no answer.

"We drove back to town and got lunch," Aunt Sheila said. "But Aubrey barely touched his."

"See, this is what I've just been finding out. I had this great big gigantic breakfast, and it's the one he fixes for people who are about to jump, and it makes everything so much better."

He looked away from his fish for the first time.

"We had breakfast already. This morning. It's the middle of the afternoon, stupid."

"So? We had breakfast for lunch. What difference does it make? Whatever time of day people come, he makes them this big hearty breakfast."

"Why?"

"Because it's the one meal he's good at. And it's sort of magic. After you eat, you feel better. Like nothing is different, but you feel like you can manage."

"Ruth," he said, like my name was some kind of excrement or fatal disease. "I eat food every day of my life. If it fixed anything, don't you think I'd know it?"

He glanced up at me for a fraction of a second, and what I saw in his eyes only made me more determined to drag him up to Hamish MacCallum to be healed. Then he looked back at his fish again.

"The breakfast is only part of it. It's the fact that he fixes it for you. It makes you feel seen."

"I don't want to feel seen," he said. "I already missed that stupid breakfast for lunch and I'm not hungry anyway and I don't want to be seen."

I realized then that I needed to leave him alone. Because he was one of the other kind. The ones whose photos would never be on the mantelpiece. Because if he was seen, like sunlight burning his eyes, he would run away and never come back again. He was one thing and I was the other.

And you can't change anybody's mind. The sooner I learned that, the happier my life would be, and now I felt like a happy life was a goal again for the first time in a long time.

And besides, all the bad things in the world start with people trying to see the world as simpler than it is. Trying to change the way life is and failing—like me thinking I could save my little brother, whether he wanted saving or not, instead of just saving me.

"Why do you have fish?" I asked him.

My voice came out soft, but as soon as I heard it, I was afraid it sounded more sympathetic than he would accept.

I put a hand on his shoulder, but he shook it off violently.

"Stop it! Because I like fish. Why shouldn't I have them?"

I looked at Aunt Sheila again, but she didn't meet my eyes.

"Well. Okay. I have to go back and say good-bye," I said, dreading the second long, breathless walk up the hill.

"Fine," he said. "Go. But hurry up this time. Don't take hours again. Some of us want to go home."

"I'm in no hurry at all," Aunt Sheila said. "Take all the time you need."

And with that, my little brother face-palmed into his own non-fish-holding hand.

———

I was puffing desperately by the time I got back up to the cottage. I rapped on the door, but he didn't get up to answer it. He just called out to me.

"Come right on in, Ruthie."

I stepped into his living room, and I looked at him and he looked at me, and we were silent for a moment, absorbing the fact that it was still just us and not Aubrey. We had tried something and failed, which was hard on me for a split second, because I wanted to think of Hamish MacCallum as someone who didn't fail.

Then I realized it was only me who had failed, because I was the only one who thought I could take what I'd found and force it into my little brother. Hamish MacCallum had even warned me I was trying to do the impossible, so that left his record suitably clean. At least, that was the conclusion I reached at the time.

Looking back I see the real, clearer message that *everybody fails*, and I see that he'd been trying to tell me that all along.

"It's not like you didn't warn me," I said, pasting on a little smile that I hoped didn't look as unnatural as it felt.

"It's not like I wasn't hoping to see him come tagging in here behind you, in spite of what I predicted."

I just stood a moment.

Then I said, "I think we need to get back now. I just wanted to say good-bye."

"If you think you're getting out o' here without a hug, Ruthie, you're more daft than I had you pegged."

He rose to his feet with some obvious effort, and I covered the ground between us and wrapped my arms around him. It was different from other hugs in my life. I'm having trouble finding a better way to say it than that. I'd hugged my friends, back when I had some, but they were my age and felt more familiar in my arms. More like hugging myself. I had hugged older people, always older relatives, but this was still different. It took me a minute to understand the difference. My older relatives grabbed me and latched onto me, and I felt like they wanted something from me. Their love felt like a demand. Then I let go and they pinched my cheeks and kissed them, and it only made me feel drained, like I had all the love and they only wanted to refill their tanks by taking some of mine.

This was the first time anybody had given me as much as—or more than—they wanted in return.

Oh. Except Isabella. But somehow that felt different because I'd known her all my life. This was a man I'd only met that day.

I stepped back and felt tears right behind my eyes, and I didn't want them. I wanted them to go away and not complicate things.

"I hate to leave," I said. "I feel like what I got here will go away again. You know . . . like . . . expire."

"But you know where I live," he said. "So there's no excuse to be a stranger anymore. And I'll write down my phone number for you. You can give my address and phone number to Aubrey, too. Tell him there's no obligation and no pressure. It's just in case he changes his mind."

He picked up his cane and shuffled over to a little white notepad by the phone. He picked up a pen that was tethered by a string—so it could never turn up anywhere else but by the phone, I assumed.

"No, I take that back," he said. "Don't give it to him, at least not yet. He'll just tear it up and throw it away. Because he only knows how he feels now. He doesn't know that feelings change over the years, because he hasn't lived enough years to see that for himself. So just tell him you have it, and it's for him, too, if he should ever change his mind."

He shuffled over and handed me the slip of paper. It had his name, postal address—which was a PO box—house address, and phone number. The letters and numbers were astonishingly neat, almost as if done by a machine that produced perfect block printing.

I wanted to hug him again, but I wasn't sure if that would sound greedy, so I never asked.

"Thank you for saving my brother Joseph," I said on my way to the door.

"Now that I can honestly say was my pleasure, Ruthie."

The minute I stepped out into the sun and closed the door behind me, the tears broke through. There was nothing I could do to hold them. I didn't even know what they were for, or exactly what had caused them. I just knew that, like the only other tears I'd cried since Joseph came home, they weren't fresh. They had been angling for their freedom for a very long time.

———

On the drive home, I sent a text to Sean's phone.

It said, *Sooner or later the reporters will get bored and wander away. Let's talk then, when I don't have to be your little secret.*

I didn't say, *Assuming you haven't wandered away by then as well.* I figured I didn't need to. When you're fifteen, the impermanence of ideas and relationships more or less goes without saying.

Part Three

Be Quiet and I'll Tell You

Remembering Summer 2004

Chapter Fourteen: Aubrey

You would think it would've all blown over a year later. Ruth swore it would.

You would be wrong. Ruth was wrong.

Yes, things sagged in between. An investigation into who said what to whom wasn't going to stay on the front page of anything for very long. Especially when the army didn't need to share all the details.

But by the following June, the court-martial had begun. And we were back into the fray.

To be much more specific, we were back at Aunt Sheila's. But I wasn't sure why. Because the reporters were totally onto us. The jackals were there, too.

Three weeks into the summer, my mom called me to freak out. I thought it was interesting that she never called until all hell broke loose. Never rang us up just to say hello. To see how we were doing.

She waited until she was ready to flatten me and then hit with both barrels.

I was lying on my back on the cot in the basement. Half watching the fish swim. Half not watching anything. Definitely not thinking anything.

My cell phone rang. I thought it was Luanne. I was waiting for her to call me with a cancellation. I mean, when she had one. I had no idea when that would be, of course. But still. Who else ever called me?

I was so sure it was her, I didn't look. I just answered. It was like leading with your glass jaw. Not even putting your fists up to guard your weakest places.

Enter Mom. Swinging.

"What the hell are you doing to us, Aubrey?"

"Mom?"

"Yes, it's your mom. What the hell do you think you're doing?"

"I . . . what? I didn't do anything. I'm just lying here."

"Who said you could keep seeing that therapist over the summer?"

Quite frankly, it had never occurred to me that anyone needed to. I thought stuff like that was exactly what everybody *wanted* me to do.

It's just impossible to keep track of what people want. What will make them happy with me. I still think so. Even now.

"I . . . I needed to talk to her. Why would you not want me to talk to her?"

"Because it costs money. *Money.* Get that? You have any idea what she costs?"

"But . . . it was your idea that I see her."

"Your principal's idea, so we went along. A year. You know? It costs a fortune. We never said we'd keep paying for it over this second summer. We had no idea until we got her bill."

"I don't . . ."

I couldn't finish the sentence. There was a big piece of the puzzle missing on my end. It was such a mystery to me. I didn't even know how to ask a question about it. I didn't even know how to get a step closer to what I needed to know.

"You don't what, Aubrey?"

"Understand. Doesn't insurance cover it?"

"No, insurance does not cover it. It's mental, not medical."

"But we had that really good coverage."

"Yes, *had*. The key word there being *had*. It cost a fortune. We had to go with a bare-bones one. No dental or visual, either. And a huge deductible."

"So I can't ever talk to her again?"

"Not unless you're independently wealthy and holding out on us."

I sat up. Looked at my fish for a moment, which had come back to Aunt Sheila's with me. Only one was an original from the previous year. They were in a bowl on one of the shelves. Surrounded by bottles. But it was too late by then. I'd been looking at them for more than a year. The bulk of the magic had been lost. You can only go to the same well just so many times, I've found. Though that's a more recent observation.

"I have to at least call her and tell her why."

"I already called her. I told her the therapy is over. Terminated."

"You *what*?" I was on my feet, pacing. But I swear I missed the moment when I stood up. I must have done it in an emotional blackout. "You humiliated me in front of her?"

"I don't have time for your ego, Aubrey. I have your father's to deal with, and he's the king of that terrain. And lay off the cell phone. I got the bill today and I nearly died. Three fifty-minute calls to her, roaming. You never thought what that would cost us? I haven't shown it to your father yet. I don't even know how to break it to him. It might just be his last straw."

"Wait," I said. "Wait, wait, wait. Wait. Wait." I seriously could not stop saying "wait." But at least she waited. "Could you please stop yelling at me? Because I honestly don't know why you're yelling at me. There was never a rule about how much I can use my phone. You didn't tell me I had to stop seeing Luanne."

"I'm telling you now."

"No, you're yelling at me for breaking a new rule you forgot to tell me about in the first place!"

Now *I* was yelling. But it had its advantages. She shut up.

I heard hurried footsteps upstairs. Someone had heard my shouting. And they were headed this way. Maybe even both someones.

I opened my mouth to say I wanted to come home. And started to cry. It twisted my mouth, which twisted my words. I had just been so unprepared for this assault. I hadn't had my guard up.

"I don't want to be here anymore," I said through tears. Humiliated, but what could I do? "It's boring here. I don't have anything to do. I don't know anybody. It was boring enough last year. I can't do it again. And the reporters are here, anyway. So what's the point? I don't even know why you sent us here again. I want to come home."

"You can't come home," she said. To her credit, she didn't yell it. "There's no home to come home to."

"I have no idea what that means."

"There's no house."

"How can there not be a house? Where's our house?"

"It's right where it always was. But it's not ours."

"You sold it?"

"Yes."

"Why?"

"Because we were about to lose it to the bank. We're lucky we found a buyer so fast. It was days to the beginning of foreclosure proceedings. We lost our shirts on it, but it was better than fore-closure. Anything is."

I looked up to see Aunt Sheila and Ruth at the bottom of the basement stairs. Staring at me. Reading my face.

"So what are we going to do?" I asked. More calmly. Because I was being watched. "Buy another?"

"You really don't get it, do you, Aubrey? If we could afford to buy a house, we would have kept the one we had."

"A smaller one."

A long silence on the line. Maybe a sigh from her. Or she might have been crying, too.

"Look. Honey. I'm sorry to break it to you this way. There's no money. Okay? There's no money. So please don't spend any money. Yes, I should have told you sooner. And that's my fault. But it's a hard thing to tell your kids. We're going to try to rent a place. An apartment, maybe. In a whole new place, where nobody knows us. But we need the summer to work it out. And please. Honey. I'm begging you. Don't send any more unexpected bills home. Okay?"

I looked up at Ruth and Aunt Sheila again. I think my mouth was hanging open.

"Right," I said. "Got it."

"I'm sorry I yelled. I know I upset you. But it's a very upsetting time here, too. I have no idea how we're going to pay for these two bills on top of everything else."

"I have my birthday money put away."

Or most of it, I thought. I didn't dare say so. I was never to have touched that money in any way. And if everything hadn't tanked with our trip to Texas the previous summer, it would've been gone.

"Save it for a dire emergency. We're not so far from one. Sorry again. It's not that I don't love you two. I hope you know that. I just . . . I didn't mean to make you cry."

"Whatever," I said. "I'll see you."

But not anytime soon. And not anyplace familiar.

I clicked off the phone.

"Did you know Mom and Dad sold the house?"

I don't know which one of them I thought I was asking. Either. Both.

"Without talking to us?" Ruth screeched.

"It was just about to be foreclosed."

"Oh, crap," Aunt Sheila said. "I had a feeling something like this could happen if Brad's clients didn't get over themselves and come back."

"Why didn't you tell us?"

It was so much the question in my head that I actually thought it had been me asking it. But it was Ruth's voice. I was just standing there with my mouth open.

"There was always a chance I could be wrong," she said. "I guess I was really hoping I was wrong."

———

I lay in the basement for hours before anybody came down to commiserate with me. When somebody finally did, I was glad it was Ruth. I didn't know how to talk to Aunt Sheila about this. Because she'd been getting by on not much money for years. How was I supposed to tell her I found the prospect horrifying?

It really wasn't that I insisted on fancy things. Or even that I wanted them. It was just scary. My mom had said, "There's no money."

What if we didn't have enough money to live *anywhere*?

Ruth came down and sat on the edge of my cot with me. I was glad, but I didn't let on. I didn't sit up.

"Kind of weird to think about," she said. "Isn't it? I never lived anyplace besides that house in my whole life."

"It's all Joseph's fault," I said.

"Maybe. But I don't see what good it does to point that out. I just keep thinking that at the end of the summer we'll go home, but we don't even know where home is."

"Mom said they're going to try to rent an apartment."

"I hope it has three bedrooms. If they say we have to share, that would suck."

"I'm not sharing," I said. "I'll sleep in the basement if I have to."

"I don't think apartments have basements. I mean, if they do, it's the basement for everybody who lives in that building, not just us."

"Oh," I said.

"And then we need another room for Isabella."

I laughed at her. Because she was so slow to catch up. I guess in hindsight, it was mean. But I was desperate for some measure of control. All I had was a little bit more information than Ruth had. And nothing else.

"She's not coming with us, Ruth. We won't be able to afford her. And we're going to be in a whole new city."

I watched her eyes go wide. And pretended it was a reaction of the weak. And that my eyes hadn't gone just as wide when I first heard. I had carefully wallpapered over the fact that I cried.

"How do you know?"

"Mom told me. She said we're going someplace where people don't know us. But as soon as we tell them our name, they will. So I don't see what good that'll do."

"What city?"

"I don't know. She didn't know. She said they needed the rest of the summer to work it out."

"Wonder where they're staying."

"No idea."

"It's weird to think about no Isabella. Mom can't even cook."

"You can say that again. But not everybody has a maid, you know."

"I know. It's not that. It's not that I need a maid. It's that I need Isabella. She's . . . like, the only one in the whole house who . . ."

But then she just faded.

"What?" I asked, when I got tired of waiting.

"Seems like she likes me."

I sat up. Looked at my sister, who wouldn't meet my eyes. Sure, I was in a surly mood. But I wasn't looking to land that kind of damage.

"I like you," I said.

"I guess I just meant who acts like they do."

"Sorry," I said.

"Don't be," she said. "I haven't been much nicer to you than you have to me. I guess it just didn't matter before this."

Then we didn't talk for a long time. Literally several minutes. Enough time that under normal circumstances, the awkwardness of not talking would have driven one of us away. But we just hung there together. Obviously not wanting to be alone. I thought it was sad that we needed each other and couldn't figure out a way to say so.

Then she spoke suddenly, and I jumped.

"I know! I have Hamish MacCallum's phone number. I'll call him."

"For what? To say what?"

"Just to ask him what we should do."

"How would he know what we should do?"

"He knows everything."

She pulled her cell phone out of her shirt pocket. I knocked it out of her hand and onto the bed.

"Don't use your cell phone if it's roaming! You want to go through what I just went through with Mom?"

"Oh. Right." Her forehead creased up, and I could see how much weight she'd put on this idea. How convinced she was that it would solve something. "I guess I could use Aunt Sheila's phone, but I have to get her permission first. I'll have to talk to him fast."

"I still have all that birthday money," I said. "You can tell her you'll pay her back."

Then her eyes came up to meet mine. For the first time.

"That's so nice. Why are you being so nice?"

"I'm nice sometimes!" I said. A little stung.

I didn't want to tell her why I made the offer. It wasn't entirely unselfish. I was beginning to think maybe Ruth was right. Maybe this guy was a source of everything. Everything we never knew where to find. Maybe I would take his address and phone number after all. Maybe I didn't have to talk to him about Joseph. Maybe I could just talk to him about all the things I didn't understand.

"Well, thanks," Ruth said. "I can't call from down here, so I'll just come back down and tell you what he said. Or do you want to come along and listen?"

"No, that's okay," I said. "I'll wait here."

I was still not willing to let on that I cared. Maybe even that I believed.

Maybe I believed because Ruth believed so strongly. Maybe because I needed to. And because there was nothing else around that I wouldn't be an idiot to believe in. No water balloon that hadn't already burst.

And left me a dripping fool.

———

Ruth was away for twenty minutes. I timed it on my watch.

I paced.

But when I heard her come back down the stairs, I threw myself on my back on the cot. Didn't let on that I'd been anxious.

"How did it go?" I asked. Like I only barely cared.

"Not quite like I thought."

She sat on the edge of the cot again. Now I wished she'd go farther away. And I wasn't even sure why. I felt like electricity at that point. I wasn't a good mix with anything else.

"Well, what did he say?"

"A lot of things. I wish you'd been there. I can't repeat them all."

"You don't have to. Just tell me what he thinks we should do."

"Nothing," she said. "There's nothing we *can* do."

Splash. Another water balloon in my unsuspecting face. Without words, without a lot of forethought, I made up my mind in that moment that I would never be unsuspecting again.

"That's *it*? I paid for a long-distance call out of my own money for *that*?"

"Well, there was more, but . . . Aubrey, there's no real answer to what we should do. We don't know where we'll be at the end of the summer. What do we do about that? Nothing. There's nothing we *can* do. There's no money. We can't fix it so Dad has money. Hamish MacCallum says we'll find out it was never about the money anyway."

"Oh. Great. So he thinks it's just fine."

"No. He didn't say that. He didn't act like it wasn't a problem. Or like we shouldn't be upset about it. He just thinks we have to accept it. We just have to wait and see what happens. He says the part that's driving us crazy is trying to fix a future that isn't even here yet. He says when it gets here, then we can figure out how to get through it. But now it's just driving us crazy because it's all unknown. So we just have to stay in the moment we're in. You know. Take things on one moment at a time."

"What an incredible waste of money. *My* money."

"Aunt Sheila says we don't have to pay her back."

"Oh," I said.

It was the first good thing anybody had told me all day. Small though it was. And it couldn't make its way in against the tide of crap. I had no space to accept it.

"Could you go away now?" I said. "No offense. I just want to be alone."

I didn't, actually. I wanted somebody around. But I wanted it to be somebody who wasn't only making everything worse.

She left without comment.

Then I felt bad. Because I knew she was having as much trouble as I was.

But I decided it was her own fault. For being stupid enough to believe an old man she'd only met once had all the answers we needed.

And worse yet, for tricking me—even for only twenty minutes—into believing it, too.

Chapter Fifteen: Ruth

————————

It was the first week in August when the media circus began to truly blossom outside Aunt Sheila's door, looking for Aubrey and me. Maybe triple or quadruple in numbers overnight. I didn't think too much about why, I guess because it seemed inevitable, like something that will always happen if given enough time.

But eventually I did ask—Aunt Sheila, that is, not the vultures. I was well trained not to engage the vultures, and I really thought Aubrey was, too. I think we all thought so.

Aunt Sheila and I were sitting at the dining-room table, which wasn't in a whole separate room from the living room. It was just sort of over in the corner. We were sitting across from each other, playing chess. We'd played anywhere from three to five games a day all summer, and I had beaten her a grand total of once. Aunt Sheila wasn't one of those older people who let you win. With her, you had to earn it.

Aubrey was slumped on the couch watching TV, one of those cartoons that's all raucous action, and the volume was too loud, and it made it hard for me to think about my chess moves. But I wasn't saying so, because any little thing could set him off by then. He had a thousand fuses, pointing in every direction, and you played with fire in his vicinity at your own risk.

"So, I haven't asked you this before, Aunt Sheila," I said, "but why are there so many reporters here all of a sudden? I mean, a few days ago it started kind of suddenly. You know. There were five or six and now there are dozens. I was thinking maybe it's because they can't find our parents to bug them."

Aunt Sheila had her hand on her queen, preparing for a move but scoping out the board one last time before jumping. When I asked, she put her hand back in her lap and sighed.

"I probably should have told you," she said. "But you guys weren't watching the news or going online, and I thought maybe it was on purpose. I thought maybe you were really happier not following the whole Joseph's trial thing. So I saved some newspaper and magazine clippings about the court-martial. I figured you could read them later just as well as you could while it was going on. If you wanted to."

"They're done court-martialing him?"

"Pretty much. They'll probably announce a sentence any time now. So I think the zoo out front is a combination of that and the fact that they can't find Brad and Janet to bug, like you said. Plus it's a big story again now, and they're desperate for anything new to put up on the screen. I'm sorry if I should have told you sooner. I wrestled with myself about it. Should I have?"

"Hmm," I said. "I'm not sure."

"You want to read what I clipped? It's not very exciting."

"No," Aubrey said, and it was the first I realized he was listening to us. "We don't care."

"Speak for yourself, Aubrey," I said. Then, to Aunt Sheila, "Maybe. I think. Maybe let me know when they have a verdict. Or a sentence. Or . . . you know. Something."

"What *verdict*?" Aubrey shouted. "What do you think the verdict's going to be, Ruth? Some big surprise that'll be. He disobeyed a direct order to go out on duty and pulled a bunch of other guys in on it with him. He never denied it. You think they're suddenly going to decide he didn't do it, even though he says he did? The only thing we're waiting for—I mean, *you're* waiting for, is the sentencing. We just don't know yet what they're going to do to him for it."

I looked at Aunt Sheila, and she had a wry half smile on her face.

"It speaks," she barely whispered, really more mouthing the words.

I burst out laughing, which I have to tell you felt like a very foreign concept. I vaguely remembered laughing, but it was like an old friend who'd moved away years ago and you didn't even think about him anymore until the moment something reminded you.

Aubrey looked up from the TV for the first time, suspiciously, to see what was so funny, or maybe just to make sure it wasn't him.

I know Aunt Sheila wasn't trying to be mean, but it was hard not to point out that Aubrey had been quite the mummy all summer. He barely moved, and he didn't speak, especially not when spoken to. He was bored here, which I didn't blame him for, but he'd attempted to solve the problem by adopting watching TV and ignoring us as his hobbies.

"Okay," Aunt Sheila said at a normal volume. "If I hear there's been a sentence handed down, I'll tell you." Then, more in Aubrey's direction, "'You' meaning Ruth and only Ruth. A brick wall doesn't have to fall on me, Aubrey."

——

It wasn't the next morning, but the morning after, when it happened.

I jumped awake to a bigger-than-usual flurry of sound out front, as though everybody had begun talking at once, too loudly and excitedly, shouting to be heard over everybody else.

I ran to the window, drew the curtain back, and looked out.

It was only just barely light, and my brother Aubrey was standing in front of them, just outside Aunt Sheila's open gate. He had his arms raised, as if commanding silence. He looked like a performer stepping out onto the stage before a huge and enthusiastic audience of his fans. I could see microphones desperately extended in his direction on the ends of anxious arms, each branded with the call letters of a radio or TV station. Cameramen struggled to keep a clear shot through the crowd, trying not to be jostled by the shoving. Two long boom mics lifted themselves over the throng and descended in the direction of my brother.

I blinked into artificial lights that bothered my eyes from all the way inside the house, and I wondered how it felt to Aubrey to have all that glare pointed right into his face. Then I remembered all his years staring at the chandelier, and I realized there was nothing you could do to his corneas that hadn't been done before. Whatever you could dish out, they'd seen worse.

At first, his body-language demand for silence had no effect, and I could hear them shouting questions at him, and I could hear words, but everybody was talking at once and they all warred with each other. But the questions all seemed to involve the words "your brother, Joseph" and "ten years."

I unlatched the old-fashioned lock on the wooden windowpane and forced the bottom half up, which wasn't easy.

"Aubrey!" I screamed through the screen. "Don't say anything!"

I have no idea if he heard me or not. I only know that a moment later, I heard his voice rise above the crowd, and he did a little shouting of his own.

"Be quiet and I'll tell you!"

Then everyone was quiet, and either Aubrey was talking in a normal voice or not talking at all, and that left me utterly powerless and unable to even follow what was going on. I knew it was a disaster, but I wanted to know exactly how much of a disaster and exactly what kind.

I hurried out of my guest bedroom and to the front door, where I ran into Aunt Sheila in her nightgown. Literally ran into her. We bumped foreheads hard and bounced off each other and looked into each other's faces while rubbing the sore spots.

"What the hell is he doing?" she asked me.

"I have no idea," I said. "I think he's lost his mind."

The door opened in, and we jumped out of the way of it, and Aubrey walked by. He honestly looked as though he thought he could go right back down to the basement without answering for anything.

"Aubrey!" Aunt Sheila yelled, and I realized I'd never heard her raise her voice in anger before.

He stopped and turned around. "What?" he asked with the kind of casual air that takes planning, not the kind that's genuine.

"What did you say to them?"

"The truth."

"What truth? The truth about what?"

"They asked me how I felt about Joseph getting ten years, and I told them the truth."

Then he turned and walked away.

I looked at Aunt Sheila and she looked at me.

"I thought you were going to tell me when Joseph got sentenced," I said.

"News to me, too, kiddo."

Then she walked into the kitchen and made a phone call, even though it was much too early to call anybody, and I pictured my mom stumbling out of bed, more than a little perturbed, to answer the phone.

I looked out the window in the front door and watched almost everybody scrambling away, gunning the engines of their news vans, slamming the doors. I pictured them racing each other back to their respective newsrooms, all vying to be the first to file the story of the words Aubrey had just given them.

Whatever words they had been.

―――――

It took me fifteen minutes to gather up the nerve to go down to the basement to confront him, and all he would say at first was "Go away, Ruth."

"Why did you even talk to them?" I asked, but he didn't answer. "What were you thinking that even made you go out there? Did you get up and go out there all on your own?"

Which was a stupid question, because clearly no one dragged him out of the house.

But he still wouldn't answer.

So I broke out the big guns.

"Mom and Dad are going to kill you. And you better hope not literally, Aubrey, because it's not out of the question."

"Too late," he said. "It's done."

I thought that was interesting, because almost everything Aubrey had said in the last few months involved the words "I don't care." But even Aubrey couldn't pretend not to care about the wrath of Brad and Janet.

"I just want to know what you said to the cameras."

"So you'll have to wait for the evening news, then," he said. "Won't you?"

―――――

Aunt Sheila and I didn't have to wait for the evening news.

We sat at the kitchen table, our chairs pushed together, shoulders nearly touching, drinking coffee and staring at her ancient laptop. She just kept refreshing the page on the news search for Joseph's trial.

And then suddenly the first hit was there—though there's no way I can account for how long we waited—and it stunned me, like it hadn't been exactly what we'd been waiting for all along.

Youngest Stellkellner: "Ten years is not enough," the headline said.

"Oh, shit," I said. "He did *not* say that."

Then I realized I never cursed in front of Aunt Sheila, or just about anybody else for that matter, but I never got a chance to back up and ask for forgiveness, because she clicked again.

I honestly think Aunt Sheila meant to click on the headline of the story, but I'm only guessing. I think she accidentally hit refresh because she'd been doing it all morning, and she was as stunned as I was, and her hand was on autopilot.

Five new versions of the same headline popped up. It was like the chicken pox, I thought—you barely have time to absorb the fact that you found the first bump, and then when you look again it's already spread like a forest fire.

She hovered the cursor over the first headline, and then we were on the page, and it was CNN, which I thought was kind of shocking, because who would ever have guessed my little brother had something to say that would end up on CNN? And there were printed words of course, and I started to try to read them without even realizing there was also video. It wasn't the kind that autoplayed, though, so if you were shocked and going fast you could mistake it for a photo and ignore it. It was the words that were pulling at me.

I got as far as:

In a surprising development, when asked what he thought about his older brother, Joseph Stellkellner, being sentenced to ten years in a federal prison, youngest sibling Aubrey Stellkellner replied, "I think it's not enough." When asked by reporters why he thought this, the young Stellkellner replied, "Because he's a coward. And he—"

That was when Aunt Sheila pressed play on the video.

We sat transfixed, watching Aubrey, his face washed out by the portable lights the cameramen shined on him, looking resolute and sure and adult . . . and really not afraid at all.

His name was written across the bottom of the screen, and it struck me again what miserable luck our last name had proven to be. Couldn't we just have been the Smiths? Then when we met people and told them our name, no connection would ever be made. It was like a nasty little joke from the universe, a sign that we had been singled out for abuse long before Joseph came home. We had been set up in an elaborate plan.

"I think it's not enough," Aubrey said. I didn't realize how completely his voice had changed until I heard it on a videotaped playback. I guess I didn't realize until that moment just how much he wasn't a kid anymore.

"Why do you say that?" a woman's voice asked from off-camera.

"Because he's a coward. And he hurts people. And they should have put him away forever, for the rest of his life. Because he deserves it. And because then he couldn't hurt anybody."

Which struck me as ironic, because Joseph had only hurt Aubrey once that I knew of, and he'd done that from his prison cell. But leave it to my little brother to propel himself more on vitriol and less on logic.

Then he just stood there, looking adult in attitude but small and slight in stature, and I thought his face looked a little whiter, but I wasn't sure. Maybe it was only the lights.

"Is there anything more you want to tell us about your brother?" a different off-camera voice asked. A man.

"No," Aubrey said. "That's everything. I just think ten years is not enough."

Then he turned and walked back through Aunt Sheila's gate, closing it behind him, and the camera stayed on him the whole walk to her front door, and that was when I realized my heartburn was back with a vengeance and I could hardly breathe around it.

The video play ran out, the image froze, and we both just sat there and stared at the screen and said nothing.

"Well, that was ugly," Aunt Sheila said after a time. "Just when you think things can't possibly get any worse."

———

When I woke up the next morning, I got dressed and wandered into the kitchen, not so much looking for breakfast as for more antacid.

I was a little surprised to see my mother sitting at the kitchen table with Aunt Sheila. Not stunned, by any means, but nobody had mentioned it was about to happen—still, it's one of those things you know in retrospect you might well have seen coming.

Before they knew I was there, I heard my mom say, "We're not blaming you, Sheila. Brad's not, either. Believe me, if anybody knows what an intractable little shit he can be, it's us. We just think they need to be where we have more control over their situation. Not that he doesn't defy us just as much, but I think he's a lot more scared of us. And then if anything goes wrong, we'll have nobody but ourselves to blame."

I was thinking about that last sentence and how it didn't match with the first one, about how they didn't blame Aunt Sheila in the first place, but I was thinking in a muddy way because I was still half-asleep. Also, I didn't think about it for long, because my mom looked up and saw me there.

"Pack your things," she said. "You kids are coming home today. And I don't mean later today. I mean now."

I didn't ask where home was, but not so much because I wanted to be cooperative and sweet. More because I was afraid of the answer.

"I had nothing to do with this," I said. "I just want you to know that."

"I do know that," she said, which was an odd vote of confidence from my mom. Or it seemed like one, at least, until she added, "We heard you on the video, yelling at him not to say anything."

"I didn't hear that on the video," I said.

"Well, there are four or five different versions of it out there now. Some are longer than others. I'm not taking you home to punish you. Your father and I just think we all need to stay closer together till this blows over. Which it should now, because there's nothing left to report. Every day in jail is like every other one, so Joseph won't stay interesting for long. Now seriously, Ruth. Chop-chop. We're clearing out of here as soon as I can get downstairs and drag your impulsive little brother out to the car by his ear."

———

I thought it had been a figurative statement—I really did—but when I got to the front door with my suitcase, there was my impulsive little brother being dragged out to the car by his ear.

All he said as he got dragged past me was, "Ow. Ow. Ow."

I thought, *Well, you wanted a reaction, Aubrey, and you got it. You wanted to go off like a nuclear weapon, so now here's your nuclear waste. You can't tell me you never saw this coming.*

I didn't say any of that out loud. I was beginning to think the best thing to say, at least 99 percent of the time, was nothing at all.

I should've known, if I ever learned anything from my little brother, it would come in the form of what *not* to do. Aubrey Stellkellner teaches Don't Let This Happen to You 101. And brings his message home in rare form.

I pictured Olympic judges holding up signs, giving Aubrey damn close to a perfect ten in man-made disaster.

Aunt Sheila followed after them with the two big duffel bags of Aubrey's stuff. I was the only one who thought of the fish.

I tried to find a plastic bag and a rubber band, but I had no idea where they were kept at Aunt Sheila's, and I couldn't get anybody's attention, so I just grabbed the bowl and poured out about a third of the water onto the lawn on my way to the car.

I was careful not to pour out any fish.

"Oh, my fish," he said when I handed them into the backseat, as though he'd forgotten them, too. "Thank you."

Thank you. From Aubrey. I took that to mean he cared. About something, even if it was just a crowd of cheap little orange fish.

Chapter Sixteen: Aubrey

The curse of the shotgun seat continued. I lost to Ruth again.

I sat in the back by myself. Trying to pretend I didn't see my mom looking at me in the rearview mirror. Every ten beats or so, she looked back. Like she might catch me in some fresh shenanigans.

Thing is, I was riding in the back of a car I'd never seen before.

It was a lot like Aunt Sheila's car, except newer. It had the ping doors. Not the thunk doors.

I didn't dare ask. I didn't dare say a word. I'd pushed my parents further than I'd ever pushed them before. Now I figured I should treat them like huge, dominant lowland gorillas in aggressive moods. Take a passive stance. Never once look them in the eye. Pray. Wait for them to get bored and move away.

Ruth asked.

"Whose car is this?"

"It's ours," my mom said.

"Oh. Do we still have the Mercedes or the SUV?"

"No."

"Oh. I just . . . I don't know. I know this one is cheaper. But the other ones . . . we already had them. I'm not sure what the advantage is of buying something new."

"They weren't paid for."

"And this is?"

"Yes, Ruth. This is. Your father took out a loan and paid . . . a couple of things that needed attention, and bought this car. We couldn't have kept the other two, anyway. There's a limit to how much your car can be worth and still keep it in a bankruptcy."

That last word stopped all conversation cold.

I wondered how the person felt who approved my father's loan, only to discover he planned to spend all the money, file for bankruptcy, and never make a payment. I didn't care much, though. At that point, I figured everybody was pretty much out to take everybody. I didn't expect better. Not even from my own family.

My cell phone let out a tone in my pocket. Someone had text-messaged me, from the sound of it. For only the second time ever.

"What was that?" my mother asked. Like a watchdog hearing a noise in the front yard.

"Nothing," I said.

I pulled it out of my pocket and looked.

It was from Luanne.

"Is that somebody calling on your cell? Because we have to pay for incoming calls, too, you know."

"No. It's not. It's a text message."

"A what? I never heard of such a thing."

It was 2004, let's not forget. Lots of people had phones with text messaging. But half of them hadn't even figured out how to use it. Or didn't even know it was there.

"It's new," I said. "Don't freak out."

I read the message. *I know you wanted to hurt him, Aubrey. You accomplished that. But I think you won't find what you're looking for in this impulsive act.*

"Who is it?" my mom asked. In that aggravating voice. Like the electric drills at the dentist's office. A wholly negative sound.

"None of your business," I said. Then I realized these were not normal times. I was down behind enemy lines. And I'd forgotten to humor my captors.

Next thing I knew, the phone disappeared from my hands. She'd reached over between the seats and snatched it.

"Dr. Gravenstein? Why would she be . . . whatever you said . . . to you?" She swerved dangerously in the road. I held my hands over the fishbowl. Then she straightened out and handed my phone to Ruth. "Here," she said. "I don't want to get us in a crash. Read that and tell me what it says."

I reached forward and grabbed for the phone. My seatbelt stopped me. And the fishbowl water sloshed. It wasn't hard for Ruth to keep it out of my reach. I watched her read the message. I waited for her to humiliate me by reading it again out loud. To betray me. Just to keep on good terms with our mom.

She didn't.

She just stalled there. Looked once over her shoulder at me. And I saw she didn't have it in her to betray me *that* badly.

I appreciated that in my sister. I did. I never said so, but I did.

"Oh, for heaven's sake," my mom said, and pulled over onto the shoulder. Even though it was the freeway. Emergency stopping only.

"Hey!" I yelled. "You're spilling the fish water!"

I'd actually spilled more grabbing for my phone. But now any spills would be her fault. Not mine.

She read it for herself. Then she handed the phone back over the seat.

"At least she was right," she said.

"I don't even understand it," I said.

"There's nothing not to understand, Aubrey. It was perfectly clear."

And with that, she pulled back into the traffic lane. Badly. Another driver had to merge left and honk.

"I wasn't looking for anything. And it wasn't impulsive."

"What? You'd been planning it for days? That would be even worse, mister. But you couldn't have been planning it, because the sentencing had just been announced, just the afternoon before."

I *had* been planning it for days. Only not in response to the sentencing. I just thought I'd say what they ought to give him for a sentence. This had been cleaner, though. This had been even better.

I didn't say any of that to my mom. I wasn't a complete idiot.

I read Luanne's text again. And I was pissed. Because she wasn't even my therapist anymore. So why did I have to hold still for her criticism? I realized I'd started to have that reaction the first time I'd read it. But things had taken a sudden turn. My pissed had been interrupted.

I texted back, *What do you care? You got to wash your hands of me. I bet you were relieved.*

A minute or two went by. I figured I'd never hear from her again. Why should she bother? She'd gotten her shot in. And she wasn't getting paid. And obviously that's all she'd ever cared about, anyway. Not me.

Then I heard another tone.

"When I get the bill," my mother said, "I better not find out that message thing costs money."

I was pretty sure it did. But how much could two messages cost? I ignored her and read the reply. *Beg to differ. Offered bottom of sliding scale. 25% normal rate. Your mother wouldn't even discuss it. But I met them 3/4 of the way.*

I looked up. Glared at the back of my mother's head.

A few seconds later, she did the Aubrey check in the rearview mirror.

"What?" she asked me.

"Nothing," I said, and slid the phone back in my pocket.

I never answered Luanne's second text.

———

It wasn't until we got onto Interstate 5 that Ruth asked the obvious question.

"Where are we going? And don't say 'home.' I know 'home.' But where? Where do we live now?"

"We rented a little place. Not an apartment. It's a house. But small. And not too fancy."

"Where?"

A pause. I knew she wished she didn't have to say.

"Bakersfield."

"Bakersfield?" Ruth and I both said at once.

"Yes. Bakersfield. What's wrong with Bakersfield?"

"I don't even know where to begin," Ruth said.

A mile of silence.

"So how did you choose Bakersfield?" Ruth asked.

"We were just looking for a place where nobody knows us. Where we could start over."

"Which would also be every other city in the United States," Ruth said.

"Your father got a little job there."

"Oh. Why didn't you say so?"

"It's not much. Just legal research for a firm. And the pay is not great. But he has to start over somewhere. Don't say anything to him about it. It's a big step down, so it's a sore subject with him. You know how your father is."

"It's all Joseph's fault," I said.

I hadn't even realized I'd been about to say it.

"Hush," my mother said.

Then nothing more on the subject. Or any other one. For quite some time.

I wanted to ask about the bedrooms. How many bedrooms? But I'd already said more than I ever meant to. Instead, I willed Ruth to ask for me. For several miles. Then, amazingly, she did.

"How many bedrooms does it have?"

"Only two. But we're going to fix the basement up for Aubrey. I don't think he'll mind. Do you?"

As if I weren't even there. But what's new?

"I think he *prefers* basements now," Ruth said.

After that, it was a long and quiet ride.

———

Around the time we pulled inside the Bakersfield city limit, she hit us again.

"There's one more thing I haven't told you," she said.

"Oh, God," Ruth muttered under her breath.

Rookie mistake. She'd let herself believe the worst was already known. I never did that. Not anymore.

"Your last name is not Stellkellner anymore."

"What?" I asked.

"It's more or less self-explanatory."

"Whose last name is not Stellkellner?" Ruth asked.

"Any of us. All four of us. Your father went to court and had it changed. Your name is Ruth Rogers. And Aubrey Rogers."

"Why?" Ruth asked.

She didn't have to ask *why Rogers*. That much was clear. Roger was our dad's middle name.

"Well, isn't it obvious, Ruth? So everybody will get off our backs and leave us alone."

"You said it was easy to find out stuff like that!"

"For the reporters, sure. For a private detective. Other regular people don't do investigations. Don't you think it would be nice to tell somebody your name and get no reaction at all?"

Silence for the rest of the ride to the new house. While we thought about that. Yeah, it would be nice to get away from the giant stain. At least keep it to myself if I chose to. And it would be easier to make new friends.

Still. It's one thing to be told there's a whole new house. A whole new city. It's another thing to be told there's a whole new *you*. And in both cases, nobody bothered to get your thoughts before deciding.

Welcome to your childhood. Until you're eighteen, it's just more of this.

————

The house was what you might call a "fixer-upper." If you were trying to be nice. Or if you were the agent trying to talk some family into renting it.

But honestly, I didn't care.

I cared more that it was entirely unfamiliar.

I cared that it contained only a few of our things. A few familiar bits of furniture. Lamps I knew. But the rest was gone, and I would never know where.

I didn't care that we would have to eat dinner in the kitchen. But I cared that there was no chandelier over the dinner table. Because I would have no place to look except at my family.

I pulled apart all my stuff in the basement. Laid it out to take inventory. It had been too hastily packed in used cartons from the grocery store. And worse yet, plastic garbage bags.

It seemed to amount to about half of what I figured I owned. Or used to own.

I never asked where everything else had gone. What difference did it make? It was gone.

The basement did have a working phone line, so I could do dial-up Internet. So I sat in the basement, on piles of clothes, and Googled my own name. My old name. And the sentence *Ten years is not enough* in quotes.

I watched the number of hits until it climbed up over a million.

I attempted to savor what I had done.

I carefully ignored the fact that it was already clear Luanne was right. The thrill of doing the unthinkable was wearing off.

I had accomplished exactly nothing.

———

That's really all I have to say about that summer of my life. Hell, that next nine years of my life.

What else can I say that's interesting?

The nice thing about my life—the *only* nice thing about my life—from May 2003 to August 2004 is that it was unique. It was hell, but it was unlike anybody else's. And it made people's eyes go wide. It made a good story. Nobody else knew how it would feel to be me. Why do you think they were crowding our gates with cameras and microphones, asking?

But our mother was right. Damn her, she was right. For once. Joseph did not continue to be interesting. So neither did we.

I resented that.

It was one thing to disrupt our lives because we mattered. It was quite another to disrupt our lives because we mattered for a split second in the great scheme of their news cycles. Disrupt and discard. Now *that* you could grow to resent.

After that, we were just like everybody else.

After that, it was just life at the Rogers household.

We had very little. We struggled to make ends meet. Four people got by on one car. When we asked for things, we were mostly told "no." We had to wear our shoes until they were too tight and our jeans until they showed too much of our ankles.

After a year or two, my dad worked his way back up to a better position. We moved into a slightly bigger house. But he never spent more than we had again. So it was still pretty different from the way it had once been.

Then our dad left our mom, and us, for a younger woman.

But even so. Let's face it. All those details—even the last one—made us anything but unique.

What's the point of telling a story that 98 percent of the people in the country could just as easily tell?

Part Four

Blindside

Spring 2013

Chapter Seventeen: Ruth

I had Maya on the diapering table and in a briefly undiapered state when my cell phone rang. Motherhood dictated that I didn't dare leave her alone for even a split second to go fetch it off the dresser, but I could see it from where I stood, and I could see who was calling. I wasn't close enough to read names or numbers, but I had it programmed to bring up a photo of most of my regular callers.

I found myself peering, at some distance, into the wrinkled and wizened, yet beautiful, face of Regina MacCallum, Ham's seventy-year-old daughter.

"Oh, shit," I said, and then clapped my one guaranteed-clean hand over my mouth. "You didn't hear that," I told Maya. "And you're not old enough to repeat the things you hear." Then, as more of a mumble to myself, "And I have to grow a filter before she *gets* old enough."

The phone was still ringing, of course. And my heart had more than sunk—it had crashed through the nursery floor.

"Sean!" I yelled out at the top of my lungs, and Maya startled and cried briefly.

"I'm in the shower!" he yelled back.

"Can you come help me? It's important!"

He stumbled in maybe thirty seconds later—dripping onto the hardwood, towel in one hand, hair still full of shampoo—but of course by then, the phone had stopped ringing and gone to voice mail.

"Can you finish diapering her? It's Regina. I have to call her back as fast as I can. I'm afraid—"

"I know what you're afraid of," he said. "Go."

I grabbed up my phone and touched the screen twice to ring back her number. It rang three times, which felt frustrating. Shouldn't she be right there beside it? She'd called like a split second ago. I prayed she wasn't marching through a list of notifications, one after the other, already having moved on to her next call. I watched Sean coo at the baby and dry himself off at the same time.

Then she picked up.

"Ruthie," she said in that beautiful Scottish voice. "First of all, I know I scared the piss out of you, so let me start by saying my father is still on this earth."

"Oh, thank God. Is he okay?"

"Not very, Ruth, no," she said, with that distinctive inflection on the *R*s. "He has pneumonia. He's in the hospital in San Fran, and the doctors are treating it. And he's a tough old bugger, you know? So he might pop up just fine, like those blow-up clown dolls you can't ever knock down for long. But I don't have to tell you that everything's a bit of a scare when you're ninety-five. Here's hoping I'm worrying you for nothing, Ruthie, but if I didn't tell you, and you'd missed the chance to see him . . . I couldn't have lived with myself over that."

I realized I had one hand to my chest, breathing in relief. I looked up at Sean, who was wrapping Maya in a clean disposable diaper, the towel around his waist, and gave him a little thumbs-up.

"No, of course, you did just the right thing, Regina. I'll come up."

"Excellent. Here's hoping I worried us all for nothing and it's just a lovely chance to visit. Haven't seen you in ages, Ruthie."

"Well, of course it's been harder with the baby . . ."

The baby. Right. Good self-reminder. It was hard to get away for a visit with the baby, and I still had one of those.

"Can you manage it now?" Regina asked, as if reading my mind.

"I'll work it out. I'll call you when I know my timing."

And we said our good-byes so I could hurry off the phone.

I looked up at Sean with a look in my eyes that I'm guessing communicated the question just fine, because he never forced me to ask it.

"How long will you need to be gone?"

"If I fly, maybe just two days," I said. "Two and a half, maybe."

"So that's three days off work for me."

"I'll take Maya."

"Into a hospital?"

"No. Right, I won't. What if I got my mother here?"

"That would help. Think she'll do it?"

"Are you kidding? She lives for her granddaughter. As she so often tells us. Just in case we were fooled into thinking her life had anything to do with us."

"Short notice, though."

"I'll call her."

"No," he said. "Go." He snapped the last snap of Maya's onesie and lifted her by her underarms, setting her on her freshly dry butt in her crib. Then he took me by both shoulders. "I'll take tomorrow off work. I'll call it in as a family emergency. I'll put the baby's car seat in my car, and Maya and I will drive out to Bakersfield and pick up your mom."

I sighed out a frightening amount of tension—I'd been in a deeply rattled panic mode without fully realizing it—and relaxed between his hands. Then I rested my temple against his bare chest.

"I don't know what I did to deserve you," I said. "But if I ever identify it, I'll do it again."

"I know what Ham means to you."

I took a deep breath and then pulled away, ready to get down to the task of packing.

At the nursery door, it hit me.

"I just had a terrible thought," I said. "Joseph is due to get out of prison in less than a month. If that's too late to see Ham again . . . if he misses him by only that much . . . can you imagine how bad he'll feel?"

Sean chewed on that for a moment, then said, "Wouldn't Ham say that's one of those life situations that's entirely out of our control?"

"Well played," I said, and got down to packing for my trip.

———

Sean dropped me at LAX, one small overnight bag on my lap.

"I'll call when I know more," I said.

"Give Ham my best. And if you feel like you need to stay longer, we'll manage."

I leaned over and grabbed him around the neck and pulled us closer together, so that I was more or less hugging his head.

"You're amazing. And appreciated."

I kissed him on the temple and then pulled away, leaving him smiling shyly as if I'd embarrassed him in front of a crowd.

I jumped out, then opened the back door and leaned in and gave Maya a kiss on her smooth, soft-haired, sweet-smelling baby head.

"You be a good girl for your daddy," I said.

I had a flash of the future—the not-too-distant future—when she'd be old enough to call me "Mommy." Would I even be able to walk away with her voice calling out to me, appealing to me by my sudden new name?

I pushed the thought away again and slammed the door, waving as they drove away.

Then I pulled my phone out of my pocket, mostly to see if I'd missed an update from the airline. So far there had been no flight delays, but I wasn't entirely sure I believed in the concept of an undelayed flight.

There was one voice mail, and it was from Regina. I froze, feeling my heart fall again. And I don't mean a light sag. I just kept feeling it, and it just kept going down. With half-paralyzed fingers, I played back the message.

"Ruthie, it's Regina, and it's not bad news." I filled my lungs with a much-needed new breath. "Notice how fast I said that? It's actually good news. They've released him, and we're taking him home right now. So don't catch a cab and go to the hospital. That would be pointless. Just go to the curb and I'll pick you up. Or somebody will. I'll make sure I get you a ride."

I saved the message, though I'm not sure why I thought I'd need it again, and then stood there like a statue for three breaths, just enjoying the sense of relief. But I didn't have much time to waste.

I got myself into the vast and unruly security line as fast as I could trot.

———

I paced the curb at San Francisco International for fifteen or twenty minutes, wishing I knew more about what I was waiting for. Regina's car I would know on sight, but if she sent somebody else, would I know the somebody else? Could I trust the somebody else to know me?

She will've given them your cell number, I thought. *Stop worrying.*

Then I saw Regina's car a good way down the line, surrounded by buses and airport shuttles. It was an old powder-blue four-door Mercedes, maybe twenty or twenty-five years old, with custom plates: "GR SCOT."

It was close enough now that I could read the plates and also see that it wasn't Regina driving. It was a man I hadn't met before, in a big-brimmed Australian outback hat and dark sunglasses, maybe thirtysomething.

Just for a moment, I regretted the prospect of having to make conversation with a stranger.

He pulled over as soon as he saw me, before I could even raise my arms to wave, so that was interesting. He must have seen a photo of me or something.

I opened the back door and threw my bag in, then dropped into the passenger seat.

"Ruth Rogers," I said, and held my hand out for him to shake.

He just stared at it, which made for a strange moment. I probably could have counted to fifteen slowly while I sat there and wondered what was up.

"Duck," he said. "It's me."

Then I was the one who just sat quietly and stared.

He lifted his hat and pulled down his sunglasses, then gave me a shy smile, and I saw that he was afraid of this meeting.

"Joseph?" I asked, my voice hushed with surprise. "I didn't recognize you."

"It's my horse-ranch disguise," he said, setting the hat and glasses back into place.

"Not just that. You used to be a skinny little guy."

He was wearing a salmon-colored T-shirt that showed off his broad shoulders, and his bulky upper arms stretched the short sleeves, causing them to rise up.

"Well, you know that cliché about guys working out in prison," he said.

A sharp rap on the driver's window made us both jump. We looked over to see a uniformed traffic cop, who signaled Joseph to get moving.

"Right," he said, mostly to me. "Time to go."

He pulled away from the curb, and we drove in silence through the curved maze of airport lanes, headed for the exit and the 101 freeway.

"I didn't even know you were out," I said. "When did you get out?"

"March," he said. No elaboration.

"I thought you were getting out in May."

"No. March."

"But they put you in pretrial confinement in May of 2003. And I heard they were going to give you credit for that time served. So that would be May of this year."

"There was a little time off for good behavior."

"Oh. I didn't know the army gave time off for good behavior."

"They do. If they didn't normally, I'm sure Brad's hotshot lawyer would have pressed for it. Since they do, he mostly concentrated on getting me a release date while I was still younger than Hammy is now."

"Brad got you a lawyer?"

"You didn't know?"

"No. And I'm amazed. Because he was so tight with money. And he was busy going broke at the time."

"Mom's idea, I'm sure."

I thought it was interesting that he'd called her "Janet" when he was younger, but called her "Mom" now. Maybe people get dearer during a ten-year prison sentence. Maybe even Janet. Or maybe, as you get older, your parents come back around to being your parents. Maybe that independent moment when you push them away is only a phase.

"I still can't figure out where he got all that—"

But then I could. It sounds like a lot to be able to remember ten years later, but it was just one of those odd mysteries that gets stuck in your head. I'd never forgotten our mom telling us how, at some point before filing bankruptcy, Brad had borrowed a bunch of money and paid something that needed paying and bought that cheap car. I could feel at the time that she'd papered over something, some expenditure she didn't care to talk about. Now I knew.

"Never mind," I said. "I think I've got it."

We rode in silence for a minute or two, and he pulled onto the freeway ramp going south. I wondered if he knew where to cut over to Highway 1. I sure didn't. I wondered how often he'd come here, and by what means, and why I had never known.

"I still can't get used to the Rogers thing," he said.

"But you knew about it."

"Yeah, Hammy told me. Just recently, because I was talking about trying to find you. In general, he's not much of a conduit of information, as I'm sure you've noticed. He doesn't like to repeat what's been told to him. He just assumes everything you say to him is in confidence. So I didn't ask him a lot of questions about the family. But he couldn't let me go off and try to contact you using the wrong last name."

"How did it make you feel?"

"Well, let me see. My entire family went to court and changed their names so as not to be associated with me in any way. So I'll go with . . . joyful?"

"Okay. It was a stupid question. Sorry I asked. And by the way, the whole family didn't go to court and change their names. Brad went to court and got all of our names changed without even running it by us first. Aubrey and I were pretty shocked."

I saw a reaction to Aubrey's name spoken out loud, a kind of flinch—which is hard to explain, because Joseph's face was still buried in the hat and sunglasses. But I know what I saw. Maybe it was something that happened more in the energy surrounding him. But I know I wasn't wrong.

"How *is* testy old Brad?" he asked, veering off in a new direction.

"I have no idea. I haven't seen him or talked to him in years."

"Well, that's a neat trick. How do you see Janet and not Brad?"

"Joseph, he's gone. He's been gone for five or six years. He left Mom for a twenty-eight-year-old paralegal. Speaking of clichés."

Silence. For digestion, I suppose.

Then he said, "Yeah, well . . . they're clichés for a reason, I guess."

Another couple of miles in silence. I wished he'd take off the hat and glasses so I could really see him. I wanted to look into his face and chart what had changed, what had stayed the same. I wanted to see his face clearly and really absorb into every cell of myself that this was my brother Joseph, whom I hadn't seen in a decade.

Even more to the point, I wanted to have more to say to him. After ten years apart, there must have been more words, but I couldn't locate them, and not for lack of trying. Something was dragging on the conversation, like a prisoner with a ball and chain on his ankle, though I regretted that choice of metaphors the moment it came into my head. I could feel a sense of exhaustion caused by the pressure of trying to fight my way through that moment.

He broke the silence.

"I notice you kept the name, though."

"Rogers?"

"Yes. That."

"I thought about it when I left home. But all my ID was in that name."

"Right," he said. "Right. Got it."

"Okay, it was more than that, but it wasn't an insult to you, I swear it wasn't. Let me think how to say this. The name 'Rogers' meant something to me by then. Something positive. It was like a badge of courage. It meant we could get through anything and come out the other side in one piece."

He didn't answer.

"I guess maybe it would be better not to stress how hard a time that was for us," I said.

"Say whatever you need to," he said quietly, and took the turn-off for the 280 South toward Daly City. "Otherwise it'll be like it was when we were kids."

Right, the silences. No one had ever referenced them out loud, as far as I could recall. I guess that was what made them the silences.

"I didn't blame you for it, though," I said. "I blamed that incredibly sick media machine. It's like a monster that serves up all news, all the time—whatever people want to have slapped on their plate so they can judge it and feel superior. I never thought that was your fault."

"Aubrey did, though," he said.

"Aubrey was just hurt because you wouldn't see us. He thought you didn't love him anymore. You know how he is."

I watched the side of his face and saw little lines form outside the edges of his sunglasses as he squeezed his eyes shut. Just for a second. Then he looked at the road again.

"The reason I wouldn't see you is because Brad told me in very clear terms that I was to stay away from both of you indefinitely."

"Yeah, we thought that might've been the case, but I guess Aubrey felt like you'd always disobeyed him before."

"Duck," he said. "Think about it. If he'd pulled that attorney out from under me, I could have been in there for life. And I don't mean 'life' as in your first parole hearing is in seven years. I mean 'life' as in die in a jail cell an old man. That's what they wanted for me. That's what would have happened most likely if I hadn't had good outside counsel. Brad held all the cards, Duck."

"Oh," I said. And then I almost couldn't finish my thought, because I so wanted to call Aubrey and tell him this immediately. "He actually held that over your head."

"You don't think he's capable?"

"Oh, no. I totally do. I'm just taking this in. It's kind of . . . a revelation. We tried so hard to think of a good reason why you wouldn't see us. But we never thought of that. But still, after you were sentenced . . ."

"You think I should have taken his money, taken the lawyer, and then the minute I was through with him, totally flown in the face of the deal? I realize there's not a person in the whole country who would probably believe this, Duck, but I do have some sense of honor. Brad thought I was a bad influence on you guys. I guess at that point, I wasn't so sure he was wrong."

Silence for a time.

Then he added, "If I'd known Brad had ditched you guys five or six years ago, I would've tried to contact you the minute he left. But nobody told me. There wasn't exactly a flow of information going back and forth. It was more like the family walled itself off with me on the outside."

We rode in silence for a long time. Half an hour. Maybe even forty-five minutes. We wound our way to the coast through some very upscale areas I'd never seen before. I had always come up from the south.

I looked down at the phone in my hand and couldn't remember having taken it out of my pocket. I was rubbing one thumb over the screen, and I knew it was because I was itching to call

Aubrey, to fill him in on these new developments, even though I knew he didn't want them. Even though I knew he would reject them. But old habits die hard in my family, and I wanted him to see the past in a new light, the way I was doing now.

But I wasn't going to make that call in front of Joseph, because I knew the rage and hatred would come through to my end of the connection—even if Aubrey kept his voice down, which wasn't likely.

"I heard you got married," Joseph said, breaking a whole new brand of modern silence.

"Yeah. Four years ago."

"Are you happy?"

"We are."

"Good. Good for you. Who'd you marry?"

"Sean Acheson."

"Are you kidding me? Isn't that the guy you kept hoping would ask you out when you were fifteen?"

"One and the same."

"I guess he finally did."

"Yeah. It was bumpy for a while there, but we kept in touch. Even after we moved to Bakersfield. We texted and talked on the phone. The funny thing is that we didn't actually go on a date until we were twenty. After I moved back to Southern California."

"Hammy says you have a baby."

I felt my heart fill, just being reminded about her, and at the same time I missed her so much it physically hurt.

"I do. Maya, her name is. She's amazing."

"And gorgeous. Hammy showed me a picture of her."

"If I'd known Ham would be home from the hospital, I'd have brought her."

"I wish you had. I'm dying to meet her."

Right around that moment, just as it struck me that we were small-talking like strangers, he got somewhat real again.

"So why isn't your name Ruth Acheson?"

"Oh. That. I'm too progressive, I guess. I hate that thing where your name disappears and you sort of become your husband. Reminds me of the old days, the fifties—not that I remember them personally—but remember on *I Love Lucy* how they referred to themselves as Mrs. Ricky Ricardo and Mrs. Fred Mertz? And then the children always got their father's name, like they were all him and no her. And, trust me, Sean's part of Maya was the easy one. We hyphenated for Maya's last name."

I looked up, surprised to see the old dusty-green house up ahead, perched on the bluff. "We're here already? I thought it was, like, an hour and a half south of the city."

"It is," he said. "It's been, like, an hour and a half."

I thought it was interesting how the intense awkwardness of our first adult meeting had created a black hole of time. I thought it should have been just the opposite—that every minute would feel like an hour. Instead, it seemed as though whole sections of the experience had just up and disappeared.

"I'm so glad you connected with Hammy while I was gone," he said, pulling into the long driveway. "It was the only news into that prison that made me genuinely happy. I'd given up thinking I had anything to offer you, but if I could have given you anything I had, it would have been Ham. I love that guy. I don't know what I'm going to do without him."

"Joseph. He's better. He's home."

"He's ninety-five, Duck. How old do you think he'll live to be? A hundred? Maybe. He could pull that off if anybody could. But, Duck . . . that's only five years."

Then there was no more time to discuss it, because we were parked just outside the front door. And just as well, I thought, because it was the last thing on the planet I wanted to talk about, anyway.

Chapter Eighteen: Aubrey

My cell phone rang. It was a little after one o'clock in the morning. It woke me up.

Sounds like more or less a given. But I was not supposed to be asleep. I could've lost my job for it.

I was in the computer room in a tiny corner of the observatory, in an old typist's chair. Asleep with my head dropped back. When I straightened out my neck, I couldn't help saying "Ow." Out loud. Necks had never been intended for that position.

The phone sounded farther away than it should have been. I needed to remember where I'd left it. But I couldn't. Because I couldn't pull my brain out of sleep.

"Damn it, Jenny," I said, also out loud. "You know when I'm working, it's not a good time."

We'd been fighting when I'd left the apartment earlier that night. I figured she'd thought of another name to call me.

I looked around. Tried to pinpoint the sound.

Just to be honest about my circumstances here, this job was maybe not what anyone will be picturing. It's romantic and comforting to think of an astronomer alone in the night with a massive telescope. Puffing on a pipe. Narrowing his brow thoughtfully at what he sees in the heavens. Maybe saying "Hmm" now and then.

I was not allowed into the main area that housed the telescope. Very few people were. The guys responsible for its settings were not astronomers at all, but highly trained engineers.

Tiny me, I worked in a tiny room with a bank of eleven computer monitors. I took readings at intervals all night and transmitted them to actual astronomers who had actually completed their education.

Most of the readings had to do with the weather.

I guess to be honest, I'd have to say part of me was grateful for the work and part of me resented it. I didn't want to be a weatherman. I wanted to develop my own theories about dwarf galaxies and failed stars. But first I had to finish graduate school.

I found the phone on a counter by the outside door. By then the call had long since gone to voice mail.

I poured myself a cup of coffee from the big double-pot machine on the counter. Even though the smell told me it was bitter and old.

There was a window that composed the whole top half of the door. Through it I saw the night sky.

I opened it and stepped out.

I'll say this for the job: I might not have had anything to do with the telescope, but I got to share the mountaintop with it. And it sat up here for a reason. And so did I. Because this is where you go to see the stars.

I was told the job came with the option to monitor from a remote location. I chose the drive up the mountain.

I dropped my head back, massaging my sore neck. Stared at the band formed by the edge of the Milky Way. It was the night of a new moon, which left the scene on the ground blankly dark. Just the way I liked it.

"Save me from Jenny, great vast universe," I said.

Then I looked back down to my phone. Rang up my voice mail. It wasn't Jenny. It was my sister.

I got a bad feeling, right off. I called Ruth three or four times a month. She called me . . . well, rarely. Usually when there was something going on that I needed to know. Or that *she* thought I needed to know. The actual need was most often debatable.

I pressed "1" to play the message.

"Aubrey," she said. "You'll never guess who I ran into completely by surprise. Joseph is out of prison."

I won't say she sounded merry. Or as though I should be happy about this new development. Her voice seemed to grasp the subtext of the situation. Still, here she was telling me about it. Which seemed like an offense all in itself. The world is full of ugly, corrosive things. But that doesn't mean you should drag any of them onto my welcome mat.

"Aubrey, I found out something that you absolutely need to—"

That was the end of the message. For me.

I clicked "Delete."

———

Jenny was gone to work when I got back to the apartment.

I scarfed down the fast-food breakfast I'd brought home with me, and then it was past time for my weekly Skype session with Luanne. Just a couple minutes past, but still.

I opened the lid on my MacBook, which was awake and turned on. I wondered if that meant Jenny had been on my computer. And, if so, looking for what?

My Skype icon bounced and rang. Which is odd. Because normally I called in to her. I hit the "Answer" button, and Luanne's face filled the small video window.

"I thought you might have fallen asleep," she said. "I thought if I called you, it might wake you up."

"No, I'm awake. I just got in."

I watched one of her eyebrows move slightly. Up.

My shift ended at 4:00 a.m. It was a fifty-minute drive. And it was now 9:04 a.m.

Sometimes when I'm upset, I like to drive around on my motorcycle.

She knew that. After ten years, she knew me so well.

"So what happened?" she asked.

"I got into a fight with Jenny."

"I mean, what happened that doesn't happen every day?"

"I can't see the fish," I said, ignoring her little dig. "Can you move your laptop back and kind of angle it so I can see at least one of the tanks?"

"You want any of me on the monitor at all?"

It was not a genuine question. It was sarcasm. But I answered it like a genuine question.

"Yeah. Of course. You're good, too."

"Aubrey."

"What?"

"You're surrounded by your own fish."

I looked around the bedroom.

It's not that I hadn't known. But I still looked. I felt a bit defensive. Also a bit apologetic toward my own fish, for feeling as though they didn't count. Didn't measure up. They were fulfilling their role, after all. They were being fish. What more could they do?

I had only four tanks to Luanne's eight. She'd added one more about two years earlier.

"Your fish are better," I said.

"How so?"

"Well, they're your fish. And besides, I'm tired of mine."

She sighed deeply. "Aubrey. How about you tell me what you're putting off telling me?"

"My sister called."

"Okay."

"Joseph's out of prison."

"Okay."

"That's all? Just 'okay'? That's all you've got?"

"You knew he would be. Pretty soon now."

"I know. But I thought I had a few weeks. It's not that, though. I feel like Ruth blindsided me. I feel like she's playing head games."

"That doesn't sound like Ruth," she said.

I didn't speak for a long time. She didn't push me.

My eyes locked onto a school of silver hatchet fish in one of my own tanks. After a minute, Luanne took pity on me and angled her computer so her built-in camera showed not only her but the clown-fish tank.

I wondered if they were the same clown fish she'd had when I'd first walked into her office all those years ago. But then I knew they probably couldn't be. Those tiny fish couldn't live ten years, right? Still, I hoped I was wrong somehow. It felt like a comfort, to think they'd listened to my troubles since I was thirteen. And never breathed a word to anyone.

That's the lovely thing about fish. They never do. They also never call you and tell you your brother's out of prison.

I still wasn't talking. She got bored after a time. Pushed harder.

"Sell me on the fact that Ruth is playing mind games."

"Well, like trying to tell me she ran into him by accident. How is that even possible?"

"She said it was an accident?"

"I think she said it was a surprise. But still. She was walking down the street and bumped into him? She expects me to believe that?"

"You could ask her how it happened. What else?"

"Oh, crap. I don't know, Luanne. She made it sound like she had this big piece of information."

"But she wouldn't tell you? That *is* a little odd. When did she say she'd tell you?"

"Well, it was just a voice mail."

"Tell me everything she said in the voice mail, then. Because there's something here that's still missing for me."

"Just that she'd run into him unexpectedly. And that he was out. And that she'd found out something I needed to know."

"And then she asked you to call her back? That doesn't sound too diabolical."

"I don't know. I don't know if she asked me to call or if she went ahead and told me the big info."

"You didn't listen to the whole message."

"No."

A freighted silence. During which I felt guilt. Because I knew it was a side of me that exasperated her. Even though she never said.

"Why don't you listen to it now, then?"

"Because I deleted it."

She squeezed her eyes shut. Just for a brief second. Then she opened them, and I could see her try to clear her facial expression. Bring it back to blank.

"I realize this is a radical thought," she said, "but you could always return her call."

"What am I supposed to do if he tries to contact me?"

"What are you afraid of?" she asked in reply.

Answering a question with another question. Not my favorite quality in a person. I had a flash of a thought that if I bombed out of graduate school, I could get a job as a park ranger. The ones who sit up on the tops of mountains in fire-watch towers. For months on end. Alone with the stars.

Nobody around who answers questions with other questions.

Nobody around at all.

And Joseph would never find me.

"How did the concept of fear even get into this, Luanne?"

"I added it. Because it's a question that doesn't make sense at face value. It only makes sense if you add that subtext."

"It makes perfect sense at face value."

"Really? Aubrey, you're an educated man. You're a scientist. You're in graduate school studying astronomy, and you just asked me a question a grade-school student could answer. What do you do if he contacts you? Well, it's not complicated. If he writes to you, you write back or don't. If he comes to the door, you let him in or don't. If he calls you, you hang up or don't. That can't be what you're asking. You have to be asking how you'll live through it emotionally if it happens. So again, I ask: What are you afraid of?"

I was suddenly aware of my own breathing. It felt like it wasn't happening automatically. Suddenly I was breathing manually. And it felt unnatural. Like it was not the way I'd always breathed before. And like I was trying to go back to the old way, but I couldn't remember how that used to go.

"I don't know," I said. "What do *you* think it is?"

"Isn't it more important what you think? You're you. I'm not."

"But I'm trying to tell you I literally, actually don't know. So it would help me to hear your guesses."

"Okay," she said. "I can think of two things. One, you're afraid you were right about him. That all your worst fears will be borne out. He's a monster and he doesn't care about you at all. But that's not a very likely scenario, because if he were somehow less than human—some uncaring, unfeeling monster—you would have known that about him. And you wouldn't have adored him so much."

"I never adored him."

"Aubrey. Please. I was there. Remember?"

A silence. She filled it.

"Besides, if he didn't care about you, he wouldn't try to contact you. Then there's the more likely scenario. The one where you find out you were wrong about him. That he's not a monster, and he does care about you. And that you hurt somebody who didn't deserve it as much as you thought he did."

"Sometimes I wonder why I pay you money to have this stuff shoved in my face," I said.

I watched an ironic half smile form at the corner of her mouth.

"If it helps to be reminded, Aubrey, you don't pay me much."

––––––

I slept for part of the morning. A couple of hours, at least. Then when I woke up, I'd missed my first class. And if I didn't get dressed fast, I'd be late for my second.

The phone rang. That figured. Because it was the worst possible time.

I figured it would be Ruth. And because of that assumption, when it turned out to be Jenny, it was actually a relief.

"I'm kind of in a hurry," I said, instead of "hello."

"Why didn't you come home?"

"I just drove around."

"I'm not sure I believe that."

"I don't have time to convince you, Jenny. I'm late for class."

"You only drive around when you're upset. Assuming you're telling me the truth, what happened?"

"I found out my brother, Joseph, is out of prison. Now if you'll excuse me, I'm really late."

––––––

Halfway to the university, I got a text from her. I shouldn't have read it while I was driving. I did anyway.

It said, *Pls pack what's mine. Leave in living room. I'll pick up while you're at work 2night.*

Without pulling over, I texted back, *Why?*

Answer: *Know how obsessed u r with him when he's in. Don't want to know what u r like when he's out.*

Chapter Nineteen: Ruth

––––––––––––––

When I woke up the light hurt my eyes, it was after eleven a.m. according to my watch, and I had no idea where I was. But it took only seconds to remember Ham's little cottage. I was sleeping on the couch, because it didn't have a second bedroom. I had no idea where Joseph had slept, and I didn't even know if Regina was still around.

I sat up and cleared my head for a moment and rubbed my face briskly.

There was food cooking. I could smell it. It smelled like Ham's lifesaving famous signature breakfast. Normally I'd have been nearly onto lunch by eleven a.m., but I'd had trouble sleeping, and besides, I reminded myself, the signature breakfast could be served at any time of day—though I couldn't imagine Ham felt good enough to get up and cook it the day after being released from the hospital.

I stumbled into the kitchen to see that it was my brother Joseph doing the cooking. I looked over his shoulder into the skillets.

"Looks and smells just like what Ham makes."

"It is," he said. "It's a pretty damn good facsimile if I do say so myself."

"How did you learn to do that?"

"I was here every summer, remember?"

"Oh, that's right. You making it for him? Or for yourself? Or for me?"

"Yes," he said. "All of the above."

It didn't really look like enough for three, which is why I'd asked, but I figured Ham wasn't nearly back to full appetite yet. Or maybe his appetite had been shrinking as long as I'd known him. Ninety-five-year-olds aren't famous for eating gigantic meals.

"So he's awake. Good. I'm going to go in and say hi."

But by the time I rapped on the jamb of the open bedroom door and peeked in, he must have drifted off again.

"Not quite," I said when I got back to the kitchen.

"No point waking him until it's ready."

I sat down at the table and played nervously with the Mr. and Mrs. Santa salt and pepper shakers, which I'd long ago learned were out all year round—maybe by the same logic that dictated breakfast can always be the appropriate meal. I could feel that I still wasn't 100 percent awake.

And I still wasn't 100 percent comfortable being alone with Joseph, but I really had no mental justification as to why that would be. I just knew I wished Ham were here to keep everything balanced, especially me.

"I didn't mean to sleep so late," I said. "But I didn't fall asleep until something like five or six."

"I had trouble sleeping, too. Wish I'd known. We could've sat outside and caught up."

"Where did you sleep? I lost track of you before I bunked down on the couch."

"In Hammy's room. In a sleeping bag on the floor. I thought it might be good to have someone close by. In case he had trouble breathing or anything."

Silence, a long one, and again it struck me as strange that two people could live together for fifteen years, then spend ten apart . . . and not have much to say to each other while reuniting.

"Where's Regina?" I asked when it felt awkward.

"She had to go back to Portland. That was all the time she could take off work."

"I'm amazed she hasn't retired."

"No, you're not. You're amazed that a seventy-year-old in general hasn't retired. But you couldn't be amazed about her."

"True," I said.

Then we fell silent again, and the awkwardness and pressure began to feel nearly unmanageable.

"So, where do you live?" I asked, finally.

"Colorado."

"Really? What's in Colorado?"

"Me," he said. He was sliding raw eggs from a saucer into simmering water to poach, one at a time. "I got a job on a horse ranch there. A guy who was in with me hooked me up with the job for when I got out."

"Like it?"

"I do. A lot. It's in the foothills of the Rockies. The air is clean. It's really beautiful."

"But . . . since when do you know anything about horses?"

"Since I got the job, I guess. It's kind of a learn-as-you-go proposition."

More terrible silence.

"You should come out and visit me," he said, which allowed me to see that he felt the pressure of the silences, too. "All three of you. I'd love to meet Sean and Maya."

"We will," I said. "We absolutely will."

And, you know, I actually wasn't lying—at least, as far as I knew. I could picture a visit with Joseph with Sean to hold up half of our end of the conversation and Maya as the constant focus. It was the one-on-one that was getting us mired up, and I wanted to get past that. I swear I did.

"You know what's weird?" I asked, because once you identify that you want to move beyond something, I find it's best to start moving. "We haven't seen each other in a decade, and I feel like all we've really done is small talk. I'm not blaming you, because I'm doing it, too. I'm just not sure how to stop."

"Well, let's just get real, then," he said, getting down three plates from the cupboard.

"I'll start," I surprised myself by saying. "Can I ask you a question?"

"Okay."

"Did you come here when you were twelve to seriously jump off that cliff?"

I watched the gears turn in his head for a second or two, thinking he seemed a little off balance. Or maybe that was me.

"That was *so* not the question I was expecting," he said, and he came and sat across the table from me. "Honest answer, I swear: I don't know. I know how it felt, and it felt so real inside me. I think I really believed at the time that I was serious. But I'd just read that article about Hammy. And now that I look back on it, I can also feel how his reaching out to people was a very real draw for me at the exact same time. So I know it sounds like a yes or no question. And I swear I'm not ducking it. But I don't have a better answer for you than that."

"That one'll do," I said.

"Besides, I'm about to burn the bacon."

He got up and turned back to the stove, where he began dishing the food up onto plates. All except the eggs, which he checked, but left simmering. He pushed the lever on the four-slice toaster, and three slices of bread disappeared into it.

"I have one for you, too," he said. "Does Aubrey know I'm out?"

"*I* didn't even know till yesterday."

"But that doesn't really answer the question, Duck. Because that was yesterday."

Then I felt a little ashamed, because he was right—I was evading.

"I called him," I said. "But I had to leave a message. And he hasn't called me back."

I watched him use a slotted spoon to rescue the eggs one at a time and set them on paper towels to drain.

"So I guess my real question, then," he said, "is whether I should even try to contact him."

"That would be the sixty-four-dollar question, all right."

"Why do you think I'm asking?"

"I'd have to say no. I'd say let him come to you."

"But will he ever? Come to me?"

"No," I said. "I don't suppose he will."

"I'm going to go wake Hammy and get him out to the table," he said.

And that was the end of that—both the small talk and our first attempt at getting real.

———

Joseph walked Ham to the kitchen table with one arm hooked through his. My old friend looked even shorter than I remembered him—which was not necessarily an illusion—and he'd lost more weight. Maybe I just wasn't used to seeing him in pajamas, but he looked bone thin. But his face was bright, his smile unchanged.

He was just very weak.

"Oh, poor Ham," I said. "We should've brought breakfast in to you."

"Don't think I didn't try," Joseph said. "Hammy's not the breakfast-in-bed type."

"Especially when you've been sick," Ham said, reaching one thin arm out to steady himself on the back of a kitchen chair. Then Joseph helped him ease into it. "Makes you feel better to be up and around. Lying there feeling sick is not always the best path to feeling well again."

I sat next to him at the table and was shocked to realize I could hear the wet rasp of his breathing—actually hear what was happening down in his poor embattled lungs.

"How do you feel today?" I asked.

"Better. Thank you, love. They have me on those strong antibiotics, so we'll get the best o' this bugger yet. Meanwhile, Ruthie, I sure hope you came here to see your dear brother Joe and not just me, because I'll be on my feet in no time, love. I'm just an old man with a bad cough. Nothing interesting about that. Like they say in the cop movies: 'Move along, show's over. Nothing more to see here.' No reason to spend hours flying just to hear me struggle to clear my old lungs."

Then, as if on cue, he launched into a coughing fit. Joseph handed him a handful of tissues, and I carefully looked the other way as he hawked phlegm up into them and wiped his mouth.

Joseph served our breakfasts.

"No, I came to see *you*," I said. Then I bit off half a slice of bacon in one enormous bite. "I didn't even know Joseph would be here," I added, mouth still full. "I didn't even know he was out."

"Regina didn't tell you?"

"No. Not a word."

I glanced over at Joseph to see if he was following the subtext I was trying—and failing—to hide. But I should have known. Joseph was not a stupid man.

"She's always up to something," Ham said. "Now, tell the truth, Ruthie. How's it feel to see your old brother after all these years?"

"Well . . . it's great," I said. Which was the truth, but not the whole truth. In fact, if I were being completely honest, I'd have to say it was less than 5 percent of the truth.

"And that," Ham said, "no offense, Ruthie, sounds more like the story for publication."

I loaded up my mouth with fried potatoes and sighed, mostly because they were so good. I'd tried to make them at home from time to time, but they were never the same. I chewed for a moment in silence.

"Confusing," I said. "I feel like it's something I could have done a better job on if I'd had time to adjust, which I guess I always thought I would have. You know, when the time finally came. It's good to see him, but it feels sad, too, because he's in his thirties and I don't even know him as an adult, and it's hard to know how to talk to an almost-stranger who's supposed to feel like family. And also . . . it's bringing up a lot of bad memories from when I last saw him, which was when all hell was breaking loose. But I hope that wasn't too much honesty. No offense intended, Joseph."

"None taken," he said, but he looked and sounded sad, too.

"Good to get the truth out into the air," Ham said. "Everything grows best in oxygen and sunlight except secrets and guilt and regrets. They like the dank spaces. Drag them out into the light and they fail to thrive."

We ate in silence for a good half of the meal.

When Ham finally spoke, it startled me.

"So how long can you stay, Ruthie?"

"I have to leave in the morning. I have to figure out how to get back to the airport."

"Joseph can drive you in my car."

"Oh," I said. "Good."

But it didn't feel good. Another hour and a half, alone in the car together, struggling to find words to say to each other. That did not sound like a good thing at all.

———

Ham was in bed the following morning when I went in to say good-bye.

"Dear, dear Ruthie," he said, and grasped one of my hands in both of his.

And although it was an oversimplification of the man, it struck me that this was his single greatest quality: he made everybody feel dear. And the sad truth of this world is that not many people feel that way, and not much of the time.

I thought about what Joseph said, wondering how he would live without Ham. How even if Ham lived to be a hundred, that would only be five more years. I wondered what I would do without him, too.

He must have seen that on me, or felt it, because he raised my hand to his lips and kissed it and patted it, then said, "Don't be going on like that, Ruthie. This is not the last you'll see o' me. You're not shut o' this old man just yet, girl."

"How do you know?"

"I just know it, in the place in my gut that knows things. I feel it in my old bones. Mark my words, Ruthie. We're destined to meet again."

I kissed him on the cheek, mumbled something about him feeling better, and headed off to join Joseph out in the car.

But before I could get to the open bedroom doorway, he stopped me with words.

"Ruthie. If there's one thing you're never to doubt, my love, it's how much Joe is devoted to you and your brother. It's a kind of love the likes o' which I rarely see. That's why I value Joe as much as I do. Not everybody has that kind of love in him. I don't know what he's been doing with it all these years, since he couldn't give it to either one o' you directly. But mark my words, Ruthie. It's not gone."

I smiled, but I think it was a pained smile.

"But *I* need to be," I said.

And I walked away from everything I couldn't handle at the time, which was pretty much everything.

———

We small-talked almost all the way to the airport, and I think we both knew it. But we didn't say it out loud, and we didn't push each other over the line into that real place. I think we were both tired from being real—I know I was—and it was such a relief to take the pressure off myself and just chat.

I told him about Sean's job running a good-sized print shop, and I told him more about Maya than most people would hold still to hear.

He told me about the horse ranch in detail, including his favorite horses and why they were his favorites, and I promised again that I would visit, but by then I'd begun to wonder if I would really keep that promise.

When we got back onto the 101 freeway and I knew the airport couldn't be far off, I decided to dive into real just once more. Because I had something to say that I knew needed saying.

"Joseph," I said, to warn him of approaching seriousness. "There's another question about Aubrey I think you should be asking yourself. You haven't even touched on the subject of whether you *want* to contact him, under the circumstances. Whether that's the best thing for you. He's not exactly your biggest ally. He's been needlessly hurtful to you in the past, and I guarantee you he will be again if you give him the opportunity. You know how Aubrey is."

"Actually, I don't," he said. "I don't know him as an adult at all."

"You remember how he was as a kid, though, right? Well, he's just like that, only more so."

A moment of silence. During it, I thought about what Ham had said just as I was walking out the door. I knew Joseph wouldn't say, "You're right. I'll just drop it." Because then all that love would have no place to go. After ten years of no place to go, I had to figure it wanted out.

"You think I don't want to get to a place of forgiveness with him just because he said some hurtful things? He's my brother, Duck. I'm going to at least try."

"Well, it's up to you. But I think my point is, it's one thing to *want* to get to a place of forgiveness. It's another thing to look reality in the eye and accept the fact that you probably never will."

———

When Sean and Maya picked me up at the airport, I jumped into the backseat, because I couldn't bear not to hug and kiss the baby hello, and you can't idle your car at that pick-up curb for long.

"Sorry to treat you like a chauffeur," I told Sean.

I leaned forward and kissed him on the ear before putting on my seatbelt.

"How was it?" he asked as he pulled back out into traffic.

"Strange. Joseph was there."

"Joseph? Is out?"

"Yeah. Don't think it didn't surprise me, too." I stroked Maya's soft hair, and she smiled, and everything felt better. "I felt kind of blindsided."

"Blindsided by who?"

"It feels weird to say it, because I never said a word against her before, but I think Regina. She sent him to pick me up at the airport. An hour-and-a-half drive down the coast, and she forgot to mention it would be Joseph driving, and I had no idea what to say to him. I just had no time to prepare."

I caught a glimpse of his face in the rearview mirror, and he was smiling, which made me feel a little cross.

"It sounds like something I can picture Regina doing," he said.

I sighed. "Yeah. Me, too, now that I think about it. I can see her thinking, 'Here's an experience for you, Ruthie. It won't kill you; it'll make you stronger.'"

We drove in silence for a time. A minute, maybe.

Then Sean touched on that sixty-four-dollar question I mentioned earlier.

"Does Aubrey know Joseph's out?"

"I've left him four messages, but he won't call me back. My pesky little brother who calls me nearly every week to tell me his troubles suddenly wants nothing to do with me."

"You told him the news in the messages, though, right?"

"Oh, yeah."

"Well, now you know why he wants nothing to do with you. Think Joseph'll try to contact him?"

"Yes. I think he will. I tried to advise him against it, twice, but I still think he will."

"That should be interesting. We'll probably see the fireworks from two hundred miles away. So . . . did you ask him?"

"Ask him what?"

"What do you mean, 'ask him what?' Did you ask him the obvious question?"

"I don't even know what you think the obvious question is, Sean."

"Did you ask him what happened over there?"

"No. What would be the point of that?"

"Isn't that what you've wanted to know all these years?"

"Not really. I read the trial transcript. It was pretty simple. What's left to ask about it? I asked him the something I've really always wanted to know, which was whether he went to Ham's house seriously intending to jump. You know, that first day when he was twelve. He was surprised, now that I think about it. He said that was totally not the question he thought I was going to ask. I guess he expected me to ask about Baghdad, too. But what more is there to know?"

"What's missing, Ruth," he said, "is Joseph's side of the story. *Why*. Aren't you curious as to *why* he did what he did?"

"No. I think it's obvious. He was scared. Two guys died in sniper fire that night. It was dangerous work."

Silence. A long silence, but I didn't think much about it at the time. I didn't realize Sean was disgusted with me until I caught his eyes in the rearview mirror.

"What?" I asked.

"I'm surprised at you, Ruth. How can you just assume he's a coward? That's exactly what Aubrey did."

"Oh, no. Do *not* go there, Sean. Do *not* lump me in with my little brother."

"Then don't act like him."

I felt a little stunned, because Sean and I didn't argue often, and when we did I could generally see it coming. I had just been blindsided again.

"If he wasn't scared, Sean, and if he's so brave, then why did he take off when the army found out what he'd done?"

"And if he's a coward, why did he go back and turn himself in?"

"Well, why do *you* think he did it, then, Sean?"

"I have no idea. My point is not that I know. My point is that we *don't* know. So you ask. When you don't know something, you ask. You don't just assume cowardice. That's what the media did. And the kids we went to school with and their parents. And you hated that. They had no idea, they hadn't been there, they couldn't possibly know anything, but they were so sure they did. And now you're doing it, too. Here's a question. If he was just scared, why did he actually try to stop the mission? If you're scared, you just don't go, right? If others are willing to go, why stop them? Why try to shut it down?"

"I have no idea, Sean; I just know it happened. Maybe he was worried for the guys he talked to. Maybe they were his friends or something, I don't know. What else could it even *be* if it wasn't fear?"

"I have no idea, Ruth. I wasn't there. I just know these situations are always more complicated than they look from the outside. Wars sometimes force guys over the line into morally gray areas. Maybe they were asking him to do something he didn't think was right. I'm just saying you should have asked him. But I guess now it's too late."

"Not necessarily," I said. "He wants us to come visit him in Colorado. But I don't know if you'd want to do that."

"If I could get the time off work, I'd love it. The famous Joseph. I'm just dying to meet him."

"Good. Then *you* ask him why he did what he did. I don't want to wade back into that old territory, Sean, period. If I see him again, I'm moving forward. I lived through that old crap once, and I'm not going back there if I have anything to say about it."

We drove for five minutes or so in silence. Maya had a hold of my index finger and was bouncing it up and down, tugging on it.

"One more question," Sean said. "If it was so weird, and you were so uncomfortable and felt so blindsided, why didn't you call me to talk?"

"Oh," I said. "That's a good question. I'm not really sure."

I thought about it for a while and decided the situation had thrust me back into a childhood mode—made me feel like a kid again—and in that feeling, there were no tools to climb out of the discomfort, just as there had been no tools when I was young. And there was no Sean. I'd honestly felt like my teenage self while I was there.

But I didn't tell Sean that, because I was still a little mad at him for verbally jumping on me. So I kept the truth—one that might have helped him understand—to myself.

And that, I now realize, is how you start the pattern of silences. So innocently and on such a small scale, and then once you open the door for them, they barge in and take on a life of their own.

Chapter Twenty: Aubrey

———————

I didn't know what time it was. Only that it was light. And that a knock on the door was dragging me out of sleep.

I looked at the clock, and it was seven. I honestly didn't know if that was a.m. or p.m.

I got up and pulled a light robe on over my boxers. Walked to the door.

"That was everything of yours," I called through the door. "I swear. If you lost something, it's not my fault. Look elsewhere. I went over this place with a fine-tooth comb. A flea comb, actually. Everything left in this apartment is mine."

Silence.

"It's Ruth," Ruth said through the door.

"Oh," I said.

I really, really, really didn't want to open the door.

I opened the door.

She had Maya on her hip. The baby reached her baby arms out to me. My heart melted. I reached back. Took her by the armpits. Pulled her into my living room. Then I spun her around in the airplane game. It was her favorite. And she assumed the position immediately. Arms outstretched. Legs flying. She giggled, which totally dissolved all the nasty stuff I'd been feeling.

"I'm using your bathroom," Ruth said. "It was a long drive."

I stopped spinning and held Maya to my chest.

"No sh—no duh, Ruth. Why exactly did you drive two hours to get here?"

"Because you wouldn't answer my six messages," she called back on her way down the hall.

"Three words, Ruth. Take. A. Hint."

She disappeared into the bathroom without comment. I bounced Maya on my hip. And realized it would be hard for me to have the conversation Ruth and I were about to have. Because I couldn't yell with the baby here.

"Maya, Maya, Maya," I said.

She made a sound that could have been any word at all, but probably wasn't. She reached out with one tiny index finger and touched my lip. Like pointing at me would be the best answer.

Then Ruth came back.

"I called your work," she said, "and there was a new guy there. He said you quit."

"Yes. I quit."

The baby reached out to Ruth. So I handed her back.

"Why?"

"Because it was such bull . . . crap. It had so little to do with actual astronomy. I might as well flip burgers to get myself through grad school."

"Is that what you're doing?"

"No. I haven't gotten another job yet."

I knew what she was thinking. How like Aubrey to walk off one job without lining up another. She didn't say so. I expected her to say, *So, are you hitting Mom up for money?* Which I was.

But she didn't ask.

She just said, "So Jenny's gone, too." It wasn't a question. "Why?"

"Other than the fact that we fought day in and day out? She said I was so obsessed with Joseph when he was in prison that she didn't even want to know what I was like when he was out. Another loss I can chalk up to my brother."

Ruth shook her head. Sat down on my couch. The baby bounced up and down. Straightening her legs and folding them again, wired with energy, while Ruth steadied her.

"Not fair to blame that on him."

"How do you figure?"

"It's *your* obsession. You were with Jenny for a year. He came nowhere near you in that year. It's *your* feelings about Joseph she couldn't stand."

"I feel the way I do about him for a reason."

"You're hopeless," she said.

"Then why come here, Ruth? Huh? Why drive two hundred miles just to insult me? If you can't stand me, why don't you stay away?"

Maya stopped bouncing. Her face darkened as if she might be about to cry. And I knew I had to tone down the anger. Which was not my strong suit.

"Did it ever occur to you," Ruth said, "that if you don't answer six phone messages, I might start to worry about you?"

"Oh. I'm sorry," I said. I sank into the stuffed chair. The one I never sat in. Because it was lumpy. "I just didn't want anything you were selling."

"I wasn't selling anything. I was warning you."

"He's going to try to contact me, isn't he?"

"Looks that way," she said.

"Well, call him off."

"He's not my dog, Aubrey. I can't call him off. I didn't sic him on you in the first place. I told him twice not to do it."

"Well, tell him again."

"Excuse me?"

"You have his address. Or phone number. Or something. Right?"

"Well. Ham does."

"So call him up and tell him to stay the hell away from me."

Silence. I looked into her face. It seemed set hard, but I couldn't quite read it. I looked away.

"No," she said.

"What do you mean, 'no'? *You* got me into this."

"What part of 'no' don't you understand, Aubrey? You're a grown man. Tell him yourself. I didn't ask for any of this. I just went to see Ham because he was sick. Nobody told me Joseph would be there. I thought he was still in prison. I didn't get you into this—I didn't even get myself into it. You're a big boy, and if you have something to say to him, buck up and say it."

I rubbed my eyes. Briefly wondered if this could be a dream. But I knew I wouldn't get that lucky.

"Fine," I said. "But will you at least get me his address? So I can warn him away before he tries?"

"Yeah," she said. "That much I'll do."

"Thank you."

"I don't suppose it'll make a damn bit of difference to you, but it should. So I'm telling you anyway. The reason he wouldn't see us when he was in prison is because he couldn't. Because Brad made him a trade. A sort of forced deal. He paid for decent outside counsel in return for Joseph's promise that he wouldn't contact us in any way. If Joseph had broken his end of the bargain, the attorney would have disappeared, and then he could have been in prison for life."

"Is that what you kept trying to tell me on the phone?" I asked. "You're right. It doesn't make a damn bit of difference to me.

Besides, it's a load of crap. Because that was only true until after his sentencing. Which was ten years ago."

"Yeah, well, after that it was a little more complicated."

"No, Ruth. It was painfully simple. He should've broken the promise."

"He's breaking it now."

"Too late," I said. "Time's up. Game over."

Now I just had to be sure that Joseph knew that. Before it was too late.

"Okay," Ruth said, and struggled to her feet with the kid. "We're going."

"Now? Already?"

"I can't deal with you when you're like this."

"Like what, Ruth? What am I like that's so abhorrent to you?"

"He's your *brother*."

"Yeah. Got that part. The problem here is not confusion about how we're related, you know? It's a bigger deal than that."

They were halfway to the door by then. And I swear I didn't think I'd raised my voice. But Maya's face twisted into a mask of sadness. She burst into tears.

"Oh, Maya," I said. "Honey. Uncle A didn't mean to upset you."

"Forget it," Ruth said. "She'll settle down in the car."

"It's just such a long drive, you know, Ruth? Two hours each way. To sit here for ten minutes."

She stopped. Leveled me with that look that used to strike fear into my heart when I was a kid.

"My thoughts exactly, Uncle A. Very long drive. So next time I call you to talk about something you don't care to discuss, how about you shoot me a text that says 'I'm fine but I'm ignoring you.' Save me the long trip."

"Okay," I said. "Okay. I'm sorry."

"Whatever. We're out of here."

Maya looked at me over her mom's shoulder. She'd stopped crying. But her lower lip still stuck out. And she looked at me like I might be just about to kick a puppy. Which made me feel about an inch tall.

Then the door slammed and they were gone.

———

"Here," Luanne said. "Fish. Are you happy?"

And she turned her laptop computer so that she disappeared from the monitor entirely.

It was our next regularly scheduled session. I'd been tempted to try for a cancellation. Ask her to squeeze me in. Instead, I'd decided to man up. Maybe because I had trouble admitting I couldn't handle things on my own.

"Very funny," I said. "I'd like to see a little of you, please."

Exactly half of her face moved onto the right-hand side of the monitor.

I rolled my eyes but didn't comment.

"What's up?" she asked. "You look off-kilter."

"My sister was here."

"Sounds like a good thing."

"Not really. She drove all the way out here because I wasn't answering her calls. Then she dropped the bomb on me that Joseph is about to try to look me up. And—get this—when I said I didn't want that, she left after about ten minutes. Got all pissed at me. Wouldn't even stay so I could get a decent visit with the baby. She said she can't deal with me when I'm like that. She said, 'He's your brother.' Like I owe him something. It just bothered me that she's on his side, not mine."

"Then I really hate to tell you: I am, too."

"Oh, crap!" I said. And leaned back hard and hit the back of my chair. "Don't I pay you to be on my side?"

"No. You don't. You pay me to help you get better. And then you define being on your side as not challenging you in any of the ways that will help you get better. So, that's the long version. Short version: no. He *is* your brother, Aubrey. And people regret letting those relationships go. Not always, but the vast majority of the time they do. And I just don't see what it would hurt to hear him out."

"It *would* hurt me, though. It hurts me just to think about him."

"I didn't mean it wouldn't cause you discomfort. I meant it wouldn't cause any genuine harm."

"Why should I purposely walk into an experience that causes discomfort?"

"Says the man with the toothache."

"Wait," I said. And rubbed my face briskly. Like that would help. "I must've missed something. Who has a toothache?"

"It's a metaphor, Aubrey. When you go to the dentist for a root canal, or even a filling, it hurts. It's a lousy experience. When you go to a doctor to have a cancerous tumor removed or to have bypass surgery, you're going to wake up in a lot of pain. So why even do it? Because there's something wrong and it needs fixing, that's why. Everything gets worse before it gets better, Aubrey."

"There's something wrong with your metaphor," I said, "because there's nothing wrong with me. I'm fine."

"So I guess that concludes our therapy experience, then. I had no idea you were cured."

I sighed. Looked at the ceiling. Then at the fish. Looked around the room, but I had no idea why.

"You know I'm not going to talk to him, right?"

"I know you're not going to talk to him today. I was hoping you'd leave open the possibility that the future can be different."

"In a lot of ways it can," I said. "Not that way. Ruth texted me his e-mail address. And his phone number. But that was stupid, because I'm not going to call him. I'm going to e-mail him and tell him to stay away from me and leave me alone."

"You still haven't told me what it can hurt."

"I hate it," I said. "I hate that . . . you know. That thing that happens."

"No, I don't know. Lots of things happen. Specificity, Aubrey."

"When you think you know how things are. What's real. What happened. And then somebody else starts talking, and suddenly they're trying to tell you reality was something entirely different than what you saw with your own eyes. And they expect you to go back and like . . . I don't know . . . retroactively change what you think happened. And I won't know if he's lying to me. Or if I was just wrong. Or if he was just wrong. Or if reality can be two entirely different things at the same time, which sort of makes me feel like my head is about to explode."

"Or maybe your reality is your reality, and Joseph's is his."

"That's the exploding-head option," I said.

She smiled with one corner of her mouth. At least, I think she did. She showed that half smile often enough. But I could still only see half of her face on the monitor, so I couldn't say for sure.

"Why not e-mail and tell him to please not contact you until you say you're ready?"

"Okay," I said. "I can go with that."

Then we talked about Jenny for the rest of the session.

And I was good with the way we left it. Because I knew exactly when I would be ready. Never. So I'd just ask Joseph to contact me then.

———

From: mruniverse1990@gmail.com
To: theonlystellkellner@skyblue.net
April 22, 2013 1:12 a.m.

Joseph,

I'm hearing from Ruth that you're going to try to get in touch. Don't. Really, don't. I know it sounds terrible. But I feel like I learned a good lesson a long time ago: if someone hurts you, and you let him back into your life again, he'll hurt you again.

Just so you know, Ruth already told me her supposedly exculpatory message from you. How you didn't get in touch because you couldn't. But it was bullshit. You were sentenced, he'd left the family . . . you could have done anything you wanted. It didn't change my thinking one bit. It just stirred up all that very upsetting old crap that I want very badly to leave behind.

So, please. Respect me on this.

Aubrey Rogers

———

From: theonlystellkellner@skyblue.net
To: mruniverse1990@gmail.com
April 22, 2013 3:01 a.m.

Mr. Universe,
Two answers.

One, yes. I'll respect that.

Two, I'm holding out hope that you'll change your mind. Not even about me in general. Just about giving me fifteen minutes or so to get something said.

I wanted to tell you when I came home ten years ago, but the only time we got to talk was that time when I woke you up. I didn't want to make it hard for you to get back to sleep. I thought I'd have a million more chances.

I learned a good lesson a long time ago, too, Mr. Universe: never assume you'll have a million more chances.

You see, nobody asked me why I did what I did. Literally nobody. Seems odd, doesn't it? Such an obvious question. And there was a reason. A very specific reason. And it had nothing to do with fear, or with wanting to undermine the war effort as a whole. But I think everybody was so sure it did . . . I think that's why nobody asked me. They just assumed I was a coward and a traitor.

I'm not saying I didn't feel fear. I think everyone over there, if they were being honest with themselves and each other, was scared. I'm not saying I wasn't; I'm just saying I went out every night, scared or not. Until the night I didn't. And when I didn't, fear had nothing to do with it.

I don't want to tell everybody in the world this story, Mr. Universe. Only you. Because it's about you. You have a part in this story. I would tell Ruth if she wanted to know, but it's really not about Ruth, and I think when she heard it, she'd understand why.

Thing is, brother—and make no mistake, you're still my brother, no matter how much you wish you weren't—it will completely explode your idea that I didn't love you enough.

So you have to be ready to let that in.

Doesn't have to be soon. Has to be before one of us dies, though. And it pays to keep in mind that we only think we know when that will be.

Okay, I admit it. This is a long-winded, long-ass e-mail from a guy who said he'd respect your wishes. Well, I will. From this moment on.

I won't write, e-mail, call, or visit unless you tell me you've changed your mind.

Your brother,
Joseph Stellkellner

Now suddenly I had no idea if signing your last name was a perfectly acceptable practice among brothers, or if he was making fun of the times I'd done it in my letters to him.

I wrote seven responses. Didn't press send on any of them.

I knew if I did, I would just be opening up an ongoing argument that would lead to all manner of information. Ultimately, I ignored his e-mail. Argued with him in my head, instead.

In time, the fight in my head got tedious. Then it slowed down.

Then I was delightfully unperturbed by my former brother for seven calm, blissful, Joseph-free months. At least, when I didn't think about it. Which frankly was not as often as I would have liked.

Part Five

What Would Aubrey Do?

Autumn 2013

Chapter Twenty-One: Ruth

———————

I should have known something was very wrong when I first answered the door, and, well . . . I guess I did. I just didn't know what.

Sean and I had invited both Aubrey and my mother to come to our house for a family Thanksgiving. Needless to say, when I heard the doorbell on the Monday morning before, I didn't expect the unannounced visit to have anything to do with that upcoming family gathering. Who would?

I put Maya in her playpen, which had been purposely situated so she could see me while I went to the door.

I opened it, and there stood my mom. Well, actually "stood" wouldn't have been so bad—she rushed me. She charged through the door, threw her arms around me, and rocked me back and forth.

I was too stunned to say anything.

She said plenty.

"Ruth. My baby. My little girl. Oh, Ruth."

I wasn't hugging her back, because my brain was still sprinting to catch up, and I was weirdly aware of my own forehead, which was doing things I don't think it had ever done before. I was thinking, *Maybe that's how wrinkles get their foot in the door.*

I was also vaguely aware of Maya calling out "Ge-mah," a loosely woven "grandma" sort of word with a strong emphasis on the second syllable.

I gave up waiting for Janet to back up on her own, so I gently took her by both shoulders and held her out at arm's length. She had a tissue tucked in one hand, and she began carefully wiping under each eye without smearing her mascara.

"Mom, what are you doing here?"

"What do you mean, what am I doing here? You invited me for Thanksgiving."

"Right. And that's Thursday. And this is Monday. You're three days early."

She didn't answer. Just swept past me and lifted Maya out of her playpen and hugged and kissed her, which I was used to. Maya always got lots of hugs and kisses from Janet. To the best of my recollection I only once had before that day, including when I was Maya's age.

"Mom. Not to be a pest about this, but can you please go on to explain why you showed up for Thanksgiving dinner three days early? Are you planning on staying here all the way through?"

"Yes; be a doll, honey, and go get my bags out of the car. I have some presents for you kids, too. And the baby."

"Mom, it's Thanksgiving. We'll get together again at Christmas."

"God willing," she said.

She handed me her keys and tried to brush right by me into the kitchen, still holding the baby. I grabbed her by the sleeve of her expensive sweater, and when she hit the end of that tether she just kept pulling, which was indescribably strange.

"Honey. Ruth. You're stretching out the fabric."

"No, *you* are," I said. "You're supposed to stop when somebody does that."

She stopped pulling, but she continued to face the kitchen, never turning her face in my direction.

"You need to talk to me," I said. "Something's going on. What is it?"

"Oh, honey, not now. We have to wait till your brother Aubrey gets here. I simply don't have the strength to go through it twice. It'll be too difficult to say it the first time."

She still wasn't looking my way.

"That won't work," I told the back of her head. "You can't just march in here and say there's bad news and you'll tell me in three days."

"I don't want to go through it all again when Aubrey gets here."

"You have three whole days to rest up in between."

I watched her deflate and knew I'd broken her down and she was going to talk. Her head pitched forward a few inches, her shoulders rounded. She turned halfway in my direction and held Maya out to me.

"Here, take the baby," she said. "Put her back in her playpen. They understand so much, even when they don't know the words."

I noticed my old pattern with heartburn was setting up again, and when I took the baby, my hands shook slightly.

————

Just like Janet to insist on tea—also known as another few minutes of torture.

I brought everything to the living room on a tray—teapot, cups, milk and sugar, spoons, those tiny plates you can put your tea bag on when it's brewed dark enough. I never did all that—in fact, I mostly handled coffee or tea with a guest by using a simple "Well, come on into the kitchen, then."

But this was my mother, and I had watched her do this with guests for years. Social responsibility, as Joseph called it.

She dipped out three spoons of sugar and stirred in silence until I couldn't bear another second of it.

"Mom," I said. "Please."

She took a deep breath and then began wiping her eyes again. Funny thing is, I never saw a tear break loose. Like the rest of her life, she seemed to keep them just on the edge of control.

"Okay," she said. "You know how I've been having a lot of lower respiratory . . . difficulties? I thought it was chronic bronchitis."

Oh dear God, I thought, *she's dying.* I tried to remember if I'd known she was having respiratory issues, but nothing came to mind. Maybe she wasn't as good a communicator as she'd made herself out to be in her own head, or maybe I didn't listen. She went on quite a bit on the phone, and it was easy to tune her out.

"Yes," I said, so she'd go on.

"Well . . . ," she said, and seemed to stall again.

"This is killing me, Mom."

"Not such good news about that. It's cancer, and if you say one word about the fact that I started smoking again when Joseph came home . . ."

"Lung cancer?"

"Yes."

"Well. You stopped again, though, right? So you did your best with it, I guess. When did you stop?"

A long silence during which she wouldn't meet my eyes. I could hear Maya saying "Ge-mah, Ge-mah" from her playpen, but I didn't know if she'd been saying it all along.

Janet never answered.

"Okay, it was more recent, then," I said.

Still no words, still no eye contact.

"You had to've quit when the doctor said you had lung cancer," I said.

"There's very little point now, Ruthie."

"That's bullcrap!" I said, half rising to my feet.

"The baby!" she hissed. "Little pitchers have big ears."

"That was the tame version! You're just making excuses, Mom. Cancer treatment's a whole new ball game these days. There's a lot they can do for you, but you have to stop smoking."

She picked up her spoon again and stirred in utter silence, and looked only where she was stirring, and a bad sense of knowing began to creep over me.

"Unless it's already so far progressed that they're not even recommending treatment," I said, and watched her for a response.

No response.

"How bad are they saying it is, Mom?"

No answer at first, just a few tears that slipped past the guards at the gate and ran down her cheeks.

"Did they give you a prognosis, as far as . . . you know . . . time?"

She nodded, but it was a weak little thing, barely noticeable. Then I decided I was pushing her too hard, maybe making things extra-difficult for her with my impatience to know.

I picked up my cup of tea and sat back and sipped, and watched Maya watch us in openmouthed silence, which was unlike her. I thought of Janet saying, "They understand so much, even when they don't know the words." I figured she would tell me in time. I also figured it wasn't absolutely necessary that she say it out loud in words. Like Maya, I could understand a lot without them.

I drank half my tea in silence.

Then she said, "Six months, maybe."

I said, "Oh." And had no idea what should follow. I wanted to be upbeat, so I added, "What about if you beat the odds and do much better than the doctors expected?"

"That more or less *is* if I beat the odds and do much better than the doctors expect. It's very fast growing, and it's metastasized."

"I don't know what to say, Mom."

"Well, there isn't much you *can* say," she said. "I just figured this would be the last Thanksgiving for us to all be together. And that was sad, so I figured we should get started early and make the best of it. Besides, I didn't want to be alone after hearing that."

"No, of course not. You did the right thing. When did you find this out?"

"Just this morning."

"Jeez. Well. Let me go ahead and call Aubrey."

"You don't tell him something like this over the phone!" she shouted, and then the volume of her own voice made her cough.

"I wasn't going to. I was just going to see if he can get off work and get here early."

"He has a job again? Then why am I still sending him checks? That'll drive him crazy, though, Ruth. He'll be just like you were. He'll say, 'Now that I know there's something to know I have to know it right now!'"

"Good," I said. "All the better to get his butt out here."

I was on my feet and halfway to the phone when she stopped me.

"Wait," she said. "Before you call him, there's something more."

My heart and stomach fell at exactly the same time. I walked back to the couch and sat—or maybe "collapsed" would be a better word.

"Okay," I said. "What?"

"I don't want you to tell Aubrey this. If you do, he won't come. But I want Joseph here, too."

"You want Joseph *and* Aubrey."

"Yes."

"At the same table."

"Yes. And it's a final wish and I expect him to abide by it."

"I'm not sure you're going to get what you're expecting, Mom. I think when Aubrey finds out, he'll get back on his motorcycle and ride away."

"If he does . . . ," she began, anger rising in her voice. But she never finished the sentence.

"If he does, then what?" I asked as gently as possible. "I mean, how do you stop him from kicking that bike into gear and roaring away?"

Much to my shock, she began to weep openly. Maya bounced up and down in her playpen and fussed, sensing problems. I jumped up and fetched a box of tissues from the nearest bathroom and brought them to Janet.

"Thank you," she said, pulling about ten out of the box. "I can't believe what I was about to say. I was going to say if he does, I'll put him out of my life, and he'll be no part of this family. And then it hit me that I haven't even cleaned up the devastation from the last time I did that. It's just that final resort you go to, thinking they wouldn't dare call you on it, you know what I mean? But it hasn't worked out so well in the past. Oh, Ruthie. Work this out for me. Please?"

I pulled in a huge amount of air and tried to sigh it out silently.

But no pressure, I thought. Just a dying family member with a dying wish that's probably impossible, but it's my job to make it come true. No worries. Happy holidays to all.

"I'll do my best," I said.

———

Janet went down for a nap, Maya resolutely refused, and I made a series of phone calls with her on my hip.

I called Joseph first. He picked up right away, but he was clearly out in the middle of nowhere, and we could barely hear each other. But after a minute or two of sentences with every third or fourth word cut out by bad reception, I heard him say he would get to a landline and call me back.

"Fifteen minutes," he said.

"Fine!" I shouted in hopes of being heard, and Maya put her hands over her ears, which was something she'd taken to doing in imitation of me when I thought she was being too shrieky.

I hung up and called Aubrey.

"What?" he said, in place of "hello."

"Nice," I said. "Lovely phone manners. You need to get out here."

"Why?"

"Mom's already here."

"It's Monday."

"I know what day it is, Aubrey. There's some . . . stuff going on. And you need to get here early. Seriously. Like as soon as humanly possible."

"I have work."

"Tell them it's a family emergency."

"Is it?"

"Oh, yeah."

"And you're not going to tell me."

"No. Mom said not to. She wants to tell you herself when you get here."

Long silence.

Then he said, "Okay. Give me a few hours."

I started to say something—"thank you," maybe—but then I realized he'd already hung up. Maya was reaching for something, leaning her upper body out away from me, so I kept moving in the direction she was reaching, like a divining rod, and while I walked, I speed-dialed Sean at work.

As the line rang, I figured out Maya wanted her juice bottle from the bottom of the playpen, so I reached in and got it for her and she settled immediately, resting her head on my shoulder. I could hear her suckling apple juice.

"Honey," Sean said. "Hey. Can it wait? Super busy here."

For a moment, I couldn't even form an answer. All I could think was *Doesn't anybody say hello anymore?* But that didn't feel like the right one.

"I guess it can. I don't know. It's . . ."

"Uh-oh," he said. "Serious, huh? I can hear it in your voice. Give me just a second."

While I was waiting, I heard him barking orders at his assistant, Rick. Probably getting him to finish what Sean would—should—have done himself, if I hadn't called.

"Okay, sorry," he said. "I'm back."

"Now I feel guilty. Because you're busy. But I just kept thinking about the last time I went to see Ham. You asked me why I didn't call you to talk if I was so upset. So that's why I did this time."

"What's going on, Ruth?"

"Mom's here."

"It's Monday."

"I really wish people would stop telling me what day it is. I know it's Monday, Sean. But she's here. She got some very bad health news."

"How bad?"

"Bad."

"Yeah, but . . . honey, can you elaborate a little? How bad?"

"She brought presents. For Thanksgiving. I said, 'Mom, we'll get together again at Christmas.' She said, 'God willing.' That bad."

"Oh, crap," he said. "That's pretty bad."

"She wants Joseph here for Thanksgiving."

"Joseph *and* Aubrey?"

"Right. And she's pretty much put me in charge of making it happen."

"I should come home," he said.

"No, you have to finish work. Just—"

But before I could say just what, I heard the tone that meant somebody was trying to call through. I held the phone away from my ear. It was the same Colorado area code I'd just used to call Joseph.

"That's Joseph calling me back. I have to take this."

"Okay. See you after work."

I clicked through to the incoming call.

"Joseph," I said.

"Hey, Duck."

"I can hear you."

"I'm in the office in the barn."

"First of all," I said, "I have to apologize. Because here I am calling you with something big, and I realize I've had your number all this time, and I should've called you before."

"You don't have to apologize for anything, Duck," he said, his voice soft.

"I feel like I do, though. And I said we'd come out and visit you . . ."

"You don't want to come in the winter, anyway. Not so good for California folks. Too snowy. Too cold."

"But I said that back when it wasn't."

"Come in the spring, Duck," he said, ignoring the subtext of my guilt. "That's when it's most beautiful."

"Maybe I will," I said, suddenly lost in the imaginary vision of something beautiful, which felt so different from my real life in that moment.

"Now how 'bout you tell me what's going on?"

"Mom wants you here for Thanksgiving."

"She's dying," he said without missing a beat.

"How did you know that?"

"It's a pretty damned big change of heart."

"Yeah, I guess it is."

"Okay," he said. Like it was easy. Like everything in this world was. "I'll get on the road. Can I bring a plus one?"

"A what?"

"A plus one. A guest."

"Oh. Yeah. Sure."

"Okay. Can't say when I'll get in, but I'll keep you posted."

And that was that.

I hung up the phone and sat on the couch with the baby and wondered if Joseph had a girlfriend. I figured he must if he wanted to bring a guest.

Then I ran out of thoughts and came crashing into the moment.

The busywork of those phone calls had been holding me up, I now realized, keeping me together and away from what was happening. And even though I'd never been particularly emotionally close to my mother, even though I'd never been her biggest fan, I broke apart and cried.

That's the thing about mothers. If you're close, you don't want to lose that closeness, though I don't know from personal experience. If you're not, you harbor this little thread of hope that you will be someday, and you don't want to be told you've just run out of time. And that I did learn for myself. Right about then.

Maya said the word "mommy" over and over, worried about me, and that didn't help stem the tears at all.

Chapter Twenty-Two: Aubrey

I sat out on Ruth and Sean's back patio with my mom. It was mid-afternoon. We were both staring at the chiminea. This freestanding pottery fireplace that shared the brick space with us. There was no fire in it, of course. It was broad daylight. And too warm.

Mom was smoking a cigarette. Which I pretty much couldn't get over. I just kept staring at it. Watching her flick the ashes into a saucer. Ruth and Sean didn't keep ashtrays. It felt like an openmouthed stare, but I could feel that my mouth was closed. In my mind, though. In my mind, my jaw was dropped. Had been since the beginning of the conversation.

"You're not saying anything," she said.

I jumped. Neither one of us had said anything for a long time. I guess I'd been expecting the trend to last.

"It's kind of hard to know what to say."

She patted my knee, and I saw a couple of tears slip out. Hers. Not mine. I would find out later that I actually did have some. Hiding in there somewhere. In that moment, though, I just felt like a block of concrete. I had all the emotion of a rock.

"So, I hate to even bring it up, Mom. But . . ."

"What?"

"You could stop sucking on those things that got you into this mess in the first place."

"People get lung cancer even when they don't smoke."

"Rarely. Mostly they get it when they do."

"And when you've been a smoker," she said, "even after you quit, you still have a higher risk."

"But not as high as if you don't quit," I said.

"Well, risks don't really apply to me anymore," she said. "My numbers are all in."

"Still . . . ," I began. Though I swear I had no idea how I would have finished.

"Aubrey," she said. "Honey. It's too late."

I said nothing. Not accepting, exactly. Just accepting that the conversation about it was over. It *was* that way. That's what Luanne always said. "It *is* that way. Now the only question is: What are you going to do about it?"

My mom startled me again by speaking.

"So why am I still writing you checks every month if you're working?"

"I'm not working," I said, relieved that the statement had recently become technically true.

"Ruth said you were working again."

"Well, I'm not."

Silence while I waited to see if she would ask more questions. Pursue me. She didn't.

"I'm going to go see what Ruth has in mind for lunch," I said. "You hungry?"

"Not really. But you're a growing boy. So go eat."

"Mom. I'm twenty-three. I'm not still growing."

"To me, you'll always be a boy," she said.

Then we both got stuck for a moment on the sad truth of that statement. She'd never watch me turn thirty. Or see my hairline recede. If I ever became a father, she wouldn't know about it. There would be moments in the future, moments that would provide irrefutable proof that I was a grown man. She wouldn't be there for any of them.

I found Ruth in the kitchen without further comment. She had the baby on her hip and was making a peanut-butter-and-jelly sandwich with the crusts cut off.

"Hey," I said.

"This sucks," she said. "Huh?"

"I . . . don't think I've really absorbed it yet."

"No, me neither. So, are you staying? Or do you have to get back to work?"

"There's no work to get back to," I said. "I don't have that job anymore."

"Since when?"

"This morning."

"I didn't tell you to quit, Aubrey. You could've just called in a family emergency."

"I tried that. They said if I took more than three days off they'd have to replace me. So I told them to go ahead and do that then."

"I'm sorry," she said.

I just shrugged. "It was a crappy job, anyway. Waiting tables is much worse than I thought it would be. Especially in a cheap place like that. So, listen. I'm thinking about food. I skipped breakfast to get here."

"I'm not exactly prepared," she said. "I wasn't expecting company until Thursday, but if you want to get takeout, I'll pay."

"Fair enough."

She handed the sandwich to the baby. Well . . . toddler. Then she carried Maya and the sandwich over to her purse.

"So, did she tell you everything?" she asked me.

I heard it in her voice. Something. I wasn't quite sure what.

"She told me it's just a matter of months."

"Oh," Ruth said. "She didn't, then."

I felt myself go steely inside. A strange feeling, to turn from stone to steel. Sounds like there'd be no difference. There was. Stone just exists, without feeling. Steel is defensive. Deliberate. It actively stands guard. Keeps everything out.

"Oh, crap," I said, cleaning up my language on the fly for Maya. "What?"

"It's her last Thanksgiving with us. You know? It's kind of a big deal. So she gets to say how she wants it to go. She gets to make a wish."

"You invited Joseph," I said through lips that felt numb. Dead.

"It wasn't my idea. She insisted. But, Aubrey . . . I'm sorry, but you have to stay. She wants us all together. We're not even sure we'll all be together again at Christmas."

"Just give me the money for the food," I said. "Okay?"

She paused. Shook her head. Then she dug for her wallet. Which she knew how to open one-handed. I guess motherhood teaches you that.

She handed me two twenties.

"Thank you," I said.

I went out the back way. On purpose.

Our mom had just lit a fresh cigarette. She looked over her shoulder at me. With no guilt. Defiantly.

"Here's the deal," I said. "I'll stay. Just because it's your wish and you get to make one." I didn't say "your last wish." I couldn't. But I guess it went without saying. "But I'm not saying a word to him. And he's not to say a word to me. You tell him that. Got it? I won't pick fights. I won't say anything mean. I just won't say anything at all."

I waited while she took another deep drag. Watched her tip her head back to blow the smoke toward the sky. Why, I had no idea.

"That's not good enough," she said.

This time my mouth really did drop open. In real time. Not just in my head.

"That's a lot!" I said. Shouted, nearly. "That's huge for me."

"But it's not enough. I want you to be civil. You don't have to forgive everything. You don't have to like him again. But if he says hello, you say hello back. If he asks you a direct question, you answer. Same as you would with anybody. Whether you know them or not."

"Strangers are easy," I said. "This is Joseph."

"Nonetheless," she said, "that's what I want."

I waited, expecting a reaction from myself. For years it had always been the same. All my life, so far as I knew. Rage would well up. I would lash out somehow. Protect what was mine. So I waited for it. Instead everything just sagged inside. I was utterly defeated. I could feel it.

"I'm going to get some takeout for lunch," I said.

———

I tore down the street at about twice the speed limit. Enjoying the roar of the bike's engine in my ears. The vibration coming up through the seat. Now and then, I glanced at my watch. Just a few blocks short of that Thai place I liked, I entered the time window I'd been waiting for. Ten minutes to the hour.

I pulled over. Balanced the bike with my boots on the tarmac. Near the curb. Dug my cell phone out of my pocket.

I texted Luanne, *So. My mom's dying.*

I waited. For maybe a minute. Maybe two.

Then I got a text back. It said, *When did you find this out?*

I texted, *Just a few minutes ago.*

She said, *How do you feel?*

I said, *I don't.*

Right. Still the denial phase. That's normal.

There's more.

I waited. But then I realized she was waiting, too. For me to go on.

I typed, *Joseph is coming to Thanksgiving.*

How do you feel about that?

How do you think I feel? But it doesn't matter. Mom holds the cards. I have to do it.

A pause. During which I didn't hear back.

So I added, *Don't I?*

She texted, *You don't *have* to do anything. What do I always say?*

That I can do whatever I want if I'm willing to pay the bill when it comes in.

Right. But I think this one would be too expensive. Don't you?

So I have to, I repeated.

Why not think of it more like: you will?

I stuck my phone back into my pocket. Rode the rest of the way to the Thai place in silence. Even on the inside. I'd been planning to ask her if she could fit me in for a session. But I changed my mind. Right in that moment, I decided she wasn't helping at all.

Nobody could help me now.

———

Most of the rest of the day was far too tedious to relate. It involved a lot of staring. At the walls. Out the window. At the chiminea if we were sitting outside. We looked at the baby and fussed over the baby. Because it was something we all still knew how to do.

But even the baby mostly stared. Under normal circumstances, she bounced endlessly. Insisted on climbing down from her mom's lap. Toddled around using chair arms and coffee tables for supplemental balance. Ran and got toys and showed them to everyone.

That day she mostly just sat.

After a few dreadful hours, Sean came home. I thought he might unlock us somehow. Instead he caught the fever. Sat and stared with us.

Dinnertime came and Mom and Ruth weren't hungry. So Sean and I ate leftover Thai takeout in the kitchen.

"How are you going to be with Joseph here?" he asked me, halfway through the meal.

I waited again. For the rage. Still nothing. What came up was more like a profound depression. The battle was over. I had lost.

"I'm going to be just how Mom says I have to be. If he says hello, I have to say hello back. If he asks a question, I have to answer it. It's a last wish. You can't deny your own mother her last wish. And she knows it."

"I think that's a good decision," Sean said. "I think you'll look back later, after . . . you know. I think you'll be glad you did. And God knows Ruth'll be relieved to hear it. Janet pretty much put her in charge of making this work out. So the pressure is really on at her end."

"So I'm pinned twice," I said.

"It'll be over before you know it," he said. Half-jokingly. Like a doctor who says, "This won't hurt a bit." When you both know it will.

We finished eating in silence.

I purposely didn't ask when Joseph was coming.

In time, we wandered back out into the living room. Everyone was gone. We found them out on the back patio. Ruth was stoking a little wood fire in the chiminea.

We sat and stared until I couldn't stand it anymore.

"I'm going to bed," I said. Jumping up suddenly.

"Aubrey," my mom said. "It's seven."

"Well, yeah. I know." I hadn't known, actually. "I'll go to bed and read," I said.

"You brought a book?" Ruth asked. The subtext being that I wasn't big on books and she knew it.

"I'll read one of yours," I said.

But my bed was nothing but a blanket and pillow thrown on the couch. So going "to bed" didn't accomplish much. Especially after it got cold and they came back inside.

I just kept my eyes closed. Didn't interact with any of them at all.

———

In the morning, I sat up. Rubbed my eyes and cleared my throat. No one was around as far as I could see. Or hear.

I wandered into the kitchen and ran into a stranger. Almost literally.

He was old. Painfully old. Bent over a cane. Hair nearly gone. Frail. Looked like he might be a hundred. When he raised his eyes to me, I expected them to be glassy. Or cloudy. Half-dead.

Instead they pierced me like a laser. Clear and alive. I thought, *He's in there, all right. Whoever he his. He's only old on the outside.*

He broke into a toothy grin.

"And you must be Aubrey," he said. The accent was lilting. Almost old-world.

I wanted to say, *How did you know?* Started to, actually. Instead I said, "And you're Hamish MacCallum." It was obvious, really. How many ancient Scottish men were likely to turn up in Ruth's kitchen?

"See?" he said. "We practically know each other already."

He angled himself over to a chair. He looked so unsteady. Like it was such a project getting himself into it. I ended up helping.

"Thanks," he said. "Joe's about to come down and make us a big breakfast."

"Joe? Who's Joe?"

"Joe Stellkellner. Your brother."

"Nobody calls my brother 'Joe.'"

"Wrong," he said. "One person does. Me."

Then suddenly, the room was full. Sean and Ruth came in, Sean holding Maya. And my mom appeared from behind me. Sat down at the table.

I looked at both kitchen doorways. For a minute, nothing. There was no one else. No one there.

Then there was.

He looked huge. Not taller, of course, but muscle-bound. His hair was shaggy and long. He'd apparently just showered, and it was slicked back along his head. Falling to his collar in back. He was in his thirties, which seemed shocking. He never had been before. I guess that sounds like a stupid thing to say. But normally you get to watch the process. It happens slowly.

His eyes locked up with mine. I went dead inside. I felt around for a reaction. Anything. But all the lines were down.

A whole room full of people hung there in silence. Waiting.

"Aubrey," he said. In that tone of voice cowboys use. You know. In the movies. When they tip their hats to passing ladies.

I realized I was disappointed. Because he hadn't called me by my affectionate nickname. Mr. Universe.

"Joseph," I said. With no inflection at all.

And then the room breathed a sigh. Well . . . the people in the room did. Though I swear it felt like the room itself resumed breathing.

———

"*Bacon?*" my mom asked. As though it were a completely outrageous concept. "*And* eggs, *and* potatoes, *and* toast? Oh, dear God. The calories! Any idea how many calories that all adds up to?"

Nobody said a word. They'd all frozen again.

So I spoke up.

"Seriously, Mom? You're on a diet? *Now?*"

I watched her take that in. We all did. Then a strange smile spread on her face. Half-satisfied, half-sarcastic.

"Good point," she said. "Joseph, make mine double bacon. Two servings. My goodness. There's a freedom in that, isn't there?"

"Coming up, Mom," Joseph said. Like a short-order cook.

He had four pans on the stove at once. Two just to get enough bacon on for everybody. One for potatoes and another to poach the eggs.

"When did you learn to do all that?" she asked him.

The silence that followed seemed to answer her question. I watched her glance over at Hamish MacCallum. And I realized she'd been doing it all along. I just hadn't noticed the look in her eyes as she did. The silent daggers of disapproval.

"Summers," Joseph said. And no more.

Then the silence grew so suffocating that I asked a question. And only after I'd blurted it out did I realize I'd just spoken to my brother.

"How did you get here so fast?"

The room reverberated. The fact that I had addressed him bounced off the walls. Through the people. I wished like hell I could pull the words back.

"I just mean . . . ," I said, plunging in deeper as a result of my panic, "it's such a long drive from Colorado. Doesn't it take days?"

"I didn't drive from Colorado," he said, breaking eggs into a saucer. Stopping to stir the potatoes with a spatula. "I flew into San Francisco. Then I hitchhiked down to Hammy's, and we drove down here in his car. I drove all night. I figured the sooner I saw Mom, the better."

———

"My, my," Mom said. After nearly half the meal in a stony silence. "I haven't eaten this big a meal in years. It has an effect on you, doesn't it? Kind of calms everything down."

I would never have admitted it, but it was having the same effect on me. Making me believe I'd survive the breakfast. Maybe even the week.

"Nothing like some protein," the old man said in that lilting accent. "Amazing what it can do. People don't realize they haven't eaten. Or that they've just eaten sugar or chemicals or refined flour. We're like our automobiles. Can't expect any work from 'em if we don't put in some decent fuel. And that's true even if the work is just thinking straight."

I realized I'd been trying not to like him. For as long as I'd known his name. But, in a renewed sense, since discovering him in Ruth's kitchen. In that moment, I gave up the goal.

Nobody said anything, so he added, "Joe's learned to make this meal at least as well as I make it myself and almost as well as my wife, God rest her soul, made it before me."

"Joe?" my mom said, a rise in her voice. Like a trout coming up to the surface to take the bait. "Nobody calls him 'Joe.'"

"Wrong," Hamish MacCallum said.

"One person does," Ruth said.

"Him," I said, and pointed at Hamish.

Then we all fell back into silence.

―――

Sean had already peeled away early to get to work. The moment Joseph and Hamish got up and left the table, my mom lit into Ruth.

"Why did you invite him?" she asked. Her voice was a deep hiss.

"I didn't! Joseph just brought him."

"Well, he's not family. And I don't want him at our family Thanksgiving."

"I don't think you have a choice, Mom," I said. Because Ruth looked like she needed rescuing. "I don't even think he drives anymore. Joseph drove him down here. The only way he's getting out of here is if Joseph leaves, too."

"This is not the way it was supposed to be!" she said, going after Ruth again. "You said Joseph had a girlfriend."

"I said I *thought* he did. He just said he was bringing a guest, so that was what I thought."

"Well, I wanted it to be all family."

I jumped to Ruth's defense again.

"If he'd brought a girlfriend," I said, "she wouldn't be family, either."

"Oh, stay out of this, Aubrey. Okay, fine. I wanted it not to be *him*!"

"How can you not like Hammy?" Ruth asked. Her voice sounded genuinely stunned. "How can *anybody* not like Hammy?"

My mom didn't answer. She got up and left the room. Or maybe I should say her answer was to get up and leave the room.

"Use your head, Ruth," I said. "He's the one who has all the answers. Or so the story goes. He's the one everybody looks up to. Mom and Brad broke Joseph, and Hamish MacCallum patched him up and got him halfway back together again. At least well enough that he lived to grow up. You didn't think that would raise any hackles in our family?"

"I heard that!" our mom called in from the living room. Which made me wince.

I waited. But my mother chose to neither confirm nor deny. And so, in her silence, confirmed.

Chapter Twenty-Three: Ruth

I woke in the middle of the night, the way I did when I heard Maya crying, but she was silent and apparently asleep.

What had wakened me, I realized, was the sound of soft voices in the backyard. I got out of bed and walked to the window. Below me on our brick patio, I saw Mom and Joseph huddled close to the fire. They had a fire going in our little chiminea, and they had their heads close together, and my mom was talking quietly. In the years before Maya—before I'd learned that new mother's half sleep—I'm sure I never would have heard a thing.

I stood there at the window and watched for a long time, my fingers on the glass of the one window that was too high for Maya to smear with prints. But in that moment, I wasn't in housekeeper mode and I didn't really care.

I wanted to go downstairs, go closer. I wanted to hear what she was saying to Joseph, but I didn't know how to do it without alerting them and therefore breaking up the moment. Besides, it really wasn't any of my business.

Then, a moment later, she squeezed his hand, rose, and disappeared back into the house.

I just stood there for a time, waiting to see if Joseph would go inside, as well. Instead, he reached for another stick of firewood and dropped it into the chiminea.

I pulled on my robe and walked downstairs and through the back patio door, taking the chair our mom had just vacated.

"Hey, Duck," he said, turning his head just slightly.

"You don't have to tell me if you don't want," I said, feeling how much this man was a relative stranger, "but that looked like some kind of genuine moment with Mom."

"It was," he said, and threw another two sticks of wood on the flames.

"None of my business, I guess."

A long silence, long enough that I figured he agreed.

Then he said, "She's getting her affairs in order. I think you know what I mean. She had an amends to make to me. Her assessment, not mine. She was trying to tell me it was Brad who threw me out of the house, out of the family. Not her. It wasn't an amends like you'd hope, but I guess for Mom it was a lot. It kind of felt like she was trying to duck responsibility. Put it all off on Brad. But that doesn't really mean none of it was true. She was trying to explain how, in those days, she went along with him a lot when she knew she shouldn't have. Not so much because she felt subservient. More like financial insecurity. He was the breadwinner. She was afraid to make waves. She'd never been without money and it terrified her. She thought running out of money was something like dying. You know, the end of everything. Then they ran out of money anyway, and they survived. And then Brad left her and she survived. And then she felt pretty stupid. But anyway, she always regretted putting me out like that. Who knew, right? That's why she wanted me here. Wanted to see me. She wanted to ask my forgiveness."

"Did she get it?"

"Yeah, sure," he said, as if nothing could be easier. As if the whole world wasn't made up of people writhing and struggling for any kind of forgiveness, both the given and received variety. "That was nothing. I never blamed her anyway. Never really blamed Brad, either. I didn't like him, but I didn't blame him. I wasn't into blame. Maybe because I had so much of it directed at me, you know? I guess you can go one of two ways with that. You can reflect it right back out at everybody else, or you can drop out of the whole blame paradigm. I guess I chose not to play the game anymore."

"That's a lot of honest information coming from Mom," I said, skirting around all the honest information that had just come from *him*. Possibly because I had no space in me to understand not blaming people for hurting you.

"Yeah. Well. Running out of time will do that to a person. I'm watching Hammy do that now, too. Tie up all his loose ends. Thing is, he has so few. Not like Mom. He pretty much keeps his life clean as he goes. But still, you can feel it."

We watched the flames crackle for a minute or more in silence. I tried not to focus on the fact that Ham was wrapping up his life, too. And something else happened in that moment—I felt a bond with Joseph again, like we were really related. Like we'd grown up together, which of course we had, but it hadn't always felt that way. Like I'd missed him, and we still fit somehow.

"May I ask you a question, Joseph?" I asked, marveling at the formality of my phrasing.

"You may," he said, and I couldn't tell if he'd caught formality like a cold or was teasing me slightly for it.

"Why did you refuse to go out on duty that night in Baghdad? And why did you convince those other guys to do the same?"

At the corner of my eye, I saw him rock back in his chair. "That's amazing," he said under his breath.

"What's amazing?"

"How long I had to wait. I kept waiting. I kept marking time until somebody asked me that question. It seemed like such an obvious question. Never thought I'd have to wait ten and a half years."

"I'm really the first one who asked?"

"Believe me. If anybody else had, I'd have remembered."

"I guess we all thought we knew."

"You thought I was afraid."

"Right."

"I was. Of course I was. You almost had to be, over there. You were either so batshit crazy you didn't understand what was going on, or if you had a normal brain and half an instinct for self-preservation, you were afraid. Fear just came with the territory. Naturally I was afraid. But that's not why I didn't go."

I looked over at the side of his face in the half dark, and the flickering flames showed those little lines at the corner of his eye. I thought, *Where does the time go? Where do our lives go so fast?*

"You could have volunteered the story to somebody," I said.

"Wouldn't have made any difference. You do what you're told to do, and if you don't, I'm not sure the nuance of your reasoning matters. Maybe it depends on the commanding officer. I don't know. And the public had already made up their minds. But anyway, it wasn't a story for the public. It's something really only our family would understand. Maybe not even the whole family. Maybe just you and Aubrey. Anybody who doesn't know Aubrey pretty well wouldn't understand what I'm about to tell you at all."

"What does Aubrey have to do with this?"

"Everything. He has everything to do with it."

A silence, which I didn't fill, because I realized he would tell me what I wanted to know if I would just shut up and let him.

"I have to start by telling you what we were doing," he said. "What the duty in question involved. There was a strong insurgency. I'm sure you know that. The Iraqis mounted a resistance."

"Which is very dangerous," I interjected.

"Also very understandable," he said.

I was surprised. "That seems like an odd thing to say," I told him.

"Does it? Doesn't seem odd to me. We were in their country. Can you imagine how we would feel if some foreign army were occupying our country? Setting up checkpoints? Shooting up cars and the people in them if they didn't stop on command? Breaking down their doors in the middle of the night? That's what we were doing. That was the duty I finally refused. We'd go to a family's house. Break down the door. Because it was like a police raid—we couldn't let them know we were coming. Then we'd charge in, split up, and go to all four corners, every room. Get the whole family together and out on the lawn at gunpoint. The women and children would scream and cry. They were terrified. And for good reason. One false move and somebody can die really fast. One of us or one of them. You just never knew. We were trying to make sure it wasn't one of us. So we were holding guns on these civilian families. The men were absolutely humiliated and demoralized because there was nothing they could do to protect their families. Every night, that was what we had to do."

"Why? Was it just at random?"

"No, it wasn't that bad. There was a reason for it. It was a sweep for insurgents. It wasn't random. It was based on intelligence. But 'intelligence' is a loose word. It can mean somebody overheard something, or thought they did. A family can have a problem with a neighbor and just plant the rumor that an insurgent lives next door. Sometimes, I'm sure there really were insurgents in the house. Other times, I'm pretty sure there weren't. But you can't know until you go in. I'll give the army credit for one thing, though. After I left, the intelligence got much better and so did the raids. It didn't take long to figure out that breaking down doors was going to be counterproductive. And I wasn't the only one who was uneasy with it. I'm not saying *I* made the situation better. It just changed. So I guess it was my bad luck to be there when we were still finding our way."

He went silent for a time. So I tried to finish the story for him.

"So you couldn't live with the fact that maybe some of those people were innocent."

"No," he said. "I couldn't live with it either way."

"But the insurgents were killing you."

"Yes," he said. "Yes, they were. And that was very bad, when they killed us. And also we were killing them. And that was very bad, when we killed them. That's the part it's harder to get an American to see. They see one but not the other. I couldn't help but see both. But you know, I don't blame the Americans who were over there fighting with me for not seeing it that way. I'm less patient with the ones who were sitting safely at home, but I don't blame those other soldiers at all. It's very hard to empathize with an enemy while he's shooting at you. I actually think it runs counter to human nature. But my nature must be different, I guess. I feel like my brain is wired differently or something. I swear, I couldn't *not* think about it from their point of view. I just couldn't stop. I kept watching them die for opposing us, so we wouldn't die, and yes, that's very understandable, too. I get our side's position. But then the more of them we kill, the more we fuel the insurgency. And then more of us die, so we have to kill more of them. It never ends. It just keeps refueling itself."

"So what's the answer?" I asked, still wondering what all this could possibly have to do with Aubrey.

I watched his face in the flickering light for a moment, wondering if he even had an answer.

"Invade fewer countries?" he asked in time.

"But their leader was killing his own people."

"Not as many as the leaders in Rwanda. Or Sudan. But there's no national interest there for us. Which is just another way of saying no oil."

I shook that off, wanting it not to be true, or at least not so black and white.

"But some wars are unavoidable. Look at World War II."

"Why does everybody always go back to World War II?" he asked, his voice rising for the first time.

We both looked back toward the house, but nothing stirred.

"Every time I question the concept of war," he said, lowering his voice again, "people bring up World War II. Two problems with that. First off, I'm talking about starting a war by invading. So while we might not have been wrong for getting drawn in, I still say Germany and Japan were wrong to attack and invade to get it started. Second, does that mean World War II was really our last justified war?"

"This is making my head hurt," I said. "And besides, I still have no idea what this has to do with Aubrey."

"Then I'll tell you," he said. "It was about ten minutes before I was due to go out. I was lying on my cot. I had this rare moment of break time. The rest of the guys were outside smoking, but I didn't smoke. Not then. I started thinking. I started imagining. So imagine this with me, Ruth. Some Muslim nation has invaded the US. Overthrown the government, even if it wasn't a very good one. The reason I say 'Muslim nation' is so you get the full comparison. Different religion. Different language. Totally different culture. And there are soldiers with guns when you go to work or school. There are checkpoints you have to drive through, and if you don't stop for them, you'll be shot dead on the spot. And then one night, the soldiers break your door down and haul your whole family out onto the lawn at gunpoint. Because they think you have a member of the insurgency under your roof. Now, let's say for a minute you do. He's not an evildoer, as far as you're concerned. He's a member of your family. He's somebody who's seen enough innocents killed that he's ready to fight back. Protect his homeland. And then he sees a bunch more of his friends and relatives killed for protecting their homeland. Got a clear picture so far?"

"Unfortunately clear," I said, because I hated those moments when life provides no clean answers, no easy-to-follow road map of who's right and who's wrong. In fact, it was making me feel a little queasy.

"Then here's the big question for you, Ruth."

Before that night, he hadn't called me "Ruth" in as long as I could remember. Maybe ever. But I didn't point it out. I didn't say anything.

"What would Aubrey do?" Joseph asked.

I burst out laughing. I couldn't help it.

"'What would Aubrey do?'" I repeated.

"Yeah. Why is that funny?"

"It's like those people with signs on their desk that say 'WWJD?' 'What would Jesus do?' And . . . Aubrey and Jesus . . . that's the last comparison you'd expect to hear."

"But I don't mean it like that," he said. "It's a straight question. What would he do in those circumstances?"

I paused to think, but I didn't need to think for long.

"He'd defend us," I said. "Or, well . . . at least he'd defend himself. Aubrey is nothing if not defensive. He wouldn't roll over for anyone."

"Exactly," he said.

But right in that moment, I still didn't quite get it.

"I don't—" I began.

"Aubrey would be an insurgent."

And we sat in the flicker of the fire for a minute or two, with nothing being said.

"That's why you didn't go."

"I couldn't go out gunning for a bunch of young men who were more or less the Iraqi equivalent of my own little brother."

Another long silence.

"Why are you crying?" he asked.

I actually hadn't realized I was crying until he pointed it out. My mind was a million miles away, and the tears were just something going on in my absence.

"I guess I was thinking about that morning Aubrey went out and talked to the reporters in front of Aunt Sheila's house, and it seems so incredibly sad after what you just told me."

He didn't answer, and I didn't look over. Because he'd known the sadness of that moment all along, ever since it had happened, and I didn't want to know what that pain looked like.

"Why didn't you tell him?" I asked.

"I tried. But I wasn't home long. I went up into his room that first night and tried to tell him. But I left out most of the details. Because I woke him up. He had school in the morning. I didn't want to dump a bunch of stuff on him that would only keep him awake all night. So I just told him it was more of a principled stand than Brad was making it out to be. I thought I'd have plenty of time to finish the story over the next few days. Even though I was actually already AWOL. But I figured we'd be in touch, at least. Funny how sure we are about stuff like that and how wrong we can turn out to be."

"Oh, he's going to hear this," I said. "I'm going to see to it."

"Don't force it too hard. He'll just reject it. Wait until you see a crack in his armor."

"I'll make my own crack," I said. "I'll crack that little brat with my own hands."

We sat for a few moments in silence. The fire was already dwindling down. It had burned hot and now it was burning itself out. My eyes were grainy from lack of sleep, and I was thinking seriously about going back to bed. But Joseph was right about one thing: that wasn't exactly a bedtime story, what he'd just told me.

"Let me ask you one more question," I said. "Okay, so you're lying on your cot alone, and you decide this. The other guys are out smoking. Then what? How does this get from your head into the heads of three other guys? Where did the conspiracy come in? How did it turn into mutiny? Or *was* it a mutiny as far as you were concerned?"

He shook his head, and I waited, but for a while he just kept shaking it.

"God, I wish I knew," he said. "I mean, I was there. I remember every single thing that happened that night. But I just couldn't feel the moment when it crossed that line. Except I can see it looking back. You look back and it's this huge thing. But it never felt that way at the time. I swear to God I don't even understand it myself."

"Well, maybe just tell me what you remember happened, then."

"Tim came in. And he was sort of a friend of mine, and I knew he was uneasy, too, about what we were doing. So I started talking to him about what I'd decided. I didn't mention Aubrey, though. Just my feelings about the raids in general. There were guys over there, and some women, you could talk to about stuff like this, and then a whole bunch more who wouldn't have wanted to hear it. I could kind of feel which was which. I just wanted to hear how it would sound outside my own head. You know? I was bouncing stuff off him. So then Tim left the room. I didn't even know for sure if he was going to refuse to go or not. Then he ran into two other guys and told them what we'd been talking about. And that it was my idea. But what I don't know to this day is whether he *only* talked to two guys. Or if maybe he mentioned it to a third guy who turned out to be the wrong guy. Somebody he shouldn't have told. Because somebody called the media when the whole thing hit the fan."

"So Tim was really the one who started the mutiny."

"No," he said firmly. "I started it. I rolled that snowball downhill. I never thought it could get as big as a house and flatten part of a village. But I have to take responsibility for starting it rolling."

"What happened to Tim?" I asked, not sure how much I agreed or disagreed with Joseph's assessment of his own guilt.

"Bad conduct discharge."

"Why wasn't he charged with mutiny, too?"

"Because I never ratted him out."

"But he did more wrong than you did."

"It doesn't matter, Duck. If he'd gotten prison time, too, it wouldn't have made my time any shorter. Besides. That's not all there was to it. He brought the other two guys back in to talk to me. And we all four had a conversation. That was the conspiracy part, I guess. Right there. I feel stupid looking back, because it seemed so innocent. I guess I thought we were doing something good. There would be a group of us who would question the whole way we did those raids, and maybe it would change the way things were being done. We thought it was like a principled stand, but it was incredibly naïve. I see that now. I went at it totally the wrong way. I handled it all wrong. We figured if there were four of us or maybe even more who wouldn't go, our commanding officer would have to call off the raid. But he didn't. He sent it out undermanned. And two men died. And I'm responsible. And there's no weaseling out of that. I set things in motion and two men died. I should've just not gone. Taken the discharge. I should've kept my mouth shut and left everybody else out of it."

I wanted to ask him about the officer who sent the unit out undermanned, but then I remembered that I knew. There had been an investigation, but ultimately no charges against him. Joseph had taken the weight of everything that happened that night. Fairly voluntarily, from the sound of it.

He startled me by speaking again.

"Hammy says you can't unroll a snowball. Just like you can't un-ring a bell. He wasn't blaming me or trying to make me feel guilty or anything. It's just the way it is. We're responsible for what we do."

I reached over and took his hand and gave it a little squeeze. He seemed surprised—startled, even.

"I'm sorry I thought you were a coward," I said.

"Didn't know you did," he said, a little hurt from the sound of it.

"Well, I didn't mean to. But I didn't ask you why. So I guess I figured it was fear, like everybody else."

"At least you didn't say it out loud into a bank of television news cameras."

"You know how Aubrey is," I said.

"I do indeed," he said. "Our little insurgent."

I sat another moment. Then I was on my feet, but I swear it was done with no premeditation.

"Wait here," I said.

"For what?"

"I'm going to get Aubrey. And you're going to tell him."

"Hate to have you wake him up."

"Why? He doesn't have school in the morning."

I marched inside and over to the couch, where Aubrey lay snoring almost violently. It seemed like an affront to me, to everything, that he should be sleeping soundly when there was something so important he needed to know.

I kicked the bottom of the couch. He didn't so much as twitch, so I did it again. Still nothing.

Finally, I aimed a little higher and kicked *him*.

"Ow! What?" he said, jumping into a sitting position.

"Come with me."

I grabbed him by the arm and pulled him to his feet, then towed him over to the patio door.

"What?" he asked again. "I'm sleeping, Ruth. What are you doing?"

"There's something you need to hear," I said.

"Can't it wait till morning?"

"No. It can't. By morning you'll be all well rested and you won't have so many cracks in your armor."

"Wait. Am I dreaming this?"

I slid open the patio door and dragged him across the bricks.

"Talk to your brother," I said, sitting Aubrey down in the chair I'd just vacated.

"And say what?"

"I take that back. *Listen* to your brother."

Then I marched back inside. I watched them for a few minutes, just to assure myself that Aubrey wouldn't get up and storm away. He didn't. In fact, the more time went by, the less stormy he appeared, and the more he slumped in that chair as if anchored to it.

As with Joseph's talk with our mom, I couldn't hear the words, and didn't need to. Partly because they were none of my business, partly because I already knew the story my brother Aubrey was being told.

Chapter Twenty-Four: Aubrey

I drove around on my motorcycle for what felt like a couple of hours. It was cold. Don't believe that lie about Southern California always being warm.

I wasn't wearing a jacket. The wind flapped in my shirt and froze me. I didn't care.

An image kept coming into my mind. It was an image of me. On videotape. Holding court in front of the cameras regarding my brother. The big expert on my brother. Who he was. What he deserved.

Every time it came in, I pushed it away with the same resolute thought, *He had ten years in prison to make up that story.*

What better did he have to do? Lift weights. Not answer my letters. Figure out ways to win me over again when he got out.

A voice that sounded like Luanne's barged into my head. It said, *If he didn't care about you, he wouldn't be thinking up ways to win you back.*

"You stay out of this," I told her. Out loud. The wind grabbed my words away.

The thing I kept sticking on was this: If what Joseph had just told me was true, then what I'd done that August morning in front of Aunt Sheila's house was no longer a brave and justified act. It was one of the greatest tragedies imaginable. And if what Joseph had told me wasn't true, then it was a monstrous lie. Because it tried to reframe that brave act into the biggest mistake of my life.

Maybe the biggest mistake of anybody's life.

After a time, I realized I was using up too much of my gas. And I wouldn't have any left to get home after the holiday. I wasn't what you might call flowing over with money. I'd have to hit somebody up for a loan. Mom. Ruth.

The list ended there.

I turned around. Rode back. Turned the bike's engine off in the dark before coasting into the driveway. I didn't want to wake anybody up.

I ducked in through the kitchen door, my helmet under my arm.

The old man, Hamish, was awake. He was sitting at the kitchen table in no light but the glow from the stove lamp. Drinking what looked like a cup of tea.

"Aubrey boy," he said. In that accent.

"What are you doing up in the middle of the night? Couldn't you sleep?"

He tossed his chin in the direction of the clock on the microwave. It was 5:58 a.m.

"I slept fine," he said. "Just, when you get to be my age, you don't need so much."

"I've heard that."

I plunked down at the table. Rested my forehead on my folded arms. Sighed.

"You seem upset," he said.

I realized, just as he said it, that I'd purposely tipped him. I'd done a perfect pantomime of upset. Just so he would ask. The amazing part is the part where I realized it. Usually other people see things like that about me and I don't. They try to point them out. Even then, I don't see it. I tell them they're wrong. Now I knew they weren't. Probably never had been.

"Joseph told me some things," I said. "And I don't know whether to believe him or not."

"I've never known Joe to lie right to anybody's face," he said.

"I just figured he had all those years in prison to revise his own history. To figure out exactly the best story to win my forgiveness."

"Was it about that night in Baghdad?"

I looked up from the table. From the crooks of my own arms.

"Yeah," I said.

"Did he tell you the reason he didn't go out that night?"

"Yeah."

"Because the fellows he was supposed to be chasing down reminded him too much of you?"

"Yeah. But like I said. He had a lot of time to make that up."

"Except he told me the exact same thing just a couple days after he came home."

I tried to look closer into his face. To see if I could trust him. But it was too dark. I had an irritating sense that I knew, though.

"When did you even talk to him just days after he came home?"

"Where do you think he went when he left your house?"

"Oh," I said. "I didn't even think of that. I didn't know." I remembered trying to find out, though. Carrying cash to a private investigator. Like an idiot. Because I loved my brother so much. "Did you tell him to turn himself in?"

"No. I wouldn't have told him what to do. And I didn't need to. There was never any question that he would. He was always going to pay the price for what he did. He was relieved, of course, for a time there, when he thought the price was just a bad discharge. But when he found out otherwise, it never occurred to him to hide. However much they chose to charge him for what he did, he always aimed to pay it."

It made me think of Luanne. Saying, *You can do anything you want, so long as you're willing to pay the bill when it comes in.*

Except maybe that wasn't entirely true. Because sometimes other people get hurt in the bargain.

"I just keep thinking about those other two guys, though," I said. "Those two soldiers. Who died that night."

"So does Joe," he said. "On the drive down, he told me not a day's gone by in the last ten and a half years he doesn't think about them. He even tried to go and talk with their parents after he got out."

"Did they talk to him?"

"One did. One young man's mother was very kind. The other, the father wouldn't let him anywhere near."

"Oh. Wait, I have a question, though. If he's so thoughtful and trying to be honorable and he's not a coward, and if he always planned to pay the price, why did he run away when the news came out?"

"Well," Hamish said. "I'm afraid you can blame that squarely on me. That was my fault."

"What did you do?"

"I was old."

That made no sense, of course. But I didn't ask. I didn't say anything. I just waited. Blinked.

"I was eighty-five. And he was waiting to see if he'd be charged with the greater crime. When they sent him home to the US, he was only charged with disobeying a direct order to go out on duty. He was waiting to see what came out in the investigation. He went AWOL from his army base to go home and see you, because you and Ruth meant so much to him. He figured he'd spend what time he could with you and then they'd just come get him there at your family's house. But then when the full story hit the paper, he took off and came to see me one last time. Or, well . . . I guess it wasn't the last time the way it turned out, was it? But he thought it would be. Because he knew then that he was going away for a very long time. After we said our good-byes, he went straight back and turned himself in."

We fell silent again. I dropped my head back onto my arms.

A bad feeling was forming. I had no intention of saying it out loud.

Then I lifted my head and did anyway.

"So it's true, what he told me."

"It is, Aubrey boy. You've had a lot o' problems in your young life, I'll be the first to testify to that. But not being loved by your brother was never one of 'em. That you've always had."

"Oh my God," I said. "I'm such an idiot."

My brain flooded with the image again. Me, at thirteen. My voice barely done changing. My skin tone washed out by the portable lights. Telling the whole world who my brother was. When I didn't even know.

This time, I had nothing to say to scare it away.

"Oh my God. What did I do?" I asked out loud.

Then, much to my humiliation, I cried.

Hamish reached over the table and patted my arm.

"You mean that day you talked to the media?"

I nodded, unable to talk.

"I won't lie to you, Aubrey boy. It hurt him."

"What did I do?" I asked again. When my words broke loose, they were just a loop of the same words.

"I'll tell you what you did, Aubrey boy. You made a mistake. Joe made mistakes with you, too. All people make mistakes."

"What was Joseph's mistake?"

"He let your father convince him that you and Ruth were better off without him. It was a low point in his confidence, so he believed it. He shouldn't have. And if he hadn't, he would've made contact with you, and the whole thing would have played out very differently."

Before I could think of anything to say, I looked up to see my mother standing in the kitchen doorway.

"What the hell is going on in here?" she asked. In her famous high-dudgeon mode.

"Nothing," I said. "We're talking."

"Nothing doesn't make you cry your eyes out," she said. "What happened? Who made you cry?"

I noticed she turned her face toward Hamish as she spit out that last sentence.

"*I* did," I said. In a strong voice. "*I* made me cry. Now if you'll excuse us . . ."

"I want to know what happened," she said. Hands on hips. Unmovable.

"Fine. Fine, Mom. I'll tell you what happened. I walked out of Aunt Sheila's house and stood in front of the reporters and their cameras and told them Joseph was a coward who hurts people. And I was wrong."

A long silence.

"I wondered when you'd regret that," she said. "Didn't put any bets on ten years after the fact. I'm going out back for a smoke."

She slid open the glass door between the kitchen and back patio. A blast of cold air washed over me. And Hamish. I thought I saw him shiver.

Then the door closed again. With my mom on the outside. We watched her light a cigarette.

"Wow," I said. "She really won't give either one of us a break."

"Not so far," he said.

"Wait. Wait. Why did she even let Joseph spend every summer with you if she hated you so much?"

"Well," he said, "it wasn't so much of a 'let.' He ran off the first summer and came to my house. Your parents called the police to get him home. Then he ran off again. And again. And again. Pretty soon I think the police got tired o' dragging him home. And maybe your folks got tired of admitting they couldn't control him. After a while, everybody just sort of looked the other way."

He reached out for his cane, a wild motion. "Help me up, Aubrey boy," he said to me. "Help me out there. I want to talk to your mum."

"Won't you be cold?"

"Maybe," he said. "But I'll do it anyway."

I jumped up and took his arm at the elbow. Steadied his way over to the door. Opened it again. Walked him across the brick. I looked down to be sure he had something on his feet. He was wearing warm slippers.

My mom looked over her shoulder defensively. Wrapping her thick coat more tightly around her. Like it was a force field. And could save her. I settled Ham into one of the chairs. The one I'd sat in to hear my brother's story. I expected her to get up and storm away. She didn't.

Just like I hadn't.

I hurried back into the house. Grabbed my blanket off the couch. Carried it outside and wrapped it around frail old Hamish.

"Thank you, Aubrey boy," he said. "You're a thoughtful lad."

I walked back into the house to give them their privacy. I was thinking, *Really? A thoughtful lad?* If that was true, it was news to me.

———

Joseph came down about twenty minutes later. I had made coffee. He poured himself a big mug and carried it over to the stove.

"Can you stand the same breakfast as yesterday?" he asked.

"I'd *enjoy* the same breakfast as yesterday. Did me good."

"Well, I'm glad to hear it," he said. "Because it's the only thing I can make worth a damn."

I watched him pull a package of bacon and a carton of eggs from the fridge. Set three potatoes in the microwave. Start them nuking. Grab the bread from the breadbox.

He looked over his shoulder and caught me watching.

"You okay?" he asked. "You look exhausted."

"I am," I said. "Both."

"Get any sleep after we talked?"

"Not a wink."

"Sorry. It wasn't my idea to roust you in the middle of the night. That was a Ruth plan."

"I figured," I said.

Then I watched him work in silence for a few minutes more.

"How's grad school?" he asked me.

"I kind of hate it."

"Well. You'll be done soon, though. Right?"

"If I stay."

"But you want to be an astronomer."

"I thought I did. Now I'm not sure. It's not quite what I expected it to be. Not the hands-on, me-and-the-stars experience I was picturing. It might get better deeper in. But I don't think it's ever going to be what I pictured."

"Longtime dream, though." His hands stopped moving. Just froze there, one holding a pan. One braced on a countertop. His gaze was stuck on the back patio. "Is that Hammy out there, wrapped in that blanket?"

"The one and only."

"Talking to Mom?"

"I know. Weird, huh?"

"How long have they been doing that?"

"Probably close to half an hour now. I have no idea what's going on."

"Let it," he said. "Whatever's going on, just let it. Hammy has a way of winning people over."

"I'll say."

I watched him register my comment. Take it in. But he didn't address it.

He stared at the back patio for a moment longer. Then he shook his head. Like he was shaking cobwebs away. His hands moved again. And just for a minute, he was my big brother. I saw him that way. The way I'd seen him before all this happened. The way I'd looked up to him.

I thought about Luanne saying he was my brother, even back when I didn't want him to be. I thought of that e-mail from Joseph, when he said the same thing.

Now I had to go back and reframe all those years when I thought he was gone. And no relation to me. I hate reframing. Always have.

"So what are you going to do?" he asked. Knocking me out of my own head. My own past.

"About what?"

"You going to stay in school?"

"Oh. That. I'm not sure. I really want to take a month or so. Since I'm not working, anyway. Just get away. You know? Get my head together. Especially after . . . you know. All this." I tossed my head in the direction of Mom on the back patio. Joseph was part of "all this," of course. Maybe the biggest part. But I didn't toss my head in his direction. "Not sure where I would go, though. I don't have a cent. I'll be lucky if I can put enough gas in the bike to get home."

He didn't answer. At least, not for a long time. Long enough that I didn't figure he had an answer. And why would he, really? It was my life. If I couldn't figure it out, why should he?

He pulled the hot potatoes out of the microwave with his bare hands. Not bothering with oven mitts. Even though mitts were hanging a foot from his shoulder. That seemed like something I would do. One by one I watched him drop them, fast, onto the wood cutting board.

"You could come spend a month on a horse ranch in Colorado," he said.

I didn't answer for a long time.

Finally, when the silence was just about to swallow me, I said, "With you?"

"Well, it's a big place. We wouldn't be under each other's feet all day long. But yeah. Basically. Yeah. The pay sucks. But at least it pays enough that you could afford to be there."

"I'd have to think about that," I said.

Which I figured was the most polite way to say no. Or at least not likely. I heard Ruth and the baby coming down the stairs. Heard Maya's little morning coos. I knew I was almost out of time to talk to Joseph.

So I said, "Thanks for asking, though."

He looked over his shoulder at me. As though there was somebody back there he hadn't met yet.

"Open invite," he said. "At least, as long as I'm there."

Then Ruth and the baby were in the kitchen. Standing behind Joseph. Looking over his shoulder. And then Sean was there, too. Out of nowhere. And whatever moment we'd just had, Joseph and I, was gone. And I felt like I probably should have made more of it while it lasted.

"Hope you don't mind that same breakfast as yesterday," Joseph tossed over his shoulder. To exactly who, I wasn't sure. Not me, though.

"Mind?" Sean said. "It's all I've been able to think about."

They sat at the table with me, and I took Maya onto my lap. And Sean and Ruth drank the rest of the coffee I'd made. And said it was good.

They didn't notice that Mom and Hamish were still out back, lost in conversation. Or, likely, that they'd ever been. They didn't ask where those two were.

Another twenty minutes or so passed in small talk. But I didn't have to make any of it. Which was a relief.

That breakfast didn't just throw itself together. It wasn't like cereal poured into a bowl. Maybe that was part of the point of it. The ritual. The time to settle in with the company at hand.

Before he put the eggs in water to poach, Joseph ducked out back to see if Mom and Hamish were eating. That's the first Ruth and Sean realized. The first they saw the little miracle on their back patio.

"How long has that been going on?" Ruth asked.

"Nearly an hour," I said.

"Any idea what they're talking about?"

"None."

Then Joseph came back and shook his head.

"They're going to keep talking," he said. "I promised to save them some bacon and potatoes for reheating."

We all looked at each other. Then, like anything else that can't be understood, that can't be influenced, we let it go by. We turned our attention elsewhere and just let it be.

———

It was nearly eleven a.m. when my mom came back inside. Joseph had gone off to take a shower. Sean had long since gone to work. Maya was down for a nap.

Ruth and I had been sitting together in the kitchen, mostly watching. Just watching that back patio in wonder.

When our mom came to the door and slid it open, Ruth and I sat up straighter. Looked only at each other. As if we'd been caught cheating. Leaning over and looking at the wrong paper.

"Hey, Mom," Ruth said.

"Good morning, dear," she said in return. She seemed relaxed.

"You two have a good talk?" I asked.

"We did. It's very hard not to like that man. Even if you're trying."

A silence fell. Surrounding the obvious question. I wasn't sure if I should ask it. So I breathed a sigh of relief when Ruth asked for me.

"What were you two talking about all that time?"

"Oh, everything," she said. Helping herself to a mug of coffee from the morning's second pot. "Just about every aspect of being alive. But mostly we talked about the opposite. You know. Dying. I have cancer and he's ninety-six. So we have that in common."

"Thought he was ninety-five," Ruth said.

"Well, I'm sure he was, dear. But now he's ninety-six. Anyway. It was nice to just put that dying thing out on the table. I feel ever so much more settled about it now."

Just then, Maya woke up from her nap. We could hear her crying from upstairs.

"Oh, let *me*, dear," our mom said, and hurried out of the room. Abandoning her coffee. It was probably pretty old.

Ruth and I just looked at each other. Then we shook our heads.

Ruth said, "Ham told me once that the problem with people is that we forget that something unexpected can happen at any time."

I thought the last couple of days had been a pretty good example. I didn't say so.

All I said was, "I'd better go help him back inside."

———

I sat with Joseph in the kitchen while he cleaned up after their late breakfast. Sat with him on purpose. I should have offered to help. But I was frozen, and it never occurred to me at the time.

I wasn't talking. I wanted him to ask a question to open me up. *Penny for your thoughts?* Something along those lines. But that was stupid. A day earlier, I might've decked him for a question like that.

If I wanted to talk, I was just going to have to do it.

"Know what I was just thinking?" I asked at last. My voice sounded a little shaky. To me. I wasn't sure how it sounded on his side of the kitchen.

"No, but I hope you'll tell me."

"Remember that first letter I wrote to you in prison?"

"Very well. I read it a dozen times. At least. I still have it."

I could have paused. Ridden the emotional shock waves of that moment. I didn't. I plowed forward.

"I absolutely promised you I was never going to judge anybody without knowing the whole story."

"Yeah, you did," he said. With no further commentary.

"That turned out to be kind of a joke, didn't it?"

"I noticed even at the time that you were judging other people for judging. But, hey. You were thirteen."

"But now I'm not," I said.

"No. Now you're not."

Nobody said anything for a long time. I got up and grabbed a dish towel and helped him dry. Nearly shoulder to shoulder like that. We were almost exactly the same height.

"I'm not sure the message is to kick yourself for making the mistake," he said after a few plates.

"What's the message?"

"You should ask Hammy. That's more or less his specialty."

We washed and dried in silence for a few minutes more.

Then he said, "Maybe that the things we tend to criticize in other people are actually pretty easy mistakes to make. Maybe it's just something we see them falling into in that moment. And maybe we're not above doing the same. Maybe it's just our turn to fall into that mistake some other time."

"I wasn't trying to. I didn't set out to be judgmental. I think I was just trying to protect myself."

"Maybe nobody sets out to be judgmental. Maybe everybody's just trying to protect themselves. From one thing or another."

I didn't answer. Because I didn't know what to say.

We washed and dried the rest of the dishes in absolute silence. But not a particularly uncomfortable one. We didn't try to repair the world. Forever mend that flaw in human nature. We couldn't, so we just let it be. As far from ideal as we both knew it was.

We just figuratively nodded at it. And then we finished the dishes.

Chapter Twenty-Five: Ruth

The weirdest thing happened on the actual day we hosted Thanksgiving.

It went fine.

Sean and Joseph and Aubrey ducked in and out of the kitchen, providing backup services to the cook, who was me. On an informal rotating basis, one would take Maya and play with her and keep her happy while the other two chopped onions and celery and peeled potatoes and basted the turkey every few minutes.

I don't mean to make it sound idyllic, because it wasn't quite like that. Ham was exhausted and weak and barely moved—just sat in the living room and waited for the meal to be served. Sean had the football game up too loud so he could hear it in the kitchen, and I think it might have bothered Hammy, but he was too polite to say. Aubrey was a little sullen—not combative and not openly hostile to anyone, but a little too quiet, as if lost in the landscape of his own brain.

Probably the biggest flaw of the day was Mom, though it wasn't her fault and I have to give her credit for doing her best. She would try to be involved—sit in the kitchen and talk to me while I cooked, for example—but then she had to excuse herself and lock herself in the bathroom every few minutes. The sounds that emerged were strange and upsetting, like a cross between coughing and choking, and it was very clear to everyone who heard them that her health had significantly changed just in the three days since she'd showed up here. It was alarming, to say the least.

But the meal was terrific. Mom only had to excuse herself twice. Maya fussed because she didn't want to sit in her high chair, so Joseph lifted her down and took charge of her, letting her sit in his lap all through dinner and feeding her yams and mashed potatoes, and a little bit of buttered roll.

It was just like anybody else's Thanksgiving dinner, I figured, just like so many of them all across the country that day, only I guessed it was better than the majority. Nobody took the conversation in any controversial political directions. Nobody got on anybody else about their job or relationship choices. Nobody raised their voice.

We just came together with all our flaws still intact and managed to spend a few hours without using them as weapons against anybody else, keeping their sharp edges in where they wouldn't draw blood from anybody near.

Like a family.

Which felt weird to me. I guess I'd always had this loose image of what a family might look like, or how one might function, but I never imagined it had any particular relevance to my life. I knew better than to believe a family was anything like the ones you saw on TV, and my own experience was disaster oriented at almost all times, but I knew—if only from the family I'd begun to form with Sean and Maya—that there was such a thing as people functioning together. Maybe not every minute of every day, but long enough to form a decent holiday. Maybe even a decent life.

I looked over at Ham, who barely looked strong enough to hold his own fork aloft, and remembered asking him if I would screw up my kids the same way my parents had done to me. He'd said it wasn't mandatory. That I could heal myself first. I didn't think I was fully healed, not for a second, but I must have been somewhere on that road, because I loved Maya and she knew it.

It's that second part that really counts.

Near the end of the meal, Ham weakly raised his glass of wine and tapped it with a butter knife, and we all gave him our attention.

"A toast," he said, and everybody's wine glass lifted—everybody joined him except Maya, even though we had no idea where he was going with this. "To those of us who are here today . . . who won't be here next year at this time."

I watched my mom from the corner of my eye to see how she felt about all that honesty being dragged out onto the table, but she seemed fine.

"Hear, hear," she said, and took a long drink. She was on her fourth glass, which might help explain her easygoing attitude.

Then the moment passed, but the conversation never resumed. The toast plunged us into a moment of awkwardness, and nobody knew how to talk through it. I was thinking about my mom, only about my mom, and the sadness of knowing how little time we had left with her. Difficult though she may have been, with Brad long gone away, losing her amounted to orphan status for Aubrey and me.

Oh. And Joseph. Sorry. Not sure why I forgot to include him in that. Though, I must say, I thought it would be a much greater shock to Aubrey and me. I think Joseph had been feeling like an orphan for years.

It never occurred to me that Ham's toast was intended for anyone else but my mom. Looking back, that seems naïve. I'm not sure why it never broke through to me that his toast might have been aimed at both of them.

I guess you mostly see what you're ready to see.

———

"I'll help you clean up this mess," Joseph said as we pushed back from the table, "but then Hammy and I have to get back on the road."

"Oh," I said, stunned by my own disappointment. "You're not staying?"

I'd been enjoying our weird moment of normalcy, and not realizing it intended to break itself up so soon.

"Can't," he said. "Sorry. Have to drive all night again. I fly back to Colorado in the morning. I have a guy filling in for me at the ranch. I'm lucky he has no family he particularly wanted to see, but I told him I'd be back the day after the holiday. It's a lot for him to do all by himself."

Aubrey spoke up, which surprised everyone. Well, I know it surprised me, and it seemed to surprise everybody else, too, because Aubrey had been unusually silent throughout the day.

"You can take off," he said to Joseph. "I'll help Ruth get this all cleaned up. But then I'm heading back tonight, too."

I looked at my mom, not sure what I was hoping to hear her say. "Mom?"

"Yeah, I think I'll drive back tonight, too, honey. Don't think I don't know that three or four days is a lot of me. It's time I got out of you kids' hair."

But I knew we wouldn't let her go that night. Not after four glasses of wine. Sean would corral her and get her to go to bed in the guest room, because Sean was good with my mom, and she would sleep it off and head home in the morning.

"I'll help you clean up," Sean added. He knew I was off balance now—I could tell.

"Don't tell me *you're* leaving, *too*, after that," I said to him.

Everyone laughed, though maybe a little nervously, and then the room more or less emptied out. Aubrey began to clear the table. Joseph and Ham and my mom went off to get their belongings together.

Sean hung by my side for a moment, knowing I needed some reassurance.

"Don't worry," he said when we had the room to ourselves, "I'll talk her out of driving tonight."

"Thank you," I said, and pushed into the safety of his side as he put his arm around me. "That was weird," I added.

"I know it ended kind of suddenly—"

"No. All of it. The whole day was weird."

"I thought it went really well."

"Right," I said. "That's exactly what I mean."

He chewed that over for a few seconds. Then he said, "Yeah. I guess if you look at it that way, it *was* kind of weird."

———

Aubrey and I were standing shoulder to shoulder at the sink when Joseph came down to say good-bye, Aubrey washing and me drying. Joseph came up behind Aubrey and gave him a bear hug from behind, pinning his upper arms to his sides, and I wondered if he had purposely chosen a moment when Aubrey was not prepared to resist.

Aubrey had no particular reaction that I could see—he didn't welcome the embrace and he didn't resist it.

When Joseph let go, he handed a piece of paper over Aubrey's shoulder—held it there until Aubrey could see what it was. I could see it, too, though I couldn't read every word and number, but it was clearly Joseph's address and phone number in Colorado.

Aubrey only nodded in silence, dried his hands, and stuck the paper deep into his jeans pocket.

Then Joseph turned his attention to me. I faced him and took the embrace head-on, holding him tightly in return—feeling how much I had lost ten years ago, really only understanding the loss now that I had him back.

"Come out and say good-bye to Hammy," he said into my ear. "He's exhausted and I'm trying to save him all the steps I can."

I pulled out of my big brother's arms. "Think he'll be okay riding in the car all night?"

"Absolutely," he said. "Nothing puts Hammy to sleep like a moving car. He'll sleep like a baby all the way home."

We walked together to the front door, where Ham leaned on his cane, looking more stooped than I'd ever seen him.

He held his arms out to me and I gathered him up, and held him up, and we locked into each other in that singular exchange I'd never experienced until the first time I said good-bye to Ham at age fifteen.

"Ruthie," he said into my ear, and his voice sounded small and a little bit sad. Wistful, at least. "Dear, dear Ruthie. Remember the last time I bid you good-bye? I said you weren't shut o' this old man just yet. Wish I could say that again, my dear girl, but I'm thinking this might be it for us, so let's make it good."

I just held him, as instructed, feeling his words sink in. Feeling a tingle along my arms and legs as I processed the loss of him. Not that I hadn't had plenty of time to see it coming.

"I won't see you again?" I asked sheepishly, and I sounded like a child to myself—like a little girl, whining just slightly, whether she meant to or not.

"Well, maybe I'll be wrong," he said. "It's been known to happen before. But one way or another, I'll see you again, Ruthie. I'll see you on the other side, if nothing else." Then he pulled out of my embrace and pointed a bent old finger at my nose. "Just promise me you'll keep me waiting a very long time."

Then he reached out for Joseph, who took him by the arm and supported his nearly nonexistent weight all the way out to the car.

I waved.

They both waved back.

Then they were gone.

———

It was the Sunday after Thanksgiving when I had the dream, only three days after everybody packed up and returned to their very separate lives.

I dreamed I was walking south on a high cliff over the ocean—not the exact high cliff Ham lived on, but a stretch of coast very much like it—with the two-lane Highway 1 off to my left. Sometimes the road would pull farther away from my path on the cliff, and other times the two practically ran together.

A movement caught my eye, and I turned my head and saw Hammy's car parked on the shoulder of the highway, with Hammy in the passenger seat. The car was parked perpendicular to the lanes, its windshield—and occupant—facing me, which there would likely never have been room for in real life. But this was a dream.

There was nobody in the driver's seat. Ham was just sitting there, a passenger waiting to be driven . . . somewhere. I wasn't sure where.

He raised his arm and waved to me.

I assumed he was calling me over, so I left my path at the cliff edge and walked toward the car, but Ham wasn't in it anymore. The car was still there, but Hammy was gone.

I woke up and sat up in bed and looked over at Sean, who was fast asleep. I knew he had work in the morning, so I didn't wake him up to talk about my dream, even though it had felt strangely solid and real, vivid in a way I wasn't used to experiencing. Normally I didn't dream, or at least didn't remember I had, and what little I remembered tended to feel chaotic and make little, if any, sense.

But this had been as clear as water in a mountain stream, the kind that lets you look through and see every rock and grain of sand on the bottom.

In time, I managed to get back to sleep.

———

After I'd given Maya her breakfast, after Sean had gone off to work, I still couldn't get that dream out of my mind. So I called Joseph to see if Hammy was okay.

"Joseph," I said.

"Oh," he said. "Duck. It's you." His voice sounded deep, and not just in its register. It sounded emotional, from a place deep in his chest. I could also hear it perfectly, which meant he wasn't out in the field.

"I just wondered if Hammy was okay."

"How did you know?" he asked.

And then I knew. I hadn't known, except to the extent that I had—but when he asked me how I knew, everything felt laid out clearly, and I knew part of me had known all along.

"I had a dream," I said. "I saw him waving to me in a dream."

"Sounds like something he would do," Joseph said.

He didn't go on. I waited.

Then in time, I said, "So . . ."

"He died quietly in his sleep last night, Duck. Just the way he wanted to go. He wanted to be in his own house, in his own bed, at peace. So he got what he wanted."

"How did anybody even know so soon?"

"He had nursing care at the end there. I thought you knew."

"No," I said. "I didn't know."

Then neither of us said anything for a long time, and I doubted if I had anything I could bring myself to say—even something desperately simple, like "thank you" or "good-bye."

"Not to be short with you," Joseph said, "but let's talk again when I've had more time to process this. I'm kind of a mess right now, but I'll be okay. It's not like we didn't see this coming."

"What about a memorial?"

"Not sure yet," he said. "But I promise I'll let you know as soon as I know."

"Thanks," I said.

And we hung up the phone.

I stood in the living room with my eyes closed for a minute or so. Maya was making squeaky noises as she bounced in her playpen, but they were just background to the images in my brain.

I was seeing Ham in that car again, the way he'd appeared in my dream, and wondering why I hadn't waved back.

I raised my right hand—in real life, right there in my living room—and gave him the wave I owed him.

Then I opened my eyes and got back to Maya, who didn't mind that I was crying. Babies are good that way. They have lots of things they're afraid of, but it's an entirely different list than us grown-ups. The things that scare us don't make a dent in the little newcomers at all.

Chapter Twenty-Six: Aubrey

The Monday after Thanksgiving, I had a Skype session with Luanne.

"Before you even ask me any questions," I said, "before you ask me how Thanksgiving went or ask me about my mom, I have to tell you this. I found out something. And I have to tell you about it right now."

I leaned forward. Toward my computer screen. Braced my elbows on the knees of my jeans.

As much as I could remember it word for word, I told her the story. Just the way Joseph had told it to me.

I watched her face with every sentence. Watched to see what happened inside her as each word hit home. It felt unfamiliar to me, to do that. In a way I couldn't quite place. But I didn't remember ever watching her face before as we spoke. In all those many years.

She didn't let much show.

When I was done, I sat back. Hit the back of my chair with a thump.

"So what do you think about that?" I asked her.

Her eyes met mine. Or they came up to her built-in camera, anyway.

"I realize this is a very 'therapist' thing to say. But I think it's better if we stick with what *you* think about it."

"I can't even sort out my thoughts, Luanne. They're just a big jumble."

"Go to feelings, then."

I looked away from her. Briefly at the fish. Then I forced my gaze back to her.

"Guilty. Stupid. Stubborn. Blind."

A silence.

"Go on," she said.

"I was hoping you'd argue with me."

"You know better. Go on."

I sighed. Closed my eyes. Then looked right at her again.

"Before he told me that . . . I kept basing all my feelings on whether I would ever forgive him. I was waiting to hear what he would say to me. And then I'd sort of be in this high-and-mighty place. And I'd judge whether I was ready to forgive him." I thought, *There's that word "judge" again.* "Plus, I pretty much figured I wouldn't. Forgive him. Then he tells me that story. At first, I didn't believe him. But it turns out he told Hamish MacCallum the same thing a couple of days after he got back from Iraq. And then all I could think about was what I said. You know. That day. In front of the cameras. And then it hit me that it should really have been about whether *he* could forgive *me*."

"Did he seem inclined to?"

"Didn't seem like he'd ever particularly held it against me to begin with. Which is weird."

"Why is it weird?"

"You don't think it's weird?"

"I think it's the way we're supposed to operate, Aubrey."

"Well. Maybe. But nobody ever does."

"Beg to differ."

"Not in my family," I said.

I thought I saw the tiniest flicker of a smile at one corner of her mouth. "Well," she said, "Joseph was out of your family for a lot of years. That might've helped."

A long silence.

I knew I'd skipped something. Something that had a kick to my gut when I thought about it. I'd been heading for it. But then the conversation had taken a turn.

When it came back, it kicked me again.

"It hurt him, though," I said. "Hamish told me so."

I was surprised by her reaction. I guess I'd expected it would kick her, too.

"You knew that," she said. "That's why you did it." She rocked her chair back. Steepled her fingers in front of her chest. Her eyes still didn't betray much. "It was a very purposeful, premeditated action to try to hurt him," she said. "That's what made it a radical act. And I think you were the only one who didn't see the fact that, no matter how much you were hurting, Joseph had never done anything purposeful and premeditated against you. So that's why everybody was shocked except you."

"In other words, I'm an idiot."

"In other words, you were an impulsive boy, and now you're a man who's able to look back and see things more clearly than he saw them then. Better late than never."

I looked into her eyes for a minute. And she stared right back. It was almost as though we were challenging each other. Daring each other to go a step further.

"He invited me to come out and work on that horse ranch with him for a month. In Colorado."

"Would you want to take that much time off school?"

"I'm not going to Colorado," I said. "I know that much. But I did tell him I've been wanting to take some time off. Especially now that I lost that job at the restaurant. A month, maybe. That's what he offered. Also . . . I told him I wasn't sure if I wanted to go back to school. You know. Be an astronomer at all. That it was all up in the air. But I do. I mean, I am. I'm going to go back to school. I've thought about it a lot in the past few days. And I'm going to keep going. I am."

"But you still want that month off."

"But I'm not ready for that whole Colorado thing."

"Why not?"

"Look. It doesn't matter," I said. "I have no money. I had to borrow twenty dollars from Ruth to put gas in my bike. To get home from Thanksgiving. I cleaned out my bank account when I got home, and it's been barely enough to eat on. I can't afford to get to Colorado and that's that."

"But if you could?"

"But I can't."

"But if you could?"

"You really want to go around again?" I asked.

She sighed. Then she asked me to talk a little about my mother. You know. Dying.

So that's what we did for most of the rest of the session.

———

Right after she told me our time was up, just before we clicked out of the Skype call, she said this.

"Did you notice something different about today?"

I had no idea where she was going with that. Everything seemed different. It wasn't the kind of difference that could be pinned down, though, I thought. Summed up in a neat little phrase or two.

"You mean, other than the fact that my mother is dying and my brother did what he did because of me? Because that's some difference right there."

"I didn't mean content-wise."

"Oh," I said. "Okay. I give up."

"You didn't look at the fish today," she said. "You looked at me."

"Oh. Yeah, I guess I didn't notice that."

Except I *had* noticed myself noticing that. In a way. But I guess part of me didn't realize until she pointed it out. You know. That it meant as much as it probably did.

―――

After the session, I wandered out to my mailbox.

I found two bills. A pile of junk mail. A letter from my mom.

I opened the letter on the way back to my apartment.

It was a short note. Wrapped around a check for a thousand dollars. Twice what she normally sent.

Aubrey honey,

You might as well have some of this now. You and your sister will be dividing it up soon enough.

Love,
Your mother

In my head, Luanne asked her question for a third time. "But what if you could?"

―――

Mrs. Morrison answered her apartment door on the fourth knock. She was old. It was hard for her to move around.

Just for a moment, I felt bad. Asking her to look after the fish again. She just had, over Thanksgiving. And I knew it was hard for her to go up and down those stairs.

Her face lit up when she saw me. Which, I realized, it always did. And that's something. You know? That's no small moment.

"Aubrey."

"I had a thought," I said. As I said those words, I realized: yes, I had a thought, but it was a new thought. It was different from what I'd planned to say when I knocked on her door. "I'm going to go away for a while. Longer than usual. I hate to ask you to go up and down those stairs. You know. Every day. For a month. So what if I just drain those tanks? Right now. Take the fish out. Put them in bowls or something. Take most of the water out of the tanks. Carry them down here. Get them all set up again in your apartment."

I watched the wheels turn in her head. Watched her run her hands across her apron. She always wore an apron. She usually ran her hands across it. Especially when she was thinking.

"I'd love to have them, dear," she said. "But . . . so much work for you to move them. And then in a month, when you get home, having to go through that all over again . . ."

"I wouldn't, though," I said. "If you like having them, I'd just leave them with you."

Her head rocked back a little in surprise.

"Those beautiful fish? Why, you've been collecting them for years, Aubrey. All those hundreds of dollars' worth of fish and equipment. Why would you want to give all that away?"

"I feel like I'm done with them," I said. Knowing it and saying it at exactly the same time. "I always used them the wrong way, I think. To have someplace to look. You know. When I didn't want to look at what was right in front of me. They were a distraction.

I don't think I want to use distractions anymore. I think now I mostly need to look where I'm going."

———

I cashed Mom's check and just kept driving.

I'd filled a big, technical several-day backpack with clothes and a few personal items. It was strapped onto the sissy bar on the back of my bike. The one I'd bolted on because Jenny thought I accelerated too fast. Because she was scared she'd blow right off the back. The one I'd never bothered to take down.

Everything else I'd left behind for now.

How much did a person really need?

I drove all day. And then all night. The way Joseph had done on his way down from Northern California.

I didn't call ahead. Because that way I had every minute of the trip to change my mind.

———

I didn't change my mind.

Chapter Twenty-Seven: Ruth

The memorial was held in San Francisco, nearly a month later, in a church Regina had chosen.

Joseph was waiting on the front steps when I arrived, and I walked right into his arms. I wasn't sure if it was me he'd been waiting for, but I wanted to think so, and so I didn't ask.

"Hey, Duck," he said.

"Was Hammy religious?" I asked straight into his ear.

"Not so much."

"So why are we here?"

"Not sure," he said. "It's hard to pin down what Hammy believed. Regina had to choose *some*place."

He linked his arm through mine, and we walked inside. The place was a sea of flowers—that was the first news to hit my eyes. The second was the absence of a coffin. This was a memorial, rather than a funeral. Not that I really cared about a detail like that.

There were people, but not a sea of them. Really, not as many people as flowers. Maybe thirty people, but it looked as though fifty people had sent flowers.

"Why are there more flowers than people?" I asked Joseph.

"Hammy had a lot of friends and admirers. But some of them are shy. Not all of them wanted to show their face at a time like this. Or any other time, for that matter."

I wondered if he meant the people whose photos were not on the mantel, but I didn't ask.

We took a seat on one of the front-most pews and waited, Joseph's arm still hooked through mine. We didn't talk for a time. I looked around and thought I identified five or six people whose photos I'd seen that day in Ham's house. But, of course, we were all older, so it was a little hard to tell.

"I hope all these people he saved are going to get up and speak," I said, looking around for Regina but not yet seeing her.

"They're not."

"Too bad. That would have been great."

"Not really a bunch of public speakers, that lot," he said. "People who have that particular connection with Hammy don't always relish going into detail. Regina asked them. Asked us, I mean. But only one person was willing to do it. So she went with something simpler. The minister is going to speak, and then Regina is. Nothing fancy."

"Who was the one person who said yes?"

I looked around at the faces I thought I knew from their photos. With one exception, they were seated alone, somewhere between the middle and the rear of the church, looking mildly uncomfortable. I tried to figure out which one of them was brave.

"Wouldn't really be fair to tell you that," he said.

"I'll figure it out on my own."

But they all looked too shy or walled-off to me. I looked at each and counted and wondered if I was missing anybody, or if it was someone who ultimately hadn't been able to attend. Then I remembered that Joseph was a member of that group.

"Oh, wait," I said. "It was you."

He smiled, a little shyly I thought, and he never answered me, but I knew I was right.

"How's Mom?" he asked, maybe trying to change the subject.

"Not good enough to be here. I think she would have liked to come. But it's catching up with her more every day. And I called Aubrey on his cell phone. He said he had to work. Which is weird, because he never even told me he'd gotten another job. Anyway, he couldn't get the time off."

"I know," he said.

"You talked to him?"

"Face to face. Mr. Universe is doing both my work and his while I'm gone."

"You're kidding."

"I wouldn't kid about a thing like that."

"He's in Colorado with you?"

"Just for a while. A month, maybe. Then he's going back to school. He really does still want to be an astronomer."

"I didn't know there was ever a time when he didn't."

"A lot is changing for him," Joseph said.

Then I saw Regina, and she came over and gave me a big hug. She was crying, and I caught it like the flu, only with no incubation period. I held onto her for a long time.

"Not a bad life's work," she said, pulling back from me, indicating the saved ones with a nod of her head to each. "Everybody was always surprised when they found out what my father did for a living. Weren't you? Admit it. I guess it seemed ordinary. People were always guessing he was a philosopher or something more grand like that. Not an insurance claims adjuster. But look what he managed to do."

Then she ducked her head away from me and disappeared.

"Oh my God," I said, plopping down next to Joseph again. "I just had the most awful thought. And I can't believe it's the first time I've thought of it."

"The next person who walks through the fence," he said. It wasn't a question.

"He'll just go over. Won't he? Or she?"

I still couldn't believe that the thought had only now come into my head. I knew there had to be some actual suppression there, like repressed memories from a horrible childhood of abuse. A thing like that could not possibly have just slipped my mind.

"I don't know," Joseph said. "I don't know who he's leaving the house to. There's a reading of the will, and I'm supposed to be there, but it's not until next month. Knowing him, maybe he left it to somebody who's supposed to take over the job. You know, show up out back when the motion sensor goes off. Or maybe the job stops with him. He was always so realistic about what he could do and what he couldn't. He would always say, 'I can only save what I can save and no more.' Or words to that effect. It came out differently every time he said it."

"I know," I said. "I remember."

But I didn't want that to be the answer now.

I looked around again at the faces. The special faces. The ones I'd first seen on the mantel when I was fifteen. I couldn't picture the face of the next person through the fence, and I didn't want to try.

But I knew I had to accept that, if this was the sum total of the saved, it was enough. It would have to be. Ham had saved seven people, six men and one woman, who kept in touch all these years later, and I had no idea how many more who hadn't and who we could only assume had been saved.

But seven. Even if it was only seven. That's about seven more lives than most people save.

Maybe it was too much to expect that his good works would go on after his death.

"I'm going to go look at the photos," I said.

They were on an easel in front of the altar, a loving collage of Ham from a little boy in knee pants in Scotland to an ancient man in bed maybe only days before his death. The one thing they all had in common was his eyes. Clear. Intense. Never distracted. Never evasive. From the cradle to the grave, all Hammy all the time.

"It's okay either way," I told his eyes in those photos. "You did what you could do. You did great."

I wondered if I should add Aubrey and myself to the list of people he had saved, but I didn't have much time to wonder, because the service was starting, and I had to find my way back to take a seat at my brother Joseph's side.

Epilogue

You Work to Keep

a Secret Your Whole Life

Winter 2015

Ian

When I left the dorm, I took my roommate's car keys with me, and when I got out to the student parking lot, I took his truck.

Think of it as a final act of justice. *I* did.

Kevin had come to the university with a brand-new off-road four-wheel-drive truck given to him by his parents. Which is ridiculous, because who goes off-roading in San Francisco? I happened to know the bills for the registration and the insurance went to them, his parents. He even had a credit card for one of the big gas stations that billed straight to them.

Hard to have it much easier than that.

I came to the university on public transportation, and if I'd gotten a car, it would have been because I'd worked for it.

But now I had my final answer. I didn't get a car. I would never get a car.

It wasn't any kind of jealousy that made me feel justified in taking the truck. It was the extent to which I owed him one back. Because Kevin was the guy who had dealt my life its final blow.

Maybe after I was gone, they'd even file some kind of charges against him. That happened sometimes when someone got bullied right off the edge of his life. Then again, sometimes it didn't. So I thought he at least deserved to lose the truck. Just in case that was all he lost.

I got turned around three times looking for Highway 1 south, out of the city. But it was okay, because the truck had a full tank of gas. The trip was on Kevin, and it didn't matter.

———

I can't say how long I drove down the coast, because you have to have a clear head to judge time. I just remember that the truck had knobby tires that held tight around the curves. And that my phone kept buzzing.

I'd meant to leave it behind in the dorm, but there it was in my shirt pocket. And it just wouldn't stop.

And also I remember the highway didn't look the way I'd pictured it.

It was dark. I had no idea what time it was, just that it was dark. And I'd remembered Highway 1 as being all very high over the ocean, and with no guardrails anywhere. In other words, drive off any part of it you choose.

Instead, I drove long flat stretches that were more like beaches, right down at sea level, then wound up onto high cliffs with guardrails. And that damn phone just never stopped.

I stopped, though. After a time. I switched on the dome light in Kevin's truck and pulled the phone out of my pocket. To see if I was getting texts, e-mails, or actual calls.

Yes. All of the above.

I took a fast look at the texts. With my eyes partly shut, which I realize is pathetically ridiculous, because you can't see something and not see it at the same time.

Dude. Hate to be the one to tell you. But you need to see this. With a link. To the video that had just ruined my life.

Ian. I thought we were friends, man. Why didn't you just tell me?
You didn't tell anybody they could tape that, right? There should
be a law against that. They should arrest the person who did this.

I just had this forwarded to me and about fifty other people.
With a link.

I powered down the window and threw the phone out into the
road, where a passing Mercedes SUV squashed it flat.

I thought, *You work to keep a secret your whole life* . . . but then
I couldn't think of an end to the sentence. Other than maybe . . .
and you end up here.

I drove south again.

———

After a while, I saw houses. And of course there are no guardrails in front of houses. But I couldn't bring myself to go barging
through somebody's yard in a four-wheel-drive truck. It wasn't
their fault what had happened, and there was no reason to damage
their property on the way out.

Then there were no houses and no guardrails, but the bluff was
only forty or fifty feet over the rocks. And the last thing you want
to do is just hurt yourself really badly.

Then I wondered if there was a reason why every spot was the
wrong spot. Like maybe I didn't really want to do this, after all. But
it didn't feel that way. It felt like I wanted the spot but just wasn't
finding it.

Then, just like that, I did. I saw it, and I knew it was the place.

Only thing is, it wasn't a drive-through sort of proposition. So
Kevin would get his truck back. I pulled over and looked up the
hill at the gash in the chain link fence. Just made to walk through.
And I decided it was okay to leave the truck. To let him get it back.
Better, maybe. Let all the damage be caused by him. Keep my slate

clean. People could remember me as the one who didn't hurt anybody. Except himself.

I pulled half onto the shoulder and half in the road, and parked and left the keys in the ignition.

The wind was strong and whipped hair into my eyes and flapped in my shirt. And as I walked up the hill to that fence, it started to rain. Hard, and on a slant, stinging my eyes and soaking my clothes through to my skin immediately. I cursed out loud, but then it hit me that it didn't matter. The reason people don't like to get caught in the rain is because it takes so long to dry out again, if you don't have a change of clothes. And you get cold while you're waiting.

I wouldn't be doing much waiting.

I ducked through the slash in the fence and walked to the edge of the cliff. It was too dark to see down, but I could hear it. The roar of the waves, which I knew from the sound were a long way down. Plenty long enough.

Just for a second, I faltered. I thought about how people would react. How they would be sorry to lose me. And how Kevin would be sorry for what he'd done. And just in that moment, I wavered.

I wondered if that was a good enough reason. Them. Why was I doing this to show them? What about me?

But an image of that long list of texts came back into my head, and I knew I couldn't drive home and face that. My parents would see that video. Everybody would see it. Everybody already had.

I heard a voice cut through the wind. It said, "I don't want to startle you."

I whipped around toward the house, and there was a man sitting on the porch swing on the covered patio. I couldn't see him well in the dark, but I could see that he was sitting. And that was a very important factor in how things turned out. I was afraid of him, of everybody, and I didn't figure he meant me any good, and if he'd taken two or three steps in my direction, I swear I would have jumped. To get away from him. Keep myself safe. Which is almost funny in retrospect, but that was my thinking. My brain wasn't in the best working order.

But he just sat.

"I'm sorry," I said, my voice trembling. "I guess I'm trespassing. I'll just go."

"I know this will sound like a strange question," he said, still not advancing on me in any way, "but when did you last eat?"

I stood a moment, blinking into the rain.

"You're right," I said. "That sounds pretty strange."

"You don't really have anything to lose by answering it, though."

"Okay. That's true. This morning."

"This morning?" he asked. As though that couldn't be the right answer. "It's ten after two. You ate just in the last couple of hours?"

"Oh. No. I didn't know it was that late. I meant ... you know ..."

"Yesterday morning."

"Yeah."

"Well, that's not good enough," he said.

"What difference does it make?"

"Oh, it makes a difference. You'd be surprised how much of a difference it makes. Right now you're trying to run your brain on nothing at all. I think you should come inside, get into some dry clothes, and let me make us both a big breakfast. Of course, you don't have to. You can do whatever you want. But it's a suggestion. It's an invitation."

That, of course, only renewed my fear. Now I thought he was some kind of pervert or hitting on me in some way. Or at least that he wanted *something* from me, something that I couldn't identify, wouldn't like when I saw, and wasn't prepared to give.

The rain eased slightly.

"Why would I want to do that?" I asked him, my heart pounding. "I don't even know you."

"One simple reason," he said. "Because my plan is better than your plan. It's a better next thing to happen in your life than what you had in mind."

Which disarmed me, to say the least. Because I had no idea my plans were so transparent.

"How did you know I was going to jump?"

"Just about everybody who ever came through that fence had the same plan," he said. "Myself included."

I paused to take that in. He had been going to jump, too. But he was still alive. Did that mean I might be, too? But then I remembered what was driving me forward. Stopping me from going backward.

"I can't go back there," I said. "I've been publicly humiliated. Shamed. And I mean *publicly.*"

"Yeah," he said, as though I'd said I stubbed my toe. "We definitely need to trade stories."

"Okay. I get it now. So I come in. And you make breakfast. And you go off and call the police. And I sit there eating and talking until they show up. And they take me in and lock me up in a mental hospital. Right?"

"No. That's not how it works."

"How does it work?"

Something settled in me as I asked. Only slightly, but still. And it wasn't because I trusted him much more. It was because I was still alive. I was on borrowed time already, which was a dreamy feeling, like a filmy movie scene. Like a coloring book colored outside the lines.

It made me feel like I had nothing to lose.

"You eat. We talk. Then you do what you think is best."

"There has to be a catch."

"Only to the extent that once your stomach is full and you're having a talk with someone who actually seems to notice that you exist and that you hurt, what you think is best almost always changes."

I didn't say anything for a minute, and neither did he. The rain let up completely, leaving me soaked to the skin and cold in the blustery wind.

"I'm going to get up," he said, "and take a few steps in your direction. But only to offer you my hand to shake."

He did. His hand was dry against my wet one. At least, it was until I took hold of it. I still couldn't see him well in the dark, but his hair was shoulder length and shaggy, and he wasn't tall, but he looked like he worked out.

"What's your name?" he asked me.

"Ian. I don't want to tell you my last name."

"Well, that's another thing we have in common, Ian. I don't like to tell people my last name, either. So you just be Ian. And I'll just be Joe."

He turned to walk back to the house, but I just froze there. I wasn't really sure if I was supposed to follow.

He stopped. Looked over his shoulder at me. "You coming?" he asked.

"Uh. Yeah. Sure. I guess. Why not?"

"How do you feel about bacon and eggs and potatoes?"

"I feel fine about them."

"Good. Because it's the only thing I know how to make worth a damn."

As I followed him through the sliding door and into the kitchen, I was aware of an odd sensation. The moment my life had been scheduled to end was only a minute or two in the past, but it already felt faded and distant, like something that had never been real at all. Like a dream you can only barely recall, the kind that slims down into the bare bones of its plot even while you're struggling to remember. No matter how hard you try to hold it steady, the finer details slide away.

About the Author

Born in Buffalo, New York, Catherine Ryan Hyde moved to New York City shortly after graduating from high school. With a plan to do something other than writing—something that might provide a steadier paycheck—Hyde worked as a baker, pastry chef, auto mechanic, dog trainer, and tour guide. Hyde moved to a small town on California's Central Coast in the mid-1980s. After coming to terms with alcohol and drug addiction, she realized she needed to write and hunkered down. She's been clean and sober for over twenty-five years and is the author of thirty books and numerous short stories, which have won literary accolades throughout the world. Hyde's bestselling novel *Pay It Forward* was adapted into a major motion picture and translated into more than two dozen languages for distribution in over thirty countries.